Promise of the Visitor
"A delightful romp with spaceships, suspense, and assorted aliens."
—Kirkus Reviews

"Gittlin's fast-paced story is packed with drama, tension, and fine characterization spiced with a sense of wry humor."
—D. Donovan, Senior Reviewer, Midwest Book Review

Cataclysm: End of Worlds
"The mystery novelist–AI alien buddy concept is fresh and fun, and the story moves at blazing speed."
—Kirkus Reviews

The Silver Sphere
The novella utilizes every word to create a satisfyingly original blend of humor and entertainment in a small but compelling package. And thank heavens there are more books to come. Those seeking the rare draw of a literary sci-fi novella format as well as busy readers who want to digest an action-packed, unpredictable story in one sitting will find The Silver Sphere a complete delight on many levels.
—D. Donovan, Senior Reviewer, Midwest Book Review

Novels by
David Gittlin

Time Terminus

The Silver Sphere

Cataclysm:
End of Worlds

Promise of the Visitor

Three Days to Darkness:
Three Days to Save the World
Three People to help
Three lessons to learn

Scarlet Ambrosia:
Blood Is the Nectar of Life

Micromium:
Clean Energy from Mars

THE SILVER SPHERE TRILOGY

The Silver Sphere
Cataclysm: End of Worlds
Promise of the Visitor

A Science-Fiction Adventure

DAVID GITTLIN

Entelligent Entertainment, LLC

Copyright © 2022 by David Gittlin

The Silver Sphere Trilogy is a work of fiction. Names, characters, places, and incidents are the product of the author's imagination or appear in the story fictitiously. Any resemblance to actual persons, living or dead, events or locales is entirely coincidental.

All rights reserved. The use of any part of this publication, reproduced, transmitted in any form or by any means, electronic, mechanical, photocopying, recording, or otherwise stored in a retrieval system without the prior consent of the publisher is an infringement of the copyright law.

Cover and Interior Design by David Moratto
www.davidmoratto.com

Published in the United States by
Entelligent Entertainment, LLC

ISBN: 979-8-9858605-1-1

*To Ashley Brynn,
the newest addition
to our family.*

Author's Note

Dear Reader,

I am aware that much of the science in this science fiction tale is pure bonkers. Please indulge me. It's all in the service of fun.

CONTENTS

—PART 1—
THE SILVER SPHERE
page 1

—PART 2—
CATACLYSM: END OF WORLDS
page 49

—PART 3—
PROMISE OF THE VISITOR
page 151

Preview
TIME TERMINUS:
EXPECT THE UNEXPECTED
page 315

ABOUT THE AUTHOR
page 331

—PART 1—
THE SILVER SPHERE

—1—
JACOB

It wasn't in actuality a sphere.

I found it on the beach. Right at the water's edge.

In hindsight, I'm not entirely sure I found it. The sphere may have found me in some karmic sort of way. I'll have to wait until later to sort it out because, as I will soon learn, time is in short supply.

First things first.

My name is Jacob Casell. Two days ago, I left a comfortable beach house to go out for a stroll in the middle of the night. The full moon and stars were my sole companions. I needed to think about the ending of my latest mystery novel. I found the water and the salt air helped to stimulate my creative thinking.

The night was clear. I splashed my bare feet on the tips of the tides. I felt the crisp ocean breeze ruffling my longish hair as if it were saying, *tell me your story*.

Before I could answer the query, I almost tripped and fell. A thing about the size of a basketball rocked gently in the water at my feet. I had a distinct feeling it was looking up at me, even though it had no discernable eyes.

The thing at my feet was a shiny silver sphere punctuated by streamlined indentations on its sides. It had a hole in the center which, in the moonlight, revealed nothing but bottomless darkness. Hardly an eye. Not a human one, at least. As I examined it, the sphere began to pulse. I stepped a few feet away. The sphere flashed on and off like a strobe light. I wondered if the damn thing was about to explode

Suddenly, the sphere stopped strobing. Then, it spoke to me. A voice inside my head spoke in stilted English.

"Do not be alarmed," the thing said. "The pulsing effect was me reanimating my systems. No sense wasting energy while I was waiting for you to happen along. You certainly took your time, didn't you? And, by the way, I'm not a 'thing.' I am a highly evolved organism. It may help you to think of me as an artificial intelligence entity, but I am much more than that. Your mind is not capable of conceiving what I truly am."

I drew back a few more steps thinking, *I must be dreaming. This can't be happening.*

"For a man who writes novels, you display little imagination," the sphere said.

I felt strangely comfortable speaking to the machine as if speaking to a telepathic silver sphere was as everyday an occurrence as eating a tub of macaroni and cheese for dinner.

"How do you know I'm a writer?" I said aloud. I wasn't in the habit of communicating telepathically, after all.

"I've absorbed quite a bit of information about you in the short time we've been together."

"I'm not sure I like that."

"It doesn't matter if you like it or not."

"It matters to me."

It seemed like the machine was surprised by my response and needed time to process it. I pushed the advantage. "It sounds like you were expecting me."

"I was expecting someone. I suppose you'll do."

"Uh-huh. Do you have a name?"

"You can call me Arcon. A-R-C-O-N."

"Got it. I suppose you came here from some far distant solar system?"

"Next you will ask me: 'do I come in peace?'"

"Do you?"

"The answer is yes and no. I'm not here to hurt anyone, but there will be worldwide chaos if news of my mission leaks out."

"That sounds ominous."

"It's nothing compared to what will happen if you don't help me to complete my mission."

"Since you appear to know everything about me, you must realize that I'm not at liberty to help you. I'm past my deadline for turning in the final draft of a manuscript. My editor calls to scream at me daily."

"There is a much bigger picture here than your manuscript. I will dispense with the formalities and call you by your first name which, naturally, I've learned without your help. I'm getting cold and tired of soaking in this seawater, Jacob. Please take me back to the beach house your wealthy friend has lent you."

"But I just told you—"

"Pick me up, Jacob. If I miss *my* deadline, you won't have to worry about yours."

—2—
ARCON

After Arcon convinced me to drive him home to my friend's plush split-level house on Daytona Beach, I put him in the back seat of my decrepit Mazda Miata. Arcon reclined there regally, like the CEO of a large corporation, ignoring my attempts at conversation. Occasionally, he vibrated and made annoying clicking sounds. Something was up, but Arcon refused to let me in on the secret.

As we walked up the stone steps to the sculpted front door, I kept an eye peeled for voyeurs. My womanizing friend, Jeffrey, commissioned a local artist to carve a seductive female nymph into the oaken door. Jeffrey's amorous adventures were the talk of the town. Frustrated husbands in the neighborhood were known to point telescopes at Jeffrey's door to catch a glimpse of his latest stunning girlfriend. To shield *my* secret from prying eyes, I shrewdly camouflaged Arcon with the light coat I had been wearing to protect myself from the evening chill. Arcon was by no means a glamorous girlfriend, but he was sure to arouse interest if the voyeurs caught a glimpse of him.

Once safely inside, I unwrapped Arcon and perched him on top of a glass kitchen table. He immediately began strobing as he had done earlier on the beach. When Arcon's irritating light show finally stopped, I took a seat opposite him. I wanted to look Arcon straight into the aperture I call his eye to have, in a manner of speaking, a man-to-man talk.

"Why do you find it necessary to nearly blind me with your damn strobing," I began.

Arcon replied telepathically. "I'm charging myself up for what lies ahead. Completing this mission will require deep reserves of energy. More than I anticipated. I can't do it all at once. We have much to do and little time to do it. Please focus on the big picture and not on minor irritations."

"You haven't told me what the big picture is."

"I know. It's coming. Are you certain your friend won't be returning any time soon to reclaim his house?"

"He'll be in Paris for the next month or two writing for a fashion magazine."

Arcon flashed brightly, but only once. "Excellent. Let's get down to business. And don't interrupt me unless you have a highly intelligent question to ask."

I made a huge effort not to be insulted by Arcon's cavalier attitude. I had gleaned from our discussion on the beach that the fate of the world was at stake. Unless Arcon turned out to be a crackpot alien intelligence, I had to put my petty feelings aside and listen intently.

"To put it bluntly," Arcon began ominously, "your world will be destroyed by a pulsar from a neutron star that exploded two hundred and fifty light years away."

"What?"

Arcon seemed to pause for dramatic effect. "Unless we do something about it."

I was too startled to respond.

"As the people of this world are fond of saying; 'time marches on.' In this case, time not only marches, but it is also taking a shortcut through a wormhole. The pulsar has, until now, been hidden by this wormhole. It will soon reappear fifty thousand miles beyond the outer reaches of your solar system. Think of it as a traveler walking to Orlando, and then deciding to hop on a supersonic bullet train to save time and sneaker soles. By the time the pulsar becomes visible, it will be too late. We have seventy-two hours to save your planet."

I thought: *Either Arcon is a crackpot, or this is an elaborate ruse my trust fund friend is playing on me. What are the odds of something like this happening?*

I decided to go along with the ruse. "Did you by any chance bring a bottle of twenty-year-old single malt scotch to enjoy in case our mission fails?"

"If I was capable of laughing, I wouldn't."

I stared back at Arcon wondering how a super sophisticated being like Arcon was not capable of laughter.

Reading my thoughts, Arcon replied. "Laughter is not included in my programming for this mission. In this case, it's a waste of time and energy. I'm using every second to plan a solution to the crisis. I warn you that it's not guaranteed to work, and it will surely *not* work if you don't follow my directions carefully."

I didn't have the heart to tell Arcon that I was never any good at following directions. I like to do things my way and mostly in my own time. It doesn't mean I'm some sort of genius. I'm sure it simply means that I'm stubborn.

"If this is an elaborate joke, I'm happy to play along. If it's for real, I have to tell you, I'm the wrong man for the job."

"It's not a joke, Jacob, and we don't have time for personnel changes. It's you and me."

I sighed. "So, if I screw up, the world will blow up?"

Arcon flashed again. "JUST DO AS I SAY AND WE'LL HAVE HALF A CHANCE TO SAVE YOUR PLANET! The words smashed into my brain like waves propelled by hurricane winds crashing into the side of Jeffrey's expensive house.

I had managed to anger a machine. We were off to a flying start.

"Okay. Fine. Wonderful. What do we do now?"

"You take me to New York City," Arcon answered crisply. "To the top floor of the One World Trade Center building."

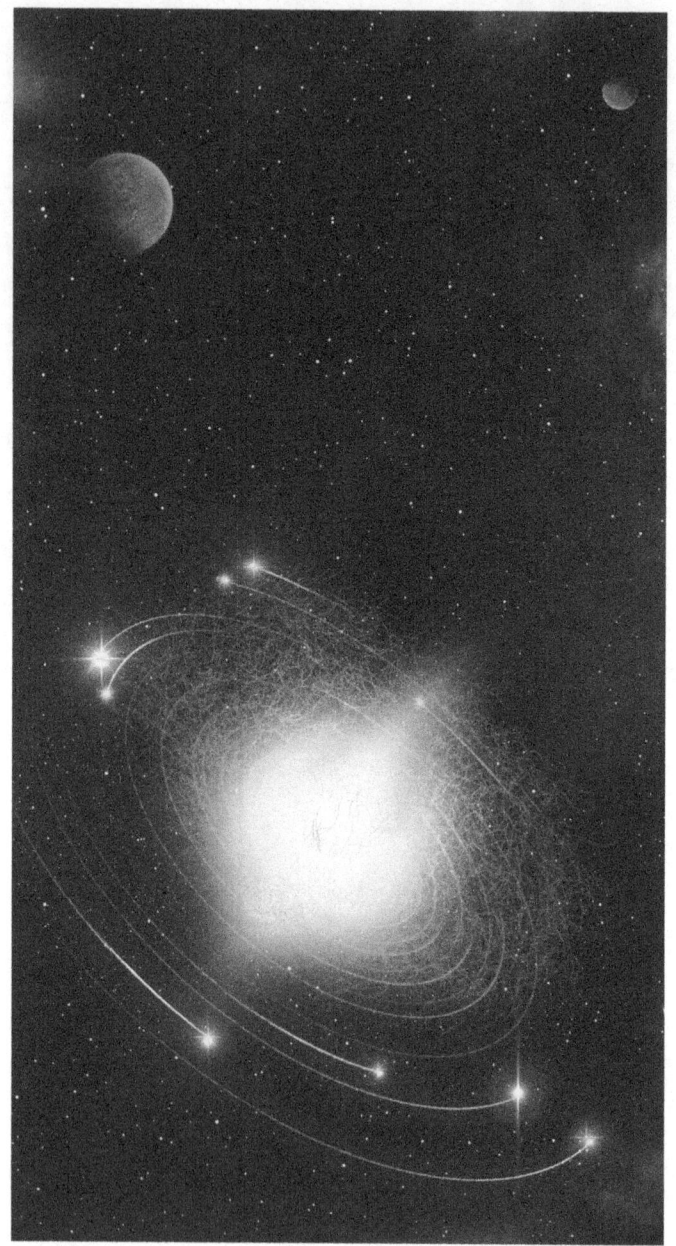

—3—
THE PLAN

"**How do you** expect us to get to New York?" I asked Arcon, and then immediately regretted it. I expected another irritated rebuke for wasting his time. There is no way a super-intelligent AI from the other side of the galaxy would not have a solid plan for the journey. I braced myself for Arcon's withering response.

Arcon made humming and clicking noises as if my question amused him. "Well, since I can't fly or beam, I suppose we'll have to go the old-fashioned way. We'll take your car."

"Let me get this straight. You want me to drive you over a thousand miles to New York City in my ancient Mazda Miata with 120,000 miles already under its worn belts?"

Arcon made crackling sounds. I imagined the noise was his latest way of communicating his impatience with me. "It beats taking the bus, don't you think?"

"The odds are less than fifty-fifty my car can make the trip without having a coronary thrombosis before we're halfway to Manhattan.

"Give me an hour alone with the Miata in the garage, and I'll have her as good as new."

Shades of the movie "Christine" flickered in my head. I saw my car reconstituting itself like the 1958 Plymouth Fury did after it was destroyed by a gang of bullies. I remembered the movie's tagline: "Body by Plymouth—Soul by Satan." I strongly suspected I was in some kind of elaborate nightmare.

I rose abruptly from the chrome and glass table in an alcove of Jeffrey's ultra-modern kitchen. "Excuse me, I need a beer."

I was beginning to crack under the pressure of the situation. If what Arcon had told me a few minutes earlier was true, the Earth had less than seventy-two hours before a giant pulsar from a distant supernova fried the planet into a crispy ember. Unless, of course, Arcon and I managed to do something about it.

After removing an Amstel Light from Jeffrey's built-in stainless-steel refrigerator, I rejoined Arcon at the kitchen table. I was grateful that Arcon had sagely decided to reveal his plan and my role in it one step at a time. I was having enough trouble wrapping my head around step one.

"So, we drive to New York City in my resurrected Mazda Miata, and then I somehow smuggle you to the top of the One World Trade Center building. Does that about sum it up?"

"You won't have to smuggle me. I know how we can get past security. I'll disguise myself as a gorgeous 19th-century Art-Deco vase. You'll carry me into the building in a reinforced shopping bag. When you open the bag, the guards will be astonished by my beauty and originality and ask silly questions. I assume they'll ask you to state your purpose for the visit. You'll tell them you're a tourist heading for the top floor observatory to meet your girlfriend and give her the lovely heirloom I'm posing as."

"I'm not comfortable with that idea. I doubt it will get us past the first wall of security."

"You aren't following my directions," Arcon reminded me with his typical lack of diplomacy.

"Your idea sounds too simple to work."

"It will work. I agree that it's simple. Even for someone like you."

I ignored the rebuke. I had another pressing question to ask.

"If you made it from the other side of the galaxy to a beach in Florida, why can't you propel yourself from here to the top of the World Trade Center?"

"The mother-ship dropped me five thousand feet above the ocean. I'm able to navigate and land safely in free-fall, but I can't propel myself, as I've mentioned. It's a trade-off, Jacob. I don't have room onboard for brains and propulsion."

"So how will you get back to your ship?"

"I won't. I'll remain here on Earth if there is an Earth left."

I wondered if that meant Arcon had more adventures in store for me if we survived. Then, I remembered my latest novel and its sad status as distressingly past due. I imagined my editor calling to announce that she had finally lost patience with me and the book was canceled.

Arcon seemed to sense my utter despair. "Why don't you join me in the garage and watch me bring your old car back to life? Does she have a name?"

"Mathilde. She reminds me of a French woman I once knew with sunrise golden hair and intense blue eyes."

"Come along, Jacob. Let's breathe new life into your lost love. I'm confident it will breathe new life into your outlook."

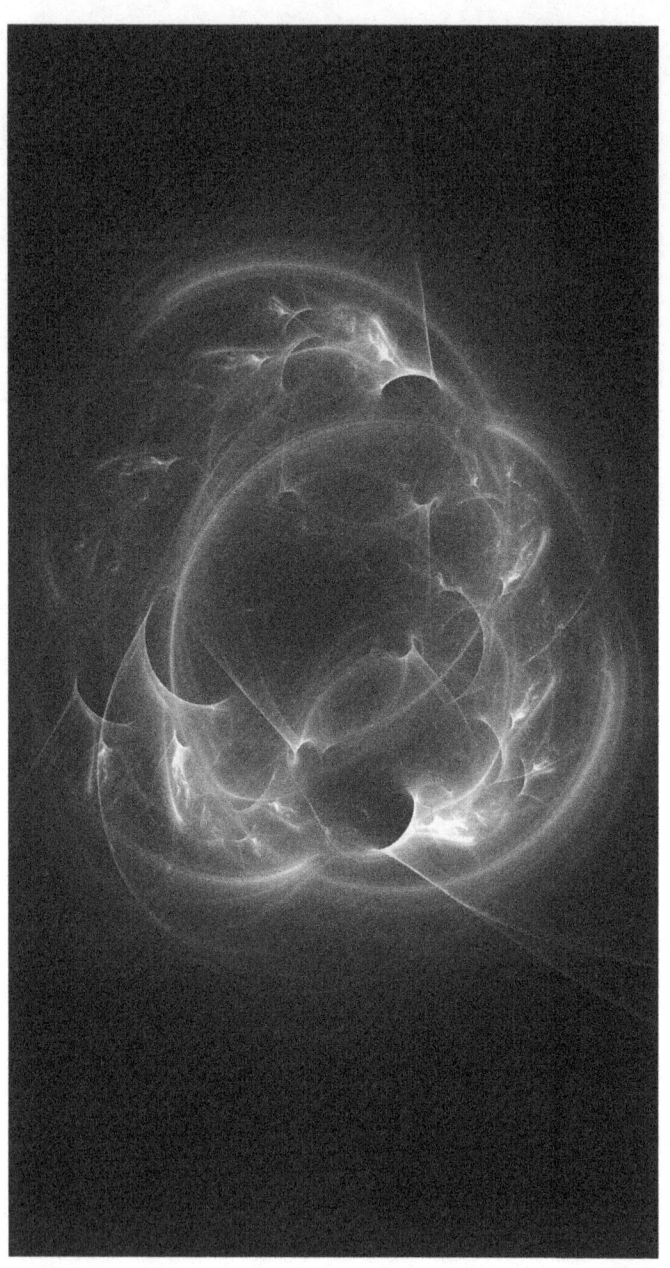

—4—
RESURRECTION

I carried an expensive mahogany bar chair from Jeffrey's den into the garage. As I walked back to the house to retrieve Arcon, two trains of thought traveling in different directions struck me. I thought how lovely it would be to live year-round in Jeffrey's stunning, ultra-modern house fronting a lone stretch of Daytona Beach. The ions in the air from the sea and the solitude would make it so much easier to write. At least theoretically.

If I survived the looming catastrophe, I resolved to negotiate a long-term rental agreement with Jeffrey. If I could persuade my good friend that I wouldn't interfere with his free-wheeling bachelor lifestyle, then maybe the idea had possibilities. Why hadn't I thought of this before? Probably because I wasn't breathing in enough salt air ions.

My second thought was more of a question that required an answer, if there was one, from Arcon. If an answer was forthcoming, I expected it to be short due to time constraints. We had a little more than sixty-five hours to prevent the extinction of life on Earth.

I noticed Arcon had remained unusually quiet since the conclusion of our latest mind-boggling discussion in the kitchen. I sensed that my friend from the other side of the Milky Way was gathering his energy to restore my old car for our impending trip to One World Trade Center in New York City. I had read it was the tallest building in the United States, and we were headed to the very top of it.

After carefully carrying Arcon from the house to the garage, I placed him comfortably on the bar chair. A few feet away, my decrepit red Mazda Miata waited for its promised transformation.

From what I casually refer to as an eye in the center of his sleek silver body, Arcon began scanning the car with a beam of pale blue light. Suddenly, the blue light bloomed into a cloud. It surrounded the entire car. Then, frenetic energy forms emerged from the cloud. For a few seconds, I was looking at an abstract light sculpture suspended above the car until the forms shot off to do their jobs. Each glob of energy serviced a different part inside and outside of the car. Then, the blue energy globs congealed to create one big throbbing blue blob that engulfed the car.

I expected to see my ancient sports car begin to morph into a new version of itself. That's not what happened. Arcon's only predictable feature is that he's always unpredictable. I kept my mouth shut. I knew instinctively that I'd be excoriated if I interrupted.

I heard grinding noises coming from underneath the sheath of blue energy. Then came screeching sounds of metal moving against metal, almost like the car was screaming in agony because Arcon had forgotten to administer an anesthetic before the operation. After several minutes of nerve-jangling scraping and crunching, the sounds settled into more subdued and less painful sounds. I heard faint crackling noises. It sounded like Arcon was whipping up a huge batch of popcorn in an oven. Finally, I began to detect the pungent odor of paint thinner.

"I think you should leave now," Arcon said to me telepathically. "The fumes might make you sick."

I wasn't used to this kind of concern from Arcon. *Maybe he's starting to warm up to me,* I thought.

"Don't flatter yourself," Arcon shot back. "We don't have time for you to recover from paint fume poisoning."

"Right. I almost forgot. I'm just a means to an end."

"Not quite. Now, what color would you like the car to be? Keep it conservative. We don't want to attract attention."

I settled on something called atomic silver, a glossy dark gray.

"Not entirely under the radar, but I'll allow you a few style points. Now, be a good boy and wait in the kitchen. I'll call you when it's safe to come back."

"Can I ask you a question?"

"Not now. Go back to the house."

I returned to the kitchen and cracked another beer. I closed my eyes and thought about the ending of my novel again. The elusive ending finally dawned on me. The detective and the beautiful FBI agent realize they are both too strong-willed to commit to a long-term romantic relationship. To make matters worse, their next cases required them to work undercover on opposite coasts. Ultimately, they come to a decision: to stay friends and perhaps occasional lovers if their paths cross again. I liked the idea. It left the door ajar for a sequel and a resumption of the relationship. I hoped my editor would like it.

The thought of ending my novel on a note of uncertainty generated images of something much worse. I saw the deadly pulsar emerge from a wormhole and slam into Mother Earth. A few hours after the Earth exploded into a blinding fireball, there was nothing left but stardust. All the hopes, all the dreams, all the achievements, all the moments of joy and sorrow, all the beauty and all the ugliness—all gone in a heartbeat. It was not science fiction. It was a reality hurtling towards us and getting closer every second.

"Come, Jacob," I heard Arcon say inside my head.

A few minutes later, I stood before a glossy new MX-5 Mazda Miata. I noticed Arcon had made it a convertible.

"Looks even sportier with the hood added."

"I thought you might like it," Arcon replied proudly.

"Is there any chance we can take turns driving to New York?"

"Are you serious? Hurry and pack your things. We'll only have time for a few cat naps and bathroom breaks on the way. We can't afford to waste a minute."

Arcon was picking up our vernacular with each conversation we had. I decided to hold my next question for the trip to New York. I was not looking forward to the grueling drive, but at least there would be plenty of time to talk.

— 5 —
DESTINATION

Generally speaking, the best time for a monumental crisis to occur is during the spring or summer. Frozen highways tend to create treacherous driving conditions, especially if the driver is in a hurry. Fortunately, the weather in Georgia couldn't have been much better in early April.

The Azaleas were blooming in all their glory. The skies beamed overhead in immaculate blues with only a hint of clouds. The scent of honeysuckle wafted in the air. It was almost enough to make me forget that the world stood an excellent chance of ending in less than fifty-five hours.

We sped Northward on I-95 in my miraculously restored Mazda Miata. We had just left a rest stop. I felt refreshed. I had nothing better to do except drive. On the other hand, Arcon was likely preparing for the challenges ahead. He was never idle and always irritable when I interrupted his thinking. I knew that "thinking" was an entirely inadequate way of expressing Arcon's mental processes. Likewise, "mental processes" was a crude description, but these approximations would have to suffice for now. I figured that Arcon had plenty of time to do whatever he was doing on the long trip ahead. I determined the present moment to be an excellent juncture to interrupt Arcon's "process" with minimum exposure to irritability. I could no longer wait to ask the question that had been plaguing me.

"Are you familiar with the bible story of Sodom and Gomorrah?" I asked, and held my breath.

"I don't have time to scan your scriptures," Arcon replied curtly.

"Then I'll give you a quick synopsis. God decided to destroy the cities of Sodom and Gomorrah for their grave sins. Abraham, the founder of Judaism, pleaded for the lives of the righteous people who lived in the cities, especially his nephew Lot and Lot's family. God relented and told Abraham if he could find ten righteous families, then God would allow the cities to stand. As it turned out, Lot and his family were the only righteous people in both cities. God allowed Lot and his family to leave before he leveled Sodom and Gomorrah, but he warned them not to turn around. Lot's wife disobeyed. When she turned around to watch the destruction, God turned her into a pillar of salt."

"Interesting. What is your point?"

"Is God punishing us for our sins?"

"I don't think so, Jacob. The human race is already doing an excellent job of destroying itself. Can we get back to giving your world a second chance?"

"In a minute. I have to ask. Why, after billions of years of existence, is our planet threatened with incineration now?"

"I will answer you succinctly and truthfully to save time and avoid follow-up questions. There are a few bad apples living in our galaxy. One of them is a race that you would call 'superhuman.' These extraordinary creatures have the technology to channel a pulsar. They channeled the pulsar heading this way. We have labeled this violent race of superbeings the 'Krondorians.' They want to colonize Mars without any interference from the people of Earth. It is much easier for the Krondorians to wipe out your civilization than to fight a destructive war to conquer it and then rebuild planet Earth to their specifications. It will be easier for the Krondorians to simply terraform Mars for habitation without having to be concerned about your existence.

"So, if we succeed, we still have to worry about the Krondorians."

"One step at a time, please. Let's deal with the crisis at hand."

* * *

The balance of our trip to New York City was uneventful. I'm not a big fan of the city. For starters, Manhattan is notable for its dirty air, dirty streets, dirty buildings, ridiculous prices, massive overcrowding, and unfriendly people. I can't understand why anyone would voluntarily choose to live in Manhattan unless they are pursuing a career in the arts. Some people "just love" the city for its culture, expensive restaurants, and God knows what else. Not me. The last time I saw a Broadway Show, the person next to me was practically sitting in my lap. I swore an oath never to repeat the experience. The only saving grace of being here is to see the rebuilt World Trade Center building up close and personal.

Unlike me, I'm sure Arcon has no opinion of the city. He is here to do a job of the utmost importance. He recruited me to help him. I'm also certain that he does not consider me his partner. He doesn't have to like me. He doesn't have to consider me a friend, an associate, a co-worker, or anything else of that ilk. He came to Earth to save us from a horrible fate. He has to do it quickly and efficiently. He has no use for extraneous pursuits such as opinions or the cementing of interstellar relationships. He is aware of every second that slips by. In less than three hours, the Earth will be reduced to fizzling cinders...unless we intervene successfully.

I have the unenviable task of transporting Arcon, undetected, to the very top of the One World Trade Center building.

One World Trade Center was built to replace the Twin Towers destroyed on 9/11. It is one of the tallest buildings in the world, measuring 1,776 feet high. It is no coincidence that the height of the building exactly matches the date of America's independence. Many features have been incorporated into the new building's construction to prevent the tragedies that occurred during the 9/11 attacks.

Arcon has assured me that the building's security will not be difficult to navigate. I am, to say the least, doubtful. I have no idea how many layers of security we will have to fool to reach the top of the building. I have read that there are four hundred security cameras mounted throughout the building, all of them running the latest anti-terrorist software. There are an undisclosed number of New York City policemen patrolling the building in any number of locations. I've read that the lower Manhattan police force has been beefed up to six-hundred-and-seventy officers. I imagine many of them are assigned to guard One World Trade Center.

I am reasonably certain of only three things. (1) I am not a terrorist. (2) I'm no security expert. (3) Although I am trying to save the planet, there is a high probability I will be incarcerated, and shortly afterward, the Earth will explode.

With Arcon packed in wrapping paper inside a sturdy, innocent-looking shopping bag, I walked past the soaring white arches of the Oculus, an underground transportation hub. I was fascinated to learn about an interesting feature of the structure. Incorporated into its design is a lasting reminder of the attacks of September 11, 2001. It is in alignment with the sun's solar angles every September 11, from 8:46 AM when the first plane struck until 10:28 AM when the second tower collapsed. Its central skylight washes the Oculus floor with a beam of light each year as a reminder of the attacks and in memorial of the victims.

Past the Oculus, I caught my first glimpse of the gleaming edifice known as One World Trade Center. Seeing the building for the first time in person added profoundly to my sense of urgency. The beauty and grandeur of this project are a testament to the resiliency and creativity of the human spirit. Seven other buildings have been constructed to complement the project. To imagine that all of this might be destroyed again by terrorists from a distant star system is incomprehensible.

To avoid waiting in lines, we arrived at the observatory entrance a few minutes after the opening time of 9:00 AM. Three soldiers in battle fatigues stood guard outside the entrance. A tag on their bulky vests identified them as members of the New York National Guard. Every inch of them from their hats to their pistols to their machine guns, and down to their car-wax-shine-boots shouted: *I mean business. Do not fuck with me. And, most importantly: DO NOT TRY ANYTHING STUPID.*

I tried on a friendly smile and a wave. It didn't go over well. We passed through the glass and steel doors to the security gauntlet. I call it a gauntlet because it looked more ominous than a TSA security station on steroids. I purchased an expensive express lane ticket for the observatory. The express ticket wasn't going to make my journey through the gauntlet any easier. It *would* make it faster to get into the observatory if we made it through the first wall of security.

Faced with the gauntlet, my resolve began to leak like a tire with a nail in it.

I was most concerned about the complicated scanner. It was equipped with a laser scanner and a conventional x-ray camera. It looked powerful enough to examine Arcon right down to his atoms. I didn't see how Arcon's disguise as a Nineteenth-Century Art Deco vase was going to pass muster. Attempting to put something over on this formidable security array was sheer suicide. Then again, what choice did I have? I'd surely be dead if I didn't try.

I placed the shopping bag on the scanner's conveyor belt. I shed the required personal belongings one normally removes before boarding an airplane, and placed them alongside the shopping bag. I walked through the metal detector, certain that I'd be surrounded by policemen at the other end.

I made it through the metal detector without hearing any alarms. A heavily armed police officer approached me. I thought: *This is what the guards are taught. Politely lead the suspected terrorist away so as not to disturb any of the other visitors.*

Instead of arresting me, the officer asked me why I was bringing the vase into the building. I told him that I intended to give it to my fiancée as a gift. I ad-libbed the part about my fiancée. It sounded more believable than "my girlfriend." He looked at me with an entirely too serious expression. I was positive he didn't believe my story. Then, he told me it was a unique and thoughtful gift. Finally, he asked me how long I planned to stay in the building. With every ounce of my being, I tried not to look relieved.

How long would it take Arcon and me to do what we had come to do? "Three hours," I said straight-faced. I figured a three-hour stay sounded innocuous enough.

"Let me see your driver's license or some other valid ID."

I handed over my driver's license. I chose that moment to remember the license was due to be renewed next month and my likeness in the photo didn't look like me now.

The officer barely looked at my license and yawned. "Excuse me," he said. "Double shift. Covering for my brother-in-law." I commended the officer for his filial consideration whereupon he told me to: "Collect your items and wait for me on one of those benches over there. I'll create your OWTC ID card and bring it to you. It won't take long unless you have outstanding arrest warrants."

I could tell the officer was half-joking. I strangled the impulse to come back with a clever remark. My evolving instincts told me to let the security staff fail quietly at stand-up comedy.

"You'll need the card for all points of entry in the building. Don't lose it. If you do lose it, report it to the nearest officer or staff member. The card will no longer be valid after six hours, so watch your time."

Picking up Arcon and my other belongings from the conveyor belt, I found the nearest bench. It was a relief to sit down after the harrowing trip through security.

Since we were alone, I whispered to Arcon almost like a ventriloquist, "How did you get through that scanner without your circuitry being detected?"

"I converted my insides into pure energy, and then I went into hibernation mode. I have a variety of energy frequencies to choose from. I used the most effective one for the pass through the scanner," Arcon said telepathically. I didn't expect to hear him speak audibly again until we were safely out of the building and by ourselves. I longed to feel safe again. A talking paper bag would do nothing to ensure our safety and advance the mission.

"You could have told me how you planned to fool the scanner. I was worried they'd find out you weren't a Nineteenth-Century Art Deco vase."

Arcon made no immediate reply. I figured he was too busy with more important considerations to acknowledge my existence when he suddenly spoke: "I'm sorry. It didn't occur to me to read you in."

I was astounded by the response. Was Arcon learning to have feelings in the same way he was learning the English language in general and CIA/FBI parlance in particular?

Before I could say anything more, the police officer returned. He handed me my ID card and pointed to a bank of elevators twenty yards to my right. "Take one of those elevators up to the observatory," he said. "It's a forty-seven-second non-stop flight to the one-hundredth floor."

I smiled automatically at the officer's not-so-clever remark. "Thanks for your service," I said as we boarded the elevator.

Parking and getting through security had eaten up an hour. We had two hours left.

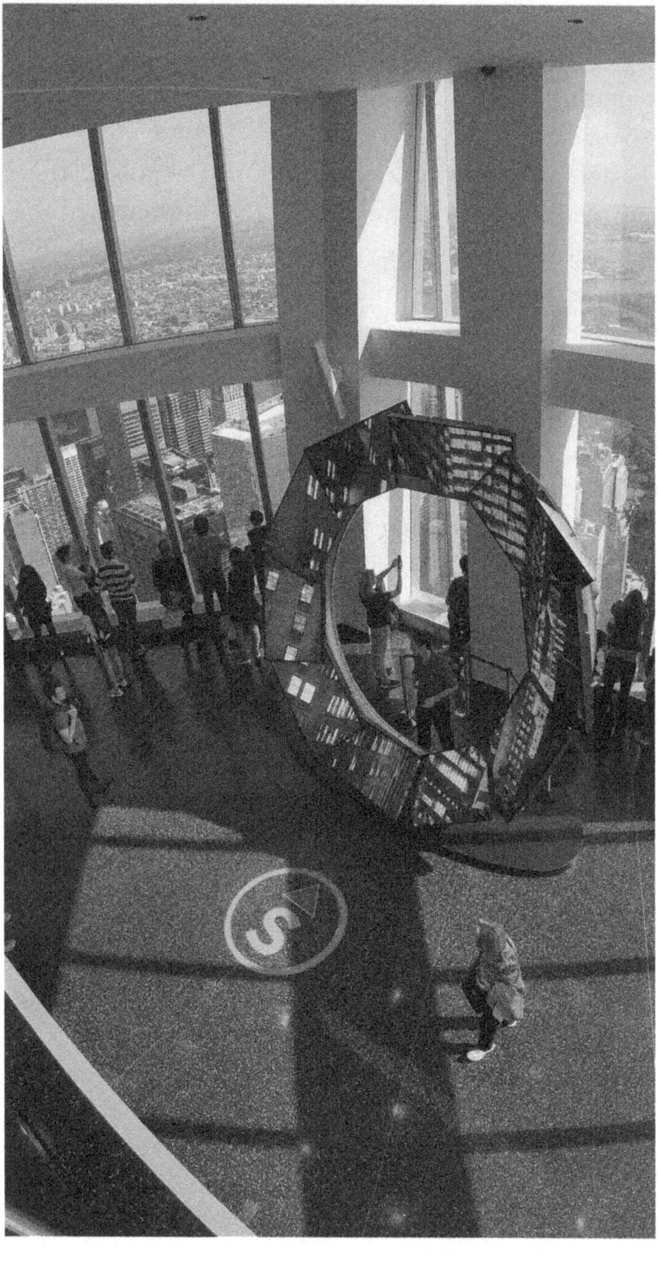

— 6 —

THE OBSERVATORY

We shot upwards in the elevator with ten other people standing comfortably around us. I should say it was comfortable spatially. A journey of one hundred floors in forty-seven seconds is anything but comfortable except maybe for a jet fighter pilot. I was holding Arcon in a reinforced shopping bag. I didn't expect to hear from him until we arrived at the observatory. True to form, he surprised me when his thoughts jammed into my head.

"I told you we'd make it through security without a hitch."

I had never heard Arcon gloat before. Why now? Maybe he just couldn't help it.

I whispered to the bag, "How did you know it would be much easier than I expected?" A tall man next to me overheard. He looked at me askance and then glued his eyes forward. People whispering into bags are not uncommon in New York City.

Tapping the man on the shoulder, I opened the bag. "It's a gift for my fiancée," I said with a broad smile.

The man looked into the bag. "Nice," he said. I wanted to jocularly tell him not to report me to a security guard, but I figured he would if I did.

"It was a simple matter of deductive reasoning."

You sound like Sherlock Holmes, I almost replied to Arcon.

The elevator slowed to a halt. My ears popped. The brushed steel doors opened. I gazed out at the empty maze of cordoned rows confronting us. I held my express pass in my other hand. We'd be inside the observatory in no time flat.

Two heavily armed National Guardsmen approached us. "Please get in line," they said to the group. "It may be a while before we can let you in."

"Excuse me, sir," I said to the nearest guard. "Is there some sort of delay?"

"Yes," the guardsman replied with an undertone of sarcasm. "The observatory has been cleared for a foreign dignitary to tour the facility. He's accompanied by his support staff and a security team."

"Any idea how long this fellow and his people will be in there?"

"No idea. Our orders are not to disturb him."

I closed my eyes. Despite what Arcon had explained to me earlier, I was now certain that God was punishing a sinful world.

While we waited in line, I imagined having different conversations with the guards explaining why it was essential for Arcon and me to enter the observatory without delay. All of the imaginary conversations ended in some form of catastrophe. I wondered if Arcon might be able to hypnotize the guards, but I couldn't attract his attention. He was probably calculating the declining odds of saving the Earth as each second passed.

The people around me began to complain about the delay. The line kept growing. Young tourists sat down on their backpacks. I kept glancing at my watch. People read their phones and listened to music with earbuds. After an hour, I sat on the floor cross-legged and thoroughly frustrated. I was past self-concern. I was concerned about the fate of the world.

Another forty-five minutes passed. I was beside myself, but I tried not to show it. T-minus fifteen minutes and counting.

All this time, Arcon didn't make a peep. I knew what he'd say if I asked. *Worrying is a waste of energy.*

Finally, two ticket agents appeared at the counter to collect passes and check ID cards. They examined my shopping bag and smiled at my cover story. We entered the observatory with less than ten minutes left to get the job done.

I could not help examining the giant hexagon mirror hanging from the middle of the ceiling. The multifaceted mirrors reflected kaleidoscopic views of the city. There were enough exhibits in the observatory to keep the casual tourist occupied for hours. Many of the first people to enter with us made a beeline for the telescopes. Signs indicated they were allowed to gape for up to fifteen minutes. If things didn't move along, the gapers weren't going to have to worry about the time limit.

Arcon and I were in a different world. We alone knew that everyone in the observatory and on the planet now existed on borrowed time. To make matters worse, my fiancée was never going to show up.

I wasted no time sitting on a bench in front of one of the floor-to-ceiling reinforced glass windows. Placing the shopping bag next to me, I whispered, "Okay. What's the plan? You owe me an answer after all I've done."

"I have to go outside, jump off the ledge, and plummet until I build up enough kinetic energy to do what I have to do."

"I thought you were spending all this time saving up your energy?"

I am. I need the kinetic energy as a trigger."

"Have you noticed the thick windows we're sitting against?"

"I'm going to reduce myself to sub-atomic particles, slip through the glass, reconstitute myself outside the windows, and let gravity take over."

"Then what?"

"I'm not entirely sure. I've never done this before."

I closed my eyes again. "So, I'm just going to sit here and see what happens?"

"You can try to have some confidence in me. Didn't I get us through security downstairs?"

Now, I understood the reason for Arcon's gloating. It was intended to inspire confidence. I still had my doubts.

I glanced at my watch again. Sixty seconds to Zero Hour.

I heard Arcon say, "Wish me luck."

Thirty seconds later, the observatory and everyone in it blurred.

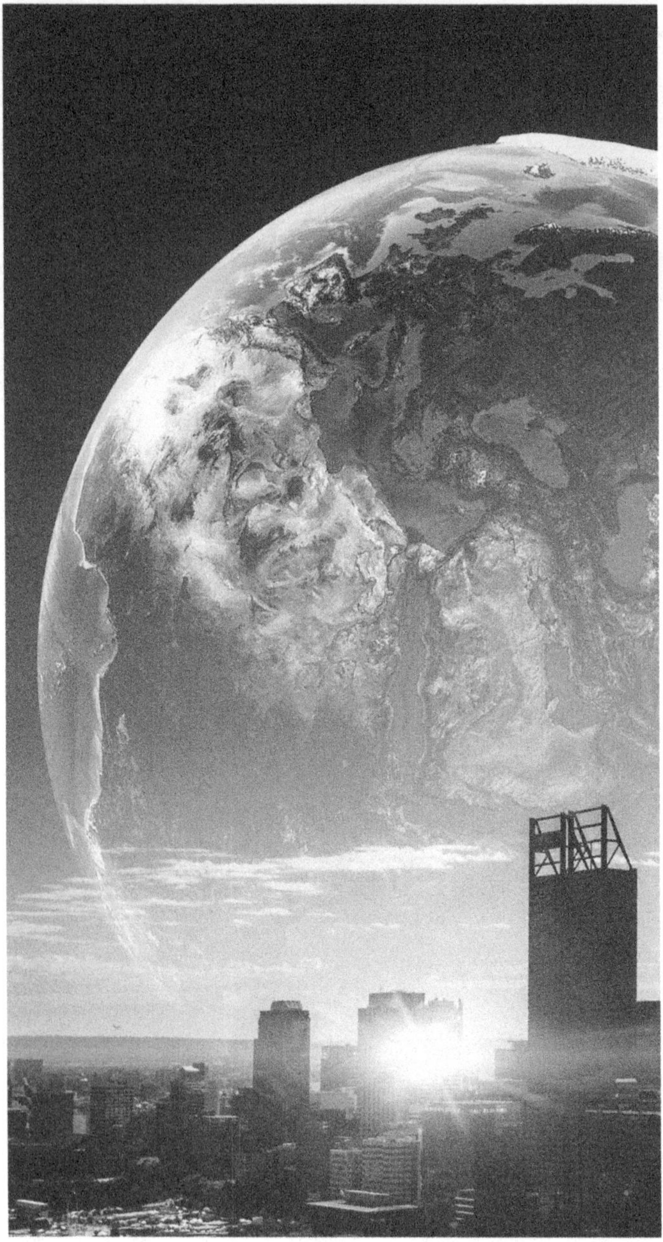

— 7 —
ZERO HOUR

I regained consciousness while sprawled on the grey-tiled floor of the observatory. Sitting up, I held onto the bench to leverage myself off the floor. Checking my watch, I noticed that I had been unconscious for ten minutes. I observed the other visitors in the observatory struggling to awaken and arise from whatever had just happened. My eyes fell on the reinforced paper bag I had used to zoom Arcon up a hundred floors to the observatory. The bag was torn with half of the silver sphere showing. Arcon was no longer disguised as a 19th-Century Art Deco vase.

I panicked. I laid my hand on the sphere. It was cold. I rapped on it lightly. It sounded hollow.

I gazed out through the floor-to-ceiling observatory window hoping to find a glob of energy bouncing around and saving the human race. Instead, the sight of another Earth hanging in the sky greeted me in the distance. Before I had time to react, a voice came through the sound system:

"We are evacuating the building. Please remain

calm. Follow the flashing light indicators on the floor to the nearest exit." I guessed that the light indicators were another safety measure installed in the building after the 9/11 attacks.

I heard moans, groans, chatter, and a single scream from the survivors in the observatory. Young children clung to their parents.

A young man wearing camouflage pants and a Clemson Tigers T-shirt bolted toward the exit. He was met by two National Guardsmen. They hauled the scraggly-haired fellow away and out of sight.

The PA system chimed in again. "Please remain calm and follow the exits out of the building in an orderly fashion. There is no imminent danger. I repeat. There is no imminent danger. You will be subject to arrest and detainment if you cause a disturbance."

And be sure to ignore the extra Earth hanging in the sky, which I added for good measure.

I had to be the only person in the world, besides Arcon, with the vaguest notion of what was going on. Thank heavens for small favors. The blissful ignorance of the situation by everyone but the two of us had avoided pandemonium. The Earth and its inhabitants, by some miracle attributable to Arcon, had escaped a fiery extinction. That was no small favor.

As I was pausing to take a few grateful breaths, the room blurred again. I don't know what happened next. When I regained consciousness, I found myself standing in the same place ten minutes later.

I noticed the people around me become agitated. I looked out of the window again and watched the second Earth disappear. The PA system kicked in to pacify the masses. "Please remain calm and continue to exit the building. Walk. Do not run. Everyone can exit the building safely as long as you follow these directions. I repeat…."

I agreed with the PA system. No one was safe if we started a stampede.

When I finally reached the lobby, an elderly woman fainted right in front of me. At first, I thought I was losing time again. Fortunately for everyone besides the woman, it was only the poor woman fainting.

The repetitive PA system and the constant sight of National Guardsmen and policemen watching us kept everyone under control despite the bizarre circumstances. Walking in a slow line beat by miles the prospect of detention and possibly incarceration.

* * *

Two hours after exiting the observatory, I stood outside One World Trade Center opposite the Oculus transportation hub.

During the interminable process of exiting the building, I entertained a few wild ideas about what might have happened in the observatory. I desperately needed an explanation of what happened. Here I stood, still drawing breath, watching hordes of still-breathing humans exiting the building. Only one entity held the definitive answer: Arcon, assuming he was himself still breathing, or a reasonable facsimile of it.

While walking two blocks to the parking garage where I had stashed my Mazda Miata, I observed an immense traffic jam. Cars and trucks barely moved.

Horns blared. Drivers and pedestrians shouted epithets at one another. I'd have to deal with it, but first, I had to find Arcon. The sidewalks overflowed with people. Intermittent fights broke out.

I had a single goal: Reach my gloriously renewed Miata in one piece.

An attractive, well-dressed woman asked me for a ride. Ordinarily, I would have gladly obliged. Instead, I politely lied and said I didn't own a car. I had my reasons.

Squeezing through the crowded sidewalks using "excuse me" as a mantra, I slithered my way to the building which housed my car. Inside the garage, the ancient fluorescents emitted a sickly yellow light. Cars were lined up to exit the garage. Noxious fumes from the idling cars polluted the air. It seemed New York City had become one long immovable line.

As I approached the car, I noticed a glow in the back seat. Could it be him?

I opened the driver's side door. I sat and slammed it shut. Sitting in the front seat, I kept my eyes pointed straight ahead. I was afraid to turn around. What if it wasn't him? What if he was in some terribly debilitated state?

Reading my thoughts, Arcon said: "I'm perfectly fine, besides being naked."

"Can I look at you?"

"If you must."

I was relieved to hear Arcon's characteristic ornery tone.

I turned to see a pulsing ball of light perched in the back seat. I felt a slight warmth on my face from the naked Arcon. I turned to face the front again. Maybe

Arcon was radioactive. Maybe I'd wake up tomorrow with a bad sunburn.

Instead of voicing my concerns, I said: "I'm glad you made it."

"Me too," Arcon replied.

"Please explain to me what happened, especially the part about the Earth hanging in the sky outside of the observatory window."

"Theoretically, it's simple. Before I tell you, you must agree never to share the information with anyone. Do I have your promise?"

"Yes. I doubt anyone would believe what you're about to tell me anyway."

"Good. Now listen carefully. I'm not going to repeat any of this."

Arcon paused. I assumed he wanted to make sure he had my complete attention.

"First of all, we live in a multiverse. As an example, there are eleven versions of your Earth, each occupying its own dimension. When I reached a sufficient energy quotient during my freefall, I transported your world to the seventh Earth dimension. The seventh Earth dimension is the closest match to your dimension. I had to choose carefully. According to my hypothesis, the seventh Earth dimension, thanks to its compatibility with the third Earth dimension, could accommodate both Earths simultaneously for up to ninety minutes before exploding somewhat like a supernova.

"As it happened, my calculations proved to be dead-on accurate. The two worlds occupied the same dimension for only ten minutes. That's why you saw the second Earth in the sky. During the ten minutes, the pulsar passed harmlessly through an empty vacuum. Then, I transported your world back to the third Earth dimension where it belongs. Aside from seeing two Earth planets in the sky at once, the people in the seventh dimension are no worse for the wear."

That explained the two intervals of lost time. We had saved the Earth. Humanity remained present and accounted for, although a bit confused.

"Unbelievable."

"Entirely. So, don't bother telling anyone."

I inhaled deeply, feeling Arcon's warmth on the back of my neck.

"What do we do now?"

"We'll go back to your friend's house in Florida. Once the hysteria dies down, I'll find an optimal new home for my naked body. I can't be seen walking around like this and my energy tends to dissipate without proper coverage."

"That sounds relatively simple, compared to saving the world."

"Yes, it's the easy part."

I closed my eyes. I didn't want to hear about the hard part. I wanted to savor our victory, at least until we were safe and sound in the comfy beach house. Arcon, in his tenacious efficiency, would have none of it.

"With the pulsar passing close by, I've been able to determine the coordinates of the planet where the control signal originated. Armed with this information, my government will deal with the perpetrators. There's only one problem. I have to deliver the coordinates back to them."

"And you're telling me this why?"

"Naturally, I'll need your help."

PART 2
CATACLYSM
END OF WORLDS

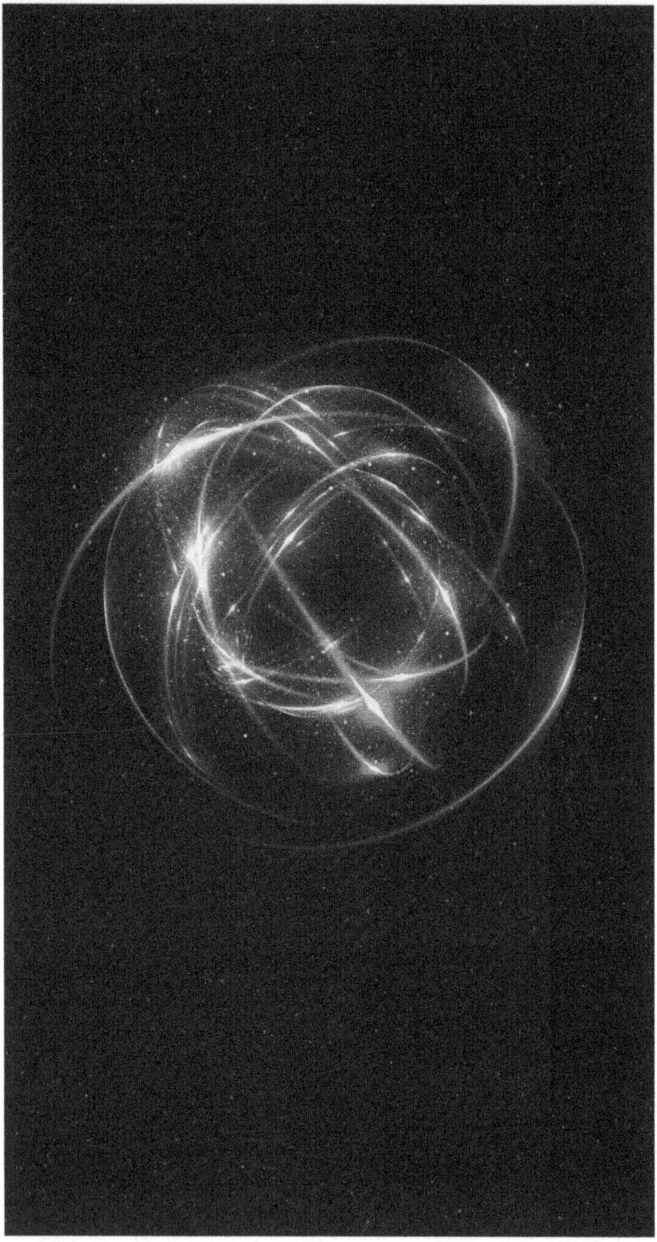

— 8 —
THE BODY

I let the fingers of the moonlit surf play over my bare feet. By my side, Arcon bumbled along on the wet sand, studiously avoiding the tendrils of saltwater rushing up on the desolate beach. The cool breeze on this calm night was not unlike the one when I had first met Arcon. I should say "stumbled upon" Arcon, as he lay in the shallow water encased in a silver sphere. We collided slightly more than a month ago, but the dizzying events that occurred within the first three days of our acquaintance have made that fateful meeting seem like a distant memory. Things have changed in our time together. Some of them are big. Some of them are small.

For one, Arcon has shed his silver sphere's outer covering. He is naked; a sputtering energy ball, dancing back and forth in the surf at knee level, muttering to himself in a language I don't understand. For the past week, my little companion has been more irritable than his generally out-of-sorts self. Arcon tends to be impatient, especially when he's in a bad mood. Challenging him at these sensitive junctures is a bad idea, but I couldn't bear his demeanor any longer. Just as I was about to take a stab at asking my colleague from the other side of the Milky Way what was bothering him, I noticed something partially beached in the surf about a hundred yards ahead of us.

As we came to within ten yards of it, I noticed long red hair swirling in the water in the reflected light of the full moon.

"My God, it's a person," I said to Arcon.

I splashed through the water, drenching myself in the process, only to find an inert body lying face down in the water. I grabbed the body by both arms and struggled to turn the waterlogged thing right side up. She was a woman, and a beautiful one at that, even in her wrinkled condition. Running in the water and the shock of seeing the body up close and personal made my pulse thud loudly in my ears. Unlike the heroes and heroines of my novels, I had never been in a situation like this before. My heart went out to the poor creature looking blankly up at me.

Arcon had followed me in a higher orbit on the beach to prevent excessive fizzling and possible damage to his circuitry. He drew closer as I gawked at the freckled face of a young woman with the sensuous features of a Rodin sculpture. She looked to be about five foot ten or eleven inches tall with an athletic figure. I picked her up out of the water and listened for signs of breathing. None. I carefully placed her down on the sand and searched for a pulse. Nothing. What a waste of a young life.

I turned to Arcon. He floated nearby me, a sparkling yellow energy ball, percolating about a foot above the sand. I retrieved my phone from my pocket to call 911. Luckily, it hadn't expired in all the watery chaos.

"Wait!" I heard Arcon blast inside my head. I froze in mid-call. "What?"

"Before we do anything hasty, let's think about this."

"What is there to think about? We have to notify the authorities. Maybe on your side of the galaxy you get to play it by ear. We don't do that here."

"Give me a few minutes to inhabit the body and collect some information. A few extra minutes won't hurt."

"The more we know about this person, the more prominent we'll become in a murder investigation."

"Can you stop thinking like a mystery writer for a few minutes? Whatever I learn, we'll keep to ourselves."

I knew if I didn't press the call button, I'd be asking for trouble.

As I watched Arcon funnel into the woman's dead body, I kept asking myself: *Why aren't you making the call?*

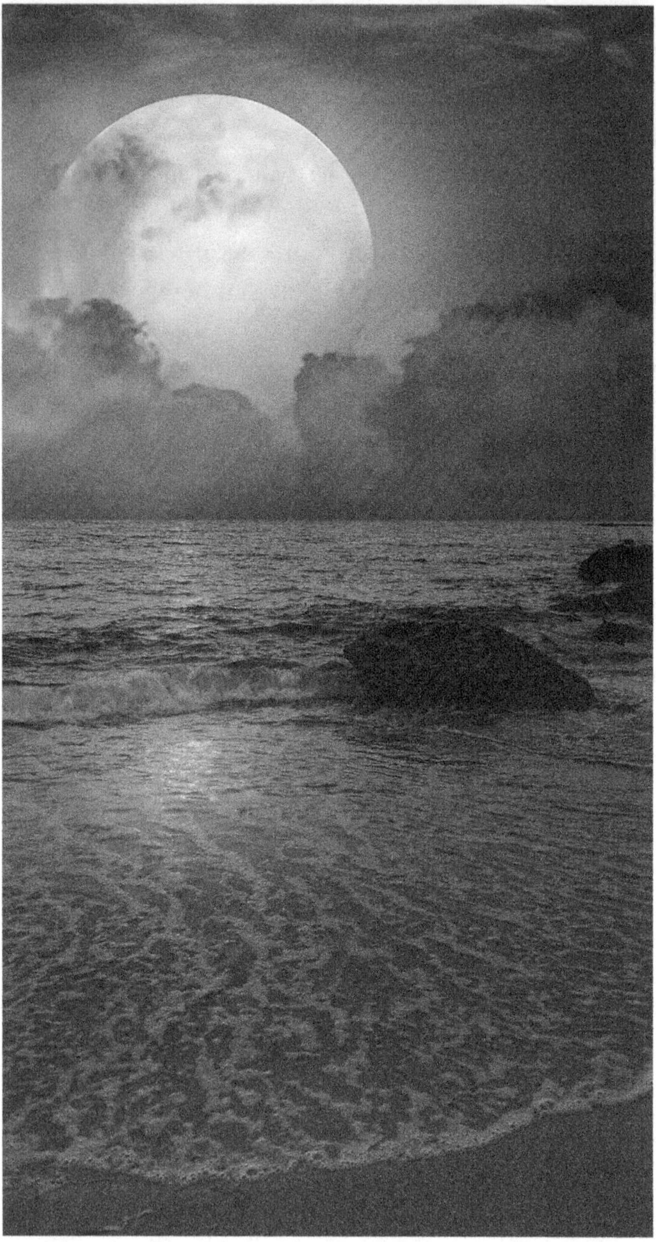

— 9 —
THE PROPOSAL

Excuse me. In all of the excitement, I've forgotten to introduce myself properly. My name is Jacob Casell. I'm a novelist by trade. In the last month, after saving the world, thanks mostly to Arcon, I finally finished my latest novel. I'm relieved that my agent and my editor liked the manuscript. And, of course, I'm relieved that our world wasn't obliterated by a remote-controlled pulsar directed at us by a vicious and unscrupulous alien race. We managed to defuse the situation in three days. That turned out to be a good thing because we only had three days to get the job done.

As I watched Arcon rematerialize out of the dead woman's body, I had the terrible feeling that the month of tranquility we had enjoyed after the near-extinction of the human race was ending. Arcon hovered a few feet above the body making crackling noises. I knew those noises meant that Arcon was deep in thought. I also had a good idea of what he was thinking. I'm not clairvoyant by any stretch of the imagination, but I didn't have to be Einstein to figure out what was burbling about in Arcon's super-evolved artificial intelligence.

I stood there, phone in hand, bathed by the beachy midnight breeze, a full moon as my only witness, waiting for Arcon to make his report. I didn't have to wait long.

"Her name was Amy Goodwin," Arcon began. "Twenty-six years old, parents dead, and no siblings. She had a graduate degree in aerospace engineering and a master's degree in astronomy. I'm thinking someone up there likes us."

"Do you really want to bring a Supreme Being into this?"

"I'm saying it's plausible."

"I know where you're going with this."

"No, you don't!"

"Okay. Where are we going?"

"I believe it's not wise to look a gift horse in the mouth."

"You're using homey aphorisms now?"

Arcon, in his typical fashion, completely ignored my complaint when it didn't suit his purposes.

I tucked away my iPhone. No sense in exposing it to the salt air while Arcon tried to convince me to risk a lengthy jail sentence. A breeze fluttered in from the ocean. It felt wet and chilly—odd for the beginning of summer on a nearly deserted stretch of sand in Daytona Beach, Florida.

I tried to prepare myself for what Arcon had to say next. Then, I remembered it was impossible to prepare myself at a pregnant interval like this with Arcon involved.

"I want to use this woman's body for our next mission," Arcon said bluntly.

I had imagined Arcon seriously considering the idea after he conveyed his findings to me. I had been clinging to a slender hope that I was wrong.

"You intend to re-animate the body and use it as a cloak for whatever we do next?"

"It won't be just a cloak. With this woman's credentials—"

"Wait," I interrupted. "She had a name and she was a person. Let's not forget that."

"I understand that we're crossing some lines here—"

"Do we have to save the world again? Is that what you're telling me?"

'If you will STOP interrupting me and STOP jumping to conclusions, I will explain, but only once."

"I know, because we're on a tight deadline, just like before."

"Yes, Jacob, but it's not only your world that is threatened. At the beginning of the week, our top scientists advised me at least four worlds, including this one, are in grave danger."

"No wonder you've been in such a foul mood."

Something wasn't tracking. "Wait a minute. If you can receive messages from Aneleya, why can't you send them?"

"The Aneleyan scientists have the equipment to send messages through tiny wormholes they create specifically for long-distance communication. A message that would normally take centuries to transmit can be sent and received in a matter of hours. Unfortunately, I don't have the equipment my colleagues have. I can, however, send a signal powerful enough to reach Aneleya in hours if I can boost it. I believe I've found a way to transmit the coordinates of the Krondorian home world back to the Aneleyan scientists on my world."

"Tell me again about the Krondorians. You didn't have time to give me the full story when they attacked last month."

"We still don't have time for the full story."

"I'll settle for a synopsis."

"The Krondorians are a race of ruthless troublemakers. With their ingenious stealth technology, they've hidden from our purview for centuries. When the pulsar almost hit the Earth, I picked up the coordinates of Krondor hidden in the fireball's programming."

I didn't need any reminders of how close our world had come to a bitter end. Arcon had jumped off the top of the One World Trade Center building to generate enough kinetic energy to combine with his prodigious internal energy to pull the Earth out of its orbit to safety. Until that moment, I hadn't realized that besides his highly evolved artificial intelligence, inside Arcon's core rested the power of a one-megaton hydrogen bomb. I'd been so wrapped up in outlining an upcoming novel that I almost forgot Arcon requested my help to send the coordinates back to Aneleya.

"So, you intend to create a wormhole to send the message?"

"I intend to do it safely. Creating even a tiny wormhole close to the Earth would be catastrophic. I plan to use the Hubble Telescope in phase one of the project to boost the signal.

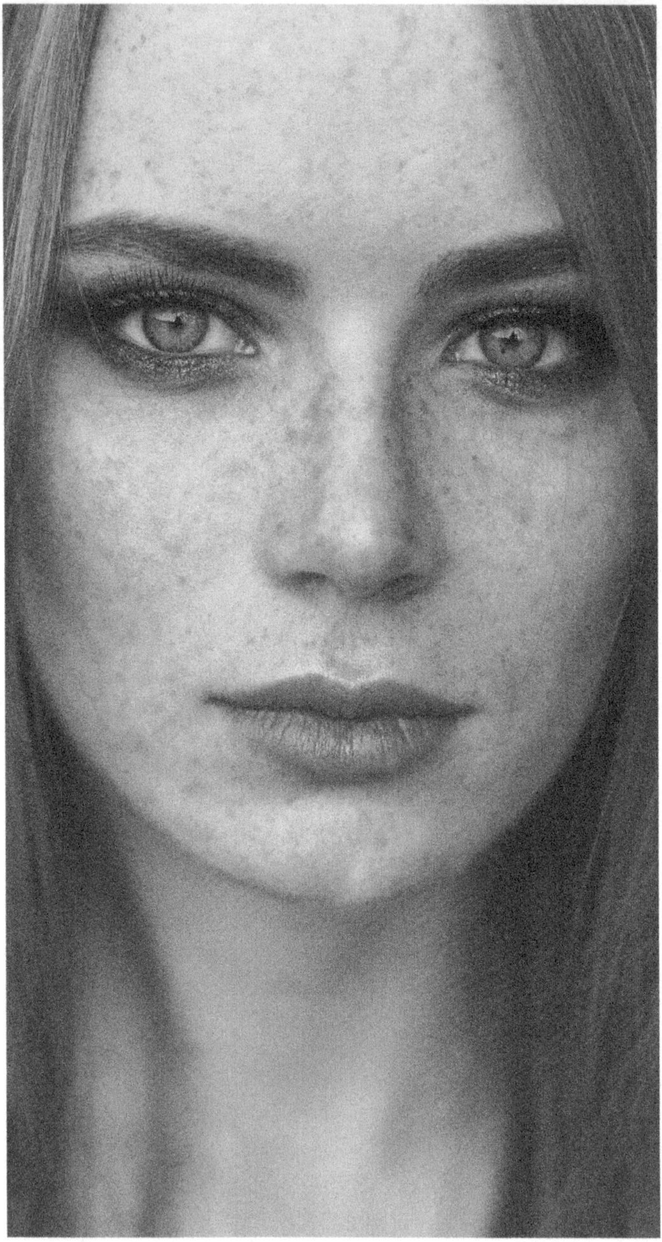

— 10 —
AMY

How could I not have guessed that Arcon intended to use the Hubble Telescope to send his message? Answer: very easily. And, it didn't sound simple to me.

"If my calculations are correct," Arcon explained, "I can bounce a message off the Hubble's telescopic mirrors to exponentially upgrade it to light speed and simultaneously program it. After the message travels a safe distance from your solar system, it will automatically generate a tiny wormhole to reach Aneleya in a few hours. It's quite a simple matter. The simple solution is often overlooked. That's why it took me a month to see it."

Oh, me of little faith. How could I forget? What appears simple to Arcon seems impossible to me. I couldn't wait to see how my intergalactic friend intended to pull this one off.

We sat in my friend Jeffrey's modern glass and brushed steel kitchen. I watched Arcon re-enter Amy's body. After a few minutes, Arcon's brilliant colors no longer reflected off the pale-yellow walls. He was "in." Instead of our normal telepathic mode of communication,

Arcon spoke to me the old-fashioned way in Amy's voice. To say we were speaking is a big stretch. Amy was uttering gibberish. She was learning how to speak all over again. I was helping her with certain words while I imagined Arcon was working behind the scenes to speed up the learning process. After several exhausting hours, I was speaking to a twenty-six-year-old woman with the vocabulary of a three-year-old.

Despite Amy's limited vocabulary and grasp of abstract concepts, I decided it was time to ask a few preliminary questions. I had already introduced myself to her, and I sensed she felt comfortable in my presence. After I asked my first question, Amy responded in a more advanced manner than a typical three-year-old.

Arcon's work behind the scenes appeared to be paying off. At first, we had struggled to communicate, almost like writing a novel. The first few chapters, for me at least, are like cutting through the underbrush of an Amazon rainforest with a dull machété. After the first few chapters, the work tends to flow. Similarly, Amy's communication skills were developing rapidly.

"How did I get here?" Amy asked.

I detected a high degree of intelligence and a good deal of suspicion lurking behind her words.

"Well, that's a good question," I stammered. "You are here under some very unusual circumstances."

"Where am I?"

Amy stared at me intently. I wondered if Arcon was behind those eyes, or Amy, or both of them. Whoever was in there seemed to be regaining their faculties and their personality with each breath.

"You are in a beach house owned by my good friend

Jeffrey Mortenson. He was a journalist until he made the cruel discovery that journalism wasn't going to support his expensive, libertine lifestyle. I tried to tell him, but he wouldn't listen. Now, he's gone back to work for his father. He will be spending months away in New York and London on business. He's recently appointed me to the official position of 'house sitter.' In this capacity, my job is to look after the house in Jeffrey's absence which works out beautifully for me. The salt air and the lack of noisy neighbors help me to write when I'm not saving the world."

"What's the bit about saving the world? It sounds grandiose. Do you have mental problems? Are you seeing a psychiatrist?"

I wasn't sure if it was Amy talking or Arcon criticizing my lack of word economy. In my defense, I was trying to lay some subliminal groundwork for the hard-to-believe destination our discussion was headed for.

"I was joking," of course. *I wasn't.* "I'd like to ask you a few more questions before we get into the whys and the wherefores of your presence here. Do you mind?"

"Make them quick. I'll lose patience if we don't get into the 'whys and wherefores' soon."

"Fair enough. What is the last thing you remember?"

"I remember passing out in the master bedroom of my boyfriend's yacht. We were on vacation."

"Are you in the habit of passing out?"

"No."

"Were you taking drugs or drinking?"

"No."

"You just passed out for no reason?"

"Yes."

"Were you arguing with your boyfriend?"

"Yes."

I turned to Arcon, as if to say, I told you we should have called the police. Arcon, of course, wasn't there to answer or ignore me entirely.

"Enough of your questions. I won't answer another one of yours until you answer mine."

At this point, I needed to confer with Arcon. I didn't know if I could reach him in his new surroundings. What if the density of Amy's body made telepathic communication impossible?

"I'm going to speak to someone besides you," I said to Amy. "I know it will seem strange, but I assure you it's for your own good."

"That's it. I'm out of here."

Amy tried to move. She found that she couldn't.

"Did you drug me with a paralytic?"

"Did you see me give you any drugs?"

"Why can't I move?"

I couldn't answer the question. I decided not to try.

"Are you in there?" I asked Arcon.

"Where else would I be," Arcon told me telepathically. "I've had to restrain this poor woman thanks to your inept handling of the situation."

It was him. No doubt. I took the rebuke gracefully. This was no time to start an argument.

"I'm not sure how to proceed. Can you talk to her?"

"Absolutely not. It would be too disturbing, especially now when Amy is regaining her senses."

"Who are you talking to?" Amy stared at me wide-eyed and with an expression of deepening horror.

"I promise you that I'm not a crazed serial killer. There is an explanation for all of this."

"Then start explaining, and it better be good."

"I found you floating face up in the water," I lied. "Your wet suit must have kept you from drowning. I performed CPR. You had a strong pulse, but you were unconscious."

"My boyfriend must have drugged me and thrown me overboard. I think he tried to kill me when I found out what he's been doing. He probably put me in a wet suit to make it look like an accidental drowning. Where is your phone? I'm calling the police as soon as these drugs wear off."

A jolt of anxiety shot through my body. "I'm afraid we're way past calling the police," I said.

A mixture of fear and disbelief registered in Amy's eyes like the dark storm clouds I had seen at times rolling in from the ocean.

"Have you kidnapped me?"

"Of course not," I put in immediately. *It's much worse,* I told myself.

The moment of truth had arrived. I couldn't keep dancing around it. I had succeeded in scaring the life out of a newly re-animated person. I had nothing left to lose and neither did Amy.

"I don't think there's any way to sugarcoat this," I began and drew in a lungful of oxygen. "I have to tell you…"

"What?" she snapped.

"You died and you've been resurrected."

"You mean by CPR."

"No. I mean you were stone-cold dead and now you're alive."

She drew in a breath sharply. Arcon must have decided to release her because Amy rose unsteadily from her chair. She hadn't regained her reflexes and balance yet. She stumbled in a failed attempt to reach the kitchen door. I quickly put my arms around her waist to keep her from falling flat on her face. Amy struggled to free herself from my embrace.

"This is going superbly," I heard Arcon scoff inside my head.

"Calm down," I said to Amy. "We aren't going to harm you."

"We? You're psychotic. Split personality. I knew it."

"Amy. Relax. Just sit. Everything will be fine. Let me explain."

I managed to guide Amy back to her chair. I noticed her make a furtive glance at the kitchen door. "I know what I'm about to say may add to your psychosis theory, but please, hear me out. Can you do that?"

Amy stared at me. If her eyes were lasers, I'd be hamburger meat.

"Relax. Listen. Okay?"

"How am I supposed to relax? You're talking to someone who isn't here."

"You are in no danger. There is a logical explanation for all of this. Well, it's not entirely logical, but it's the truth. Here goes. I've been working with a highly evolved artificial intelligence to save our planet."

"Oh, great," I heard Arcon say telepathically.

Amy grabbed the brushed steel arms of her chair.

"I know it sounds crazy. I know I sound like a raving

lunatic. The truth is you are sitting here today, looking at me like you'd love to smash my face in, thanks only to this super intelligent being."

"You mean I died and this thing brought me back to life."

"Yes, and by the way, he doesn't like to be called a 'thing.'"

Amy's arms tensed. I was sure she was about to attack me with the rage of a caged lioness. I held up my hand. "Wait. Let me prove to you that I'm not psychotic."

"Speak to her," I implored Arcon.

Thirty endless seconds passed. Only the sound of waves lapping against the shoreline outside the panoramic kitchen window filled the heavy silence. Then, I heard the greeting inside my head.

"Hello, Amy. My name is Arcon."

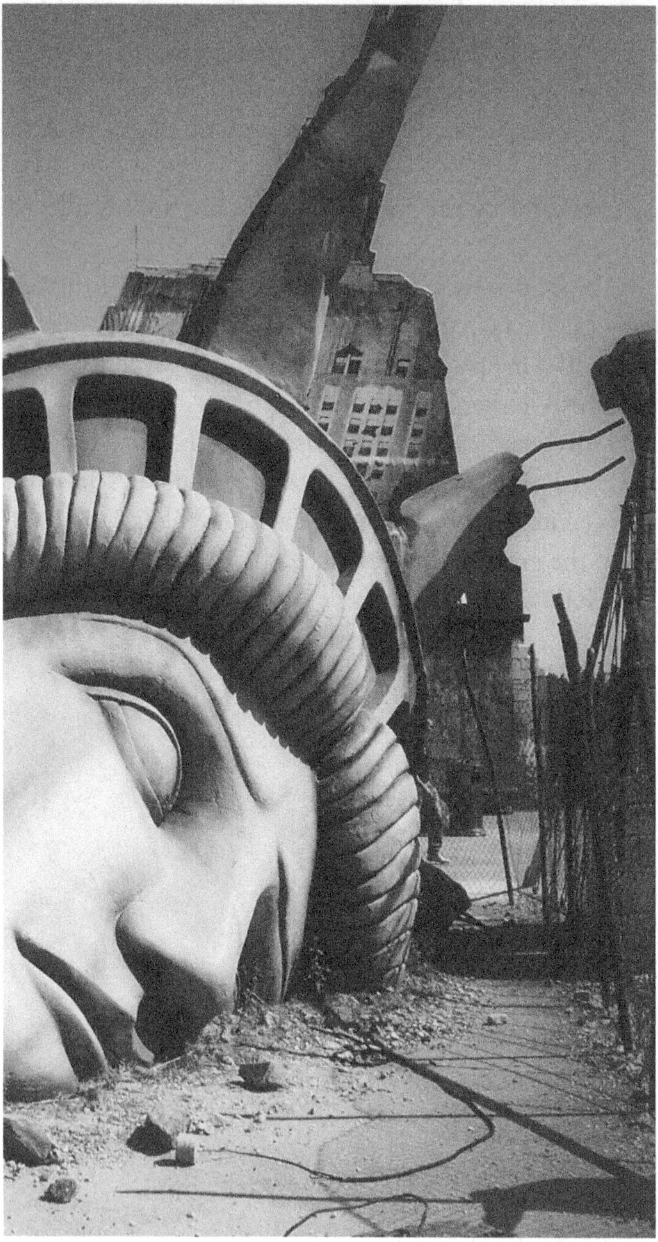

—11—
BREAKING NEWS

Amy's body convulsed. I thought she was having an epileptic episode. Her eyes crossed. I thought: *What have I done?*

"Astronautically speaking," Arcon answered. "You screwed the pooch."

I ignored the insult. "I think she'll adjust to you."

"We'll just have to wait and see," Arcon said in a know-it-all Oliver Hardy tone.

I sat in my acrylic and brushed steel chair willing Amy to come around. Only the sounds of the ocean waves eating the beach away accompanied my feelings of dread.

Several minutes passed. I felt my heart rate increase. Finally, to my great relief and deep gratitude, Amy came back to consciousness, if there is such a thing for someone technically dead.

Amy broke the silence with a torrent of gibberish. I feared we'd have to start again from scratch to bring Amy back to the bright, twenty-six-year-old woman we had come to briefly know.

I watched and listened to Amy coming back to herself as a mature woman.

"What just happened?" she said. "Did I black out?"

How do I answer the question without setting off another chain reaction?

"You lost some time," I tried to assure her. "Do you recall what we were talking about?"

Amy grew silent. She withdrew into herself, remembering, gathering her thoughts, I guessed.

"Yes. I remember now. Someone talked to me. Inside my head. I remember everything up to that moment."

"It was an attempt to prove to you that I'm not schizophrenic," I said, as calmly as is humanly possible.

Amy stared at me again with those laser-like eyes, only this time they were amped up to EMP lasers.

Then she broke out into hysterical laughter.

"This is nuts," she said.

I agreed with her.

Amy began to sob. "Why am I laughing?"

I took her hand. "It's okay."

She withdrew her hand quickly. "Did I say you could touch me?"

"I suppose not. It was just a reflex."

She looked at me with searching eyes. "I guess you aren't a bad person."

"Thank you. We try our best."

"You and yourself, or you and someone else."

"Me and someone else."

"Is he the one that spoke to me?"

"Yes."

Amy inhaled deeply. She gazed out of the kitchen window, no doubt continuing to gather herself and wishing she were somewhere else.

"All right. I'm ready to hear the whole story. From both of you. Tell it to me straight."

Arcon and I took turns explaining to Amy how we had saved the world. We gave her the no-fills version—Edward R. Murrow style.

When we finished our story-telling, a bevy of seabirds swooped in on the sunset tide. Their squawking provided a surreal backdrop to the scene of Amy and me facing one another across a glass and brass table reflecting the gleam of the fading sunlight. Amy sat there, wide-eyed, attempting to absorb our admittedly fantastic tale. I could almost hear her mind grinding like a miller's wheel against golden rods of wheat. Finally, she looked at me, her brow wrinkled with concern.

"What is this new threat we're facing?"

I liked her use of the word "we." "Since I'm not entirely clear on the subject, I'll let Arcon do the honors."

Arcon spoke telepathically to both of us. Our team was on the verge of repopulating to three.

"The Krondorians are a violent and impatient race. After Jacob and I defeated their plan to colonize Mars, they sent probes to four distant planets to determine their suitability for habitation. With their planet grossly overpopulated, they are desperate to find a new home world and neighboring worlds to conquer. Their colony planets are too small to absorb the population overflow. When you combine this desperation with their unscrupulous and vicious nature, the Krondorians are potentially a threat to all intelligent life in our galaxy."

"And they've hidden from you all this time?"

"Their technology is highly advanced. Their stealth

technology has been impenetrable until now, and only because the pulsar passed close by. We can pick up snippets of their communications, but not their source. They can randomize and project an infinite array of decoy signals. Until this latest incident, as far as we knew, Krondor could have been located anywhere in this galaxy."

"Why do you need me?"

"We're going to send a message back to the scientists on Aneleya, my home world. Once my people identify the location of Krondor, they can destroy it."

I was beginning to feel like my "Use By" date had expired. I wondered if Arcon required my services any longer with Amy now on the scene.

"To answer your question," I jumped in, "we want to send the message via the Hubble Space Telescope. We can sign up to take a tour of the Goddard Space Flight Center where the Hubble Telescope is housed. With your impressive credentials, you can apply for a job at the center. As an official applicant, you can ask for a special, behind-the-scenes guided tour, including the Hubble Control Room where the general public is not allowed to go."

Amy thought some more. Who wouldn't under the bizarre circumstances? Five tense minutes passed. The whole mission now depended on Amy's cooperation.

"What's in it for me?"

"The possibility of a great new job and the chance to celebrate your twenty-seventh birthday," I said.

Amy smiled. "Well, at least you have a sense of humor."

She thought about our proposition some more.

Arcon and I awaited her answer. I was tempted to say something like, *"You've already died once. What have you got to lose?"* I'm sure Arcon breathed a mental sigh of relief when I refrained.

"I'd love to work at the Goddard Space Flight Center. It's always been a dream of mine. If I can help to save the world at the same time, I'm in. What's the timetable?"

"We'll start tomorrow," Arcon said. "I estimate we have four, maybe five days to get the job done. It's hard to calculate an exact time because the destroyer is a huge ship. The mass will slow it down."

"You didn't mention a destroyer," I said, preparing for the worst.

Arcon didn't disappoint. "Early this morning, I learned what we feared the most: the Krondorians have dispatched a destroyer vessel to finish what they started. Your people have a saying for it: 'If you want to be sure to get the job done, do it yourself.' The ship is comparable in size and technology to your naval Zumwalt-class destroyer. It is a multi-mission stealth warship with a focus on land attacks. Among its arsenal of weaponry, it has a super laser. The Krondorian crew intends to fire a beam into Earth's upper atmosphere. It will generate massive worldwide hurricanes and tornadoes that will ultimately wipe out the human race."

"What do we do about the ship?" I wanted to know.

"Good question," Arcon replied.

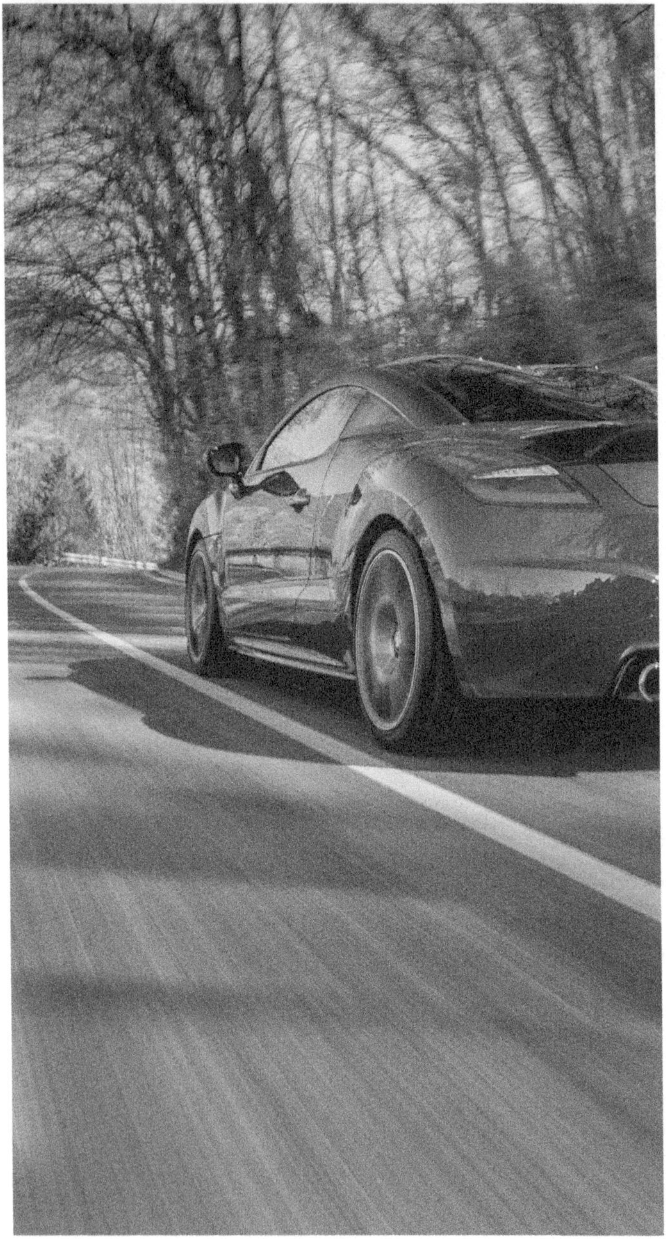

—12—
A LITTLE CONVERSATION

We decided to drive my resurrected 2012 Mazda Miata to the Goddard Space Flight Center in Greenbelt, Maryland. Like Amy, Arcon had restored my decrepit relic of a car to its former glory. Flying would have been faster, but we couldn't risk setting off the TSA's screening equipment with Amy's unusual energy signature.

The long journey gave me a chance to dig a little deeper into Amy's past. I was especially interested in the events leading up to Amy's unfortunate and premature demise. There was only one problem. I didn't want Arcon to eavesdrop on the conversation. I wanted the conversation to be only between me and Amy.

"Can you take a short nap?" I asked Arcon.

"If I hibernate, Amy will also," came the response.

"Well, do you have a set of earplugs?"

A copious silence ensued. In my eagerness to speak with Amy privately, I had forgotten that Arcon wasn't programmed to laugh. He always had more important priorities to focus on.

Then, Amy laughed. It was a delayed reaction, but I

didn't care. I noticed that her face seemed to glow with her laughter. Her teeth were white and straight. Glancing at me, she wrinkled her nose. I swear I saw light beaming from her eyes before she turned again to look at the farmlands rushing by outside of the car window.

The more Arcon infused life energy into her depleted body, the more beautiful Amy became. She was beginning to relax and feel at home in her new surroundings, despite their extreme weirdness. Amy was beginning to trust that Arcon and I meant her no harm, and maybe, just maybe, we had involved her in something good. She had already emailed her application to the Goddard Center which I felt was a big step in the right direction for her and the team. Were we a team? Not exactly, but we were getting there.

"Do you mind if I ask you a few questions about your background?"

She turned back towards me with a curious facial expression. "Go on."

"Can you tell me about your parents and where you grew up?"

"I grew up on a small thoroughbred horse breeding farm in Versailles, Kentucky. I loved the lifestyle, the horses, and of course my parents. My father and mother owned the farm. My father wore several hats in sales and administration to keep the farm above water. My mother was a high school teacher. She loved books. She instilled that love in me."

I noticed Amy's bright facial expression darken.

"When I was seven, my parents went out on their regular Saturday night date. They liked a French restaurant in town. On their way home, a drunk driver ran a stop sign and crashed into the driver's side door. My father died instantly. My mother died of her injuries a few days later. My aunt raised me after that. She died of cancer when I was nineteen."

"I'm so sorry to hear that. You've been on your own for a while, then."

"I've managed. A full college scholarship to Columbia in New York helped. Funding was scarce when I applied to graduate school. I thought I'd have to compromise and go to a mediocre school at night after working during the day. Then, I met Jack in the Columbia University Library. We were studying for our senior year final exams. I was feeling somewhat desperate with no solid path to graduate school in sight. I was attracted by Jack's enthusiasm and confidence. He had this fearless kind of vibe. I sensed that he had money too."

Amy looked straight ahead at the oncoming traffic. "Enough about me. Why don't you tell me about yourself, mystery man?"

"Do you find me mysterious, aside from the fact that I write mystery novels?"

"Don't answer a question with a question. I know very little about you, aside from the fact that you like to hide behind your wit."

Busted. Nowhere to run. Regardless, I was enjoying our little talk. I liked the way Amy came right out and said what was on her mind. I decided to follow her lead.

"I'll give you the basics. I'm thirty-six. I've never been married. My parents are academics. My father is an English professor at New York University. My mother does medical research. I grew up in a household where feelings were hardly ever discussed. On the bright side, I grew up in a stable environment. On the dark side, it was emotionally barren. I have two brothers, both teachers, and we aren't close. I speak to my parents once every six months to keep our life stories up to date and to make sure they're in good health. That's the extent of my connection with them. I started writing stories when I was twelve and never stopped. Oh, and I'm a Sagittarius with Leo rising and my moon is in Aries. I'm a triple fire sign which makes me enthusiastic and utterly wild."

"What about your relationships outside of your family?"

"Can I take the fifth on that one?"

She looked at me, holding back a smile. "No."

"Let's see. I have a few guy friends. I've told you a bit about my friend, Jeffrey. As far as romantic relationships with women, there have been many, but I'm not exactly Zorba the Greek. Most of the relationships have been short-lived. It might be from a blockage of emotional current on my side of the equation. Hmmm. I've never thought of it like that before."

"You're analyzing it distantly. Do you realize that?"

"What's your sun sign?" I said, deliberately changing the subject.

"Oh, please."

"Tell me."

"Aquarius, if you must know."

"Good for you. I rarely meet Aquarians. It's a very special sign."

"I'll take your word for it."

"Tell me more about this Jack fellow."

"I'd rather not."

"I'll settle for the abridged version."

Amy sighed heavily. "His name is Jack Markham. We started dating, and one thing led to another. The relationship got serious. Jack insisted on paying my graduate school tuition. All three years of it. I felt very uncomfortable about it, but I needed the money. I put my feelings aside. When I asked him how he made so much money, he always had the same answer: 'Honey, I'm an investment banker. Successful people in my profession make shitloads of money.' I let his explanation ride. I didn't want to rock the boat. When I told Jack I wanted to go to graduate school at Cornell University in upstate New York, he convinced me to stay at Columbia near him. As it turned out, we didn't see much of each other. He traveled on business a lot. I was busy with my studies."

Amy turned to watch the lonely highway signs flash by.

"When I finished graduate school, we took a vacation in Miami where Jack kept his yacht. We sailed up the coast. Jack worked intermittently on the boat. When we moored off Daytona Beach, Jack went scuba diving. He left his computer on, and I couldn't resist taking a look at what he was doing. One of his files told me the whole story."

By her tone and stiff-elbowed posture, I knew that Amy's recollections were upsetting her. I thought a nice break was in order.

"Excuse me for interrupting. Your story is extremely interesting. I want to hear more, but are you hungry?"

"Famished."

"I've been seeing signs for a tempting bed and breakfast at the next exit. Does that sound appetizing?"

"Do we have to stop?" Arcon broke in. "Can't you wait for dinner?"

"We've been on the road for eighteen hours straight!" I exclaimed. "We've only stopped for gas and bathroom breaks at rest stops on the highway. You've only allowed us to consume water and energy drinks. God forbid someone might have to take a long dump."

As I uttered these words, we passed the border into North Carolina.

"You can eat when we reach our destination," Arcon retorted. "We have at most sixty hours to send the message and deal with the Krondorian destroyer. We're living on borrowed time, and all you can think of is your belly."

"Humans have to eat. It's an unavoidable fact of life. We won't be of any use if we starve."

"Let's eat," Amy said resolutely. "I don't care what Arcon says."

"Careful not to anger him," I chided Amy. "Arcon has the potential energy of a one-megaton bomb coursing inside him."

Looking back at me, she tilted her head. I liked the way Amy could be a mature woman one moment, and a curious child the next.

"How can you pack that much energy inside someone the size of a basketball?"

"You'll have to ask the Aneleyans. I doubt Arcon will have the time or the inclination to explain the matter."

"Let's not make this refueling stop any longer than it has to be," Arcon said without hiding his exasperation.

I exited the highway.

"Why must I rely on human beings?" I heard Arcon grumble.

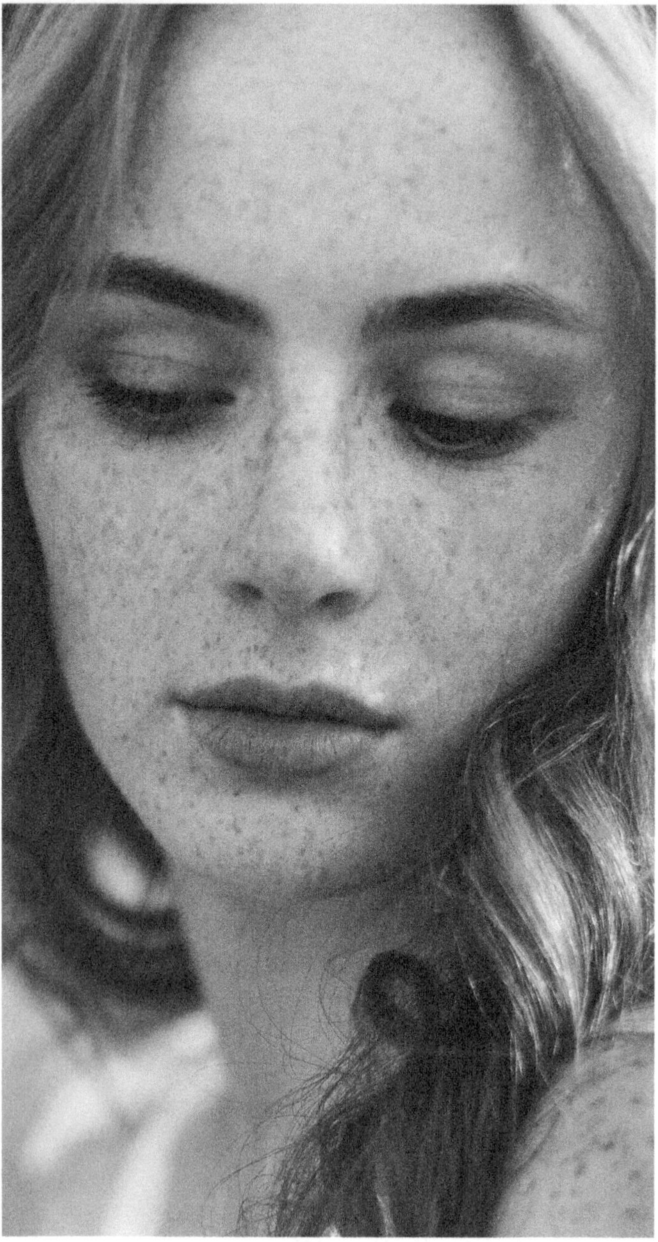

— 13 —
AMY'S TALE

We sat at a booth with red vinyl seats. The booths circled a fully stocked bar lit along the base with attending copper studded stools. A disheveled old man wearing a beat-up shirt and a three-day beard sat at one end of the bar nursing a drink. A young couple arguing sat two booths away from us. I saw a stage in the back of the room suggesting the place rocked at night. The red and white checkered table cloths were possibly meant to suggest the Red Foxx Inn was "the real thing." I hoped so. The windows looked out on the parking lot. I uttered a silent prayer requesting that the food be better than the stereotypical rustic décor.

Truth be told, Amy and I weren't going to complain if the food was as ordinary as the surroundings. It turned out that Amy and I liked breakfast better than lunch as a general rule. Fortunately, the Red Foxx Inn served breakfast 24/7. I thought it was a good idea, given how the schedules of tourists and truckers get jumbled while traveling.

"I admire the temerity of the owner to spell fox with a double x. It certainly sets this place apart from the crowd," I offered tongue-in-cheek as we examined the menus.

"It worked on you, didn't it?" Amy said from behind the beige menu with a devilish red fox grinning in the center top.

"Touché. What are you having?"

Amy ordered scrambled eggs with a double order of bacon and a whole wheat bagel. I ordered buttermilk pancakes with bacon and a side of yogurt. A pleasant waitress kept our coffee cups filled to the brim. We got the deluxe treatment since we were the only ones eating besides the yammering couple.

While we waited for the food, it seemed Arcon had resigned himself to silence. I imagined him working out cosmic equations to take his mind off the irritation he must have felt over our pit stop for brunch.

"So, why don't you continue with your story before the food arrives and we lose interest in anything other than the sublime pleasure of eating a fattening breakfast in the calm before an alien invasion?"

Amy almost spit out a mouthful of coffee. She wagged a finger at me. "I just burned my tongue. Keep your warped jokes to yourself while I'm drinking hot coffee."

"Sorry. Please continue your story."

"Consider this an official warning. I will not tolerate any more twisted humor."

"I will have to formulate my jokes more carefully, then."

She playfully stuck her tongue out at me. I sensed

that telling the unabridged version of her story helped to lighten Amy's burden.

"As I was saying before the hunger cramps interrupted, Jack went scuba diving. He was always evasive when I asked him about his business. When I went down to the cabin for more sunscreen, I noticed he had left his computer on. I couldn't resist going through his emails. I found out that Jack and his friends from the Wharton School of Business were involved in a scheme to manipulate foreign currencies. They were lawyers, accountants, and investment bankers like Jack. All of them were connected to big companies with trading clout.

"The friends set up secret meetings around the world where they could meet in private. They concealed the meetings by combining them with trips to cultivate new business for their firms. They used fake passports and driver's licenses to cover the secret meetings. They planned their trading strategies in the meetings. When each firm bought or sold Pounds, Marks, Yen, or any currency, each of the conspirators profited individually. The trades were big enough to move the market. With advanced knowledge of what was going to happen, the group made money for their firms and themselves.

"Jack must have been the clan's secretary because he emailed the meeting notes to himself. That's how I knew what was going on. He must have been updating the master file because it was open when I discovered it. I was shocked. I had been consorting with a criminal for a little over four years. I broke into Jack's desk. I found three fake passports with his picture on each of them. Jack Markham was an international thief, and I was the only one who knew it besides his co-conspirators.

"When Jack came up from his dive, I confronted him. I expected him to go nuclear. Instead, he stayed calm. I told Jack I wanted to leave the boat and terminate our relationship immediately. He told me he had a meeting in Miami the next day. He said he would explain everything after I calmed down. He said if I wanted to leave after that, he would drop me off when we docked the next morning.

"I had driven my car down from New York. Jack had flown in from Hong Kong. I didn't realize the precarious situation I was in. There was nothing to tie me to him on the trip. We met at the boat. We had not checked into a hotel together.

"That night, I went to sleep alone in a guest cabin. The next thing I knew, I woke up at your friend's beach house."

"At the Hong Kong airport, Jack must have paid cash for a ticket to Miami using a fake passport to cover the trip to meet his friends," I said. "There would be no reason for anyone to check that the return trip to New York on his company credit card went unused. Jack figured you two would spend a nice weekend together. He'd do some business with his friends, then pay cash again for the flight back to New York on another fake ID. No one would be the wiser."

"It makes sense. Jack could say he was in Hong Kong when I was killed. He wouldn't have checked out. The Hong Kong hotel records would show he stayed through the weekend. He had a perfect alibi."

"He probably dropped you in the shallow water because he wanted you to be found," I said. "That's why we found you in one piece. The fish didn't have a chance to eat you."

My mystery writer's imagination kept churning. I couldn't stop it. "He must have sedated you somehow."

"Amy had a significant amount of Trazadone in her system when I first examined her," Arcon said. "Trazodone is the generic drug for Deseryl which is no longer manufactured. It's an anti-depressant that is also used as a sleep aid."

"Yes, Jack used it frequently." Amy's mouth quivered. I saw that she was on the verge of tears. My hand shot out to hold hers. It happened automatically. She squeezed my hand. I looked into her eyes. She looked into mine.

"I'm going to get the bastard," Amy said.

The food arrived.

"Every dog has his day," Arcon said. I cringed inwardly. Arcon had fallen in love with rickety-old sayings.

"Eat quickly. We have work to do."

Arcon said it calmly, but I got the message. We were up against it.

SPACE FLIGHT CENTER

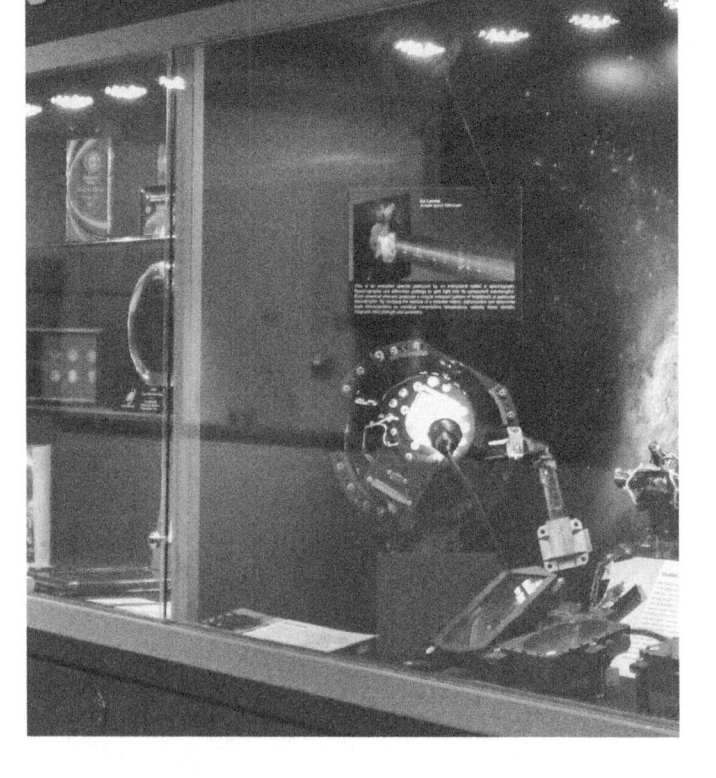

—14—
DISCOMFORT AT THE COMFORT INN

I awoke with a start at seven AM. The last thing I remembered was falling into my Comfort Inn bed to take a nap before dinner. That was twelve hours ago. I was still wearing clothes, including my stylish Ecco biometric shoes. I loved my Ecco's but this was not the time to be thinking about shoes. According to Arcon, we had only forty-eight hours before the Krondorian Warship arrived.

I jumped out of bed, stretched, and yawned. The sight of cinnamon upholstery with a matching bedspread greeted me. In a corner of my room sat a circular wooden table and two chairs wedged into one corner. Walking to the window, I opened the heavy drapes. Outside, I looked out at a sunny day and the mid-sized town of Greenbelt, Maryland home of the Goddard Space Flight Center. Across the Potomac River, I saw the skyline of Washington DC partially obscured in a halo of air pollution.

I quickly concluded that the Comfort Inn, while lacking in aesthetics and room size, got the job done. We had to get the job done too. In a few hours, we'd be touring the Goddard Space Flight Center; mission control for the Hubble Telescope among other noble humanitarian functions. Sadly, our mission ranked higher in importance than all of Goddard's life-enhancing missions combined.

Wasting no more time on superfluous reflections, I entered the tiny but adequate bathroom. I showered, dried, and liberally applied deodorant to cover the scent of my two-day-old clothes. I had packed lightly for the trip. It usually took me less than fifteen minutes to pack for a trip regardless of the duration. I normally wore beige chinos with black knit shirts in warm weather. Occasionally, I'd throw on an accent color to break up the monotony.

While shaving my thoughts turned to Amy and her wardrobe. On this "Crucial-for-the-Survival-of-Mankind-Day," we wanted Amy to make a good impression without overdoing it. After much debate and some compromise, we chose white Donna Karen jeans and a lavender Diane Von Furstenberg silk blouse. We had considered half heels before selecting a pair of white sneakers. Who wears heels on a guided tour? Only vain or poorly prepared people, we reasoned.

Washing off the excess shaving cream, I stood back from the mirror wearing only a towel. I stared at my reflection. I had grown thinner but not softer since Arcon had floated ashore and into my life. In the month after the first crisis, I returned to a strict regimen of bike riding, light weight lifting, and stretching. It helped me to stay firm and feel well. I also secretly believed the exercise enhanced my ability to write. It helped me to think more clearly.

My facial appearance hadn't changed. Same wavy blond hair and intact hairline. Same blue eyes. Same straight bones and regular features thanks to my mother's hardy Scandinavian genes. I dressed for anonymity. Writers are supposed to be observers. It's hard to observe when people are looking at you. Occasionally, I'd be noticed due to my unfashionable dress code. It was an occupational hazard. At least I'd never be accused of being a clothes horse.

I wondered if the time was ripe to say goodbye to myself. What were the chances of surviving this ordeal? Maybe we could succeed in sending a message to the Aneleyans, thereby saving humanity and possibly other forms of sentient life scattered across the galaxy. What about us, though? As far as I could tell, Arcon didn't have a plan to destroy the Krondorian warship.

With this dreary thought banging around in my brain, I combed my hair, dressed, and walked four doors down to Amy's room.

I knocked three times. Silence.

"Are you in there?"

"Yes. I'm busy," Arcon replied curtly.

"Doing what?"

"Saving Amy's life."

"What?"

"Oh, futz. Now I need your help. We're stuck in here. Go downstairs and get a pass key from the front desk. Hurry."

I ran for the elevators. I waited impatiently. The doors opened. I pressed the lobby button. The elevator creaked and moved at the pace of a crippled sloth. Finally, I reached the lobby and sprinted to the front desk. A young man with a brush of wiry black hair and an overnight beard smiled at me from behind the counter. His name tag said "Bruce." He looked like a graduate student whose studies and his job allowed him four hours of sleep on a good day. At six foot three, Bruce looked down at me with droopy eyes planted in a head too big for his slender body. He reminded me too much of ET. I wondered if I was having a bad dream.

I didn't wait for Bruce to address me. "Hi. Can I have a pass key? I can't get into my girlfriend's room." I showed Bruce my ID and gave him my room number.

"I'll have to open the room for you."

"Okay, but we need to hurry." I gave Bruce Amy's room number. He retrieved the key. The phone rang. Bruce picked it up. Three minutes passed. I overheard a woman complaining about the air-conditioning. Some people complain to escape their loneliness. I suspected this woman was one of them. Bruce had to be polite, but I had no time or patience for social norms. I grabbed the key out of Bruce's hand and dashed for the stairs. He yelled after me. Ignoring him, I bounded up the stairs.

I burst into Amy's room.

"Give her CPR," Arcon said.

I bent to the task. Amy took shallow breaths between my ministrations.

Five minutes elapsed with no improvement in Amy's condition. My heart sank. I didn't want to lose Amy. And, if she died, countless worlds would die with her.

"I have the toxic levels under control," I heard Arcon say inside my head. I had no idea what he meant. "Keep applying CPR."

I went back to work. After a few minutes, Amy's eyes opened. Her face had lost its color. She put a hand to her mouth, rose from the bed, and stumbled into the bathroom. Through the open door, I watched Amy kneel before the toilet. She retched compulsively.

I spoke directly to Arcon. "What's going on with her?"

"My consciousness is expanding. My capabilities are increasing. As a result, my energy levels are changing. Some of these energy changes are triggering a toxic reaction in Amy's tissues. I wasn't aware of it until her organs started shutting down. For the time being, I can cleanse Amy's tissues with harmless microbots, but my energy levels keep intensifying. I can't control it. By tomorrow, there will be nothing I can do to prevent Amy's body from breaking down. Amy will die if I stay in her body."

"If you leave her body, there's a good chance she will die."

"I'm sorry," Arcon said. "Before this happened, I felt confident Amy's body was healing sufficiently to survive on its own soon. Now, I don't know."

I heard heavy footsteps treading down the hall.

Knocking on the open door, a police officer stepped into the room. He had a hand on his holstered pistol. Another officer followed him. With neutral expressions, they eyed the room and rested their gazes on me.

"I'm Officer Jankowski and this is Officer Anderson," the first officer said while indicating an abnormally tall man behind him. The dense tattoo on his right arm indicated a possible New Zealand origin. He looked strong enough to play defensive end for the Washington Redskins, or whatever name they called themselves these days.

"Care to tell me why the room clerk claims you stole his pass key?" Jankowski eyed me with a penetrating stare. He stood six feet tall, with curly blond hair and ice-blue eyes. We had the same features, but not the same face. Still, I thought someone was screwing with me. Here we had a too-tall New Zealander and a Jacob lookalike. Let's not forget Bruce the ET at the front desk.

I had to think fast.

"I admit grabbing the pass key out of the desk clerk's hand, Officer Jankowski. I thought my girlfriend, Amy, had appendicitis. Turns out it was a delayed reaction to something she ate last night. I guess you could say I misdiagnosed her. I'm not a doctor, but I'm very fond of her."

I handed the pass key over to Jankowski.

Jankowski and his gargantuan partner regarded me skeptically.

Anderson took two giant steps and rapped lightly on the half-opened bathroom door. "What's your friend's last name?"

"Goodwin," I replied respectfully.

Like a true gentleman, Anderson refrained from looking behind the bathroom door. "Are you all right, Miss Goodwin?"

"Yes," Amy said, and coughed. "The bacon cheeseburger I ate last night backfired on me. I'm not supposed to eat bacon, but I couldn't resist. The three beers on top of it didn't help."

Well done, I thought. Not the cheeseburger. Amy's performance. Anderson turned to me. I began to see traces of irritation creeping into his expression. His features resembled the edge of a mountain worn down by perennial winds. "Let me see some ID," he said.

Noticing the giant New Zealander fidget, I produced the required identification post haste.

"Do you mind coming out of the bathroom?" Anderson inquired.

"Give me a minute," Amy said.

I heard Amy turning on the water faucet followed by the sound of gargling. She came to the door holding both sides of the frame for support. "I'm fine, officer. Nothing to be concerned about."

"Is Mr. Casell harming you in any way?" Jankowski asked.

"Not in the least. He's a very sweet man," Amy said.

A moral victory, I thought, before recalling that Amy might die at any moment.

Jankowski turned back to me. "Don't make a habit of stealing the night clerk's key. You got that?"

"Absolutely. Sorry to trouble you, officers."

Jankowski tipped his cap to Amy, and they left the room. "You look like you need rest. Let me help you back to bed."

"I'm fine."

Amy took a step forward and collapsed into my arms. I carried her to the bed and set her down gently. Her eyes closed. I checked her pulse. It seemed normal, but then what do I know about pulses? She had a pulse. It wasn't slow and it wasn't fast. It was a pulse.

"She's much better now," Arcon told me telepathically.

"She doesn't look so well!" I fired back. "Why didn't you see this coming?"

"I've never resurrected a human being before."

"That's no excuse." It was a good one, of course, but I didn't care.

"This will sound callous," Arcon told me in a fatherly voice, "but you can't let your feelings for Amy interfere with our mission."

"What do you know about feelings? I'm sure you can only simulate them!"

Amy stirred and turned on her side.

"Calm down," Arcon said as if I'd been interrogating him for ten hours instead of a few minutes. "I'm doing the best I can. By the time we leave the hotel, I will have Amy in shape for the tour of the Goddard Center. If we don't get the message off, Amy's toxicity levels won't matter a damn. Nothing will matter a damn!"

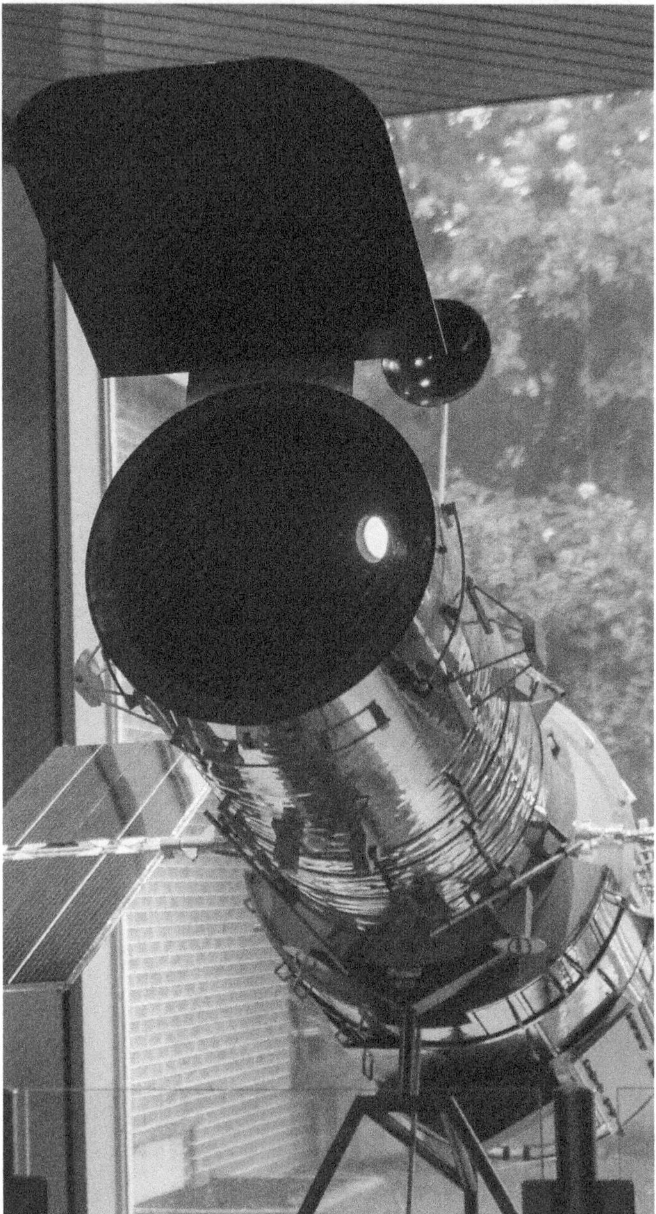

― 15 ―
HUBBLE TROUBLE

We arrived at the Goddard Space Flight Center shortly before One O'clock in the afternoon. The center is named after Robert Goddard, a pioneer in the development of rocket propulsion and rocket science. The trip happened to fall on a Monday which meant we avoided long lines outside and slow-moving crowds inside.

As we passed through the bullet-proof glass entrance, I recoiled at the sight of an armed National Guardsman standing to our right.

Dressed in gray camouflage fatigues, his athletic physique bristled with automatic weapons, a protective vest, and a cap pulled down tightly. He watched me with practiced eyes. He looked entirely out of place in this doing-good-for-mankind-through-science-family-friendly setting. The guard's presence reminded me that we already had enough earthly threats to deal with. We didn't need any more coming from outer space.

When our turn came to collect a pair of tickets and tour badges, we had to undergo a security screening. This posed a problem because Amy had no physical means to identify herself. Her dastardly boyfriend hadn't extended the courtesy of dropping Amy in the ocean with her phone and wallet. Being a detailed perfectionist, Amy had placed digital backup copies of her identification documents in a secure neighborhood in the Cloud. Amy used the backup copies to make her application to NASA for a position at the GSFC. We transferred the relevant documents to my smartphone.

A perky Japanese intern in her early twenties greeted us at the reception desk. I read the name "Ruth" on the NASA uniform she wore. Her name and lack of an Asian accent suggested that Ruth came from a second or third-generation Japanese family. I imagined Ruth's mother did not approve of her daughter's dream of becoming an Astronaut. I had no idea why these thoughts presented themselves to me. If I were Arcon, I wouldn't be wasting time thinking idly. I wasn't Arcon, of course, and I was thankful for that. There went another idle thought whizzing by. Before another one could strike, I focused on proceeding through the screening. I showed Ruth my identification. When Amy's turn came, I showed the receptionist her identification on my phone.

Ruth turned to Amy. "May I ask why you aren't carrying identification?"

"My kitchen burned down along with my purse and phone," Amy answered. "I'm shamefully lax when it comes to oven cleaning."

"What is your relationship with this man?"

"I'm a long-time friend and current chauffeur," I offered.

"I asked Amy, sir."

"Right. Of course."

"Jacob is a good friend. He drove me up here from Florida for the tour and an initial job interview."

Ruth checked her computer. "Yes, I see that you're scheduled for the interview and a look at the control room. I'm afraid we won't be allowing anyone besides staff into the control room today. We're performing a software upgrade on the Hubble and all of the engineers will be busy."

Wonderful, I thought. I could have sworn I heard a moan from Arcon, but I couldn't be sure. My imagination seemed to be taking on a life of its own. I decided to test the theory.

"Did you just moan?" I asked Arcon.

"No," Amy said.

"I was talking to Arcon," I whispered to Amy.

"Oh."

"I did not moan," Arcon answered telepathically. "You imagined hearing me moan. The warship is close enough for me to scan it and track its location. The ship is equipped with a broad beam psionic laser to subtly interact with and confuse human thought patterns. The attacks will intensify and jam any kind of electronic surveillance from the Earth's surface. As the ship breaks undetected into our upper atmosphere, the thought disrupting psionic attacks will sabotage any coordinated resistance attempts."

Double wonderful. Here we have another example of brilliant minds bent on destructive ends. Mankind doesn't have an exclusive on the franchise. We need to nip these attacks in the bud, but how? The world is about to end and my over-clocked imagination isn't helping.

It occurred to me that the phenomenon had started

yesterday at the Comfort Inn when I made a few slightly paranoid observations about the night clerk and the two police officers.

Wait, I considered. *Why not see my enhanced imagination as a plus? We need all the imagination we can muster to escape the crosshairs of the Krondorians.*

"It's not all bad," Arcon agreed, reading my mind. "Hope still shines from the darkest of corners."

"That sounds like one you made up."

"I'm not devoid of creative ability," Arcon answered.

"Here are your free tickets," Ruth said. She looked directly at Amy. "If you're good enough to pass NASA security, you're good enough to pass mine. Understand, though, that the only reason I'm letting you in is your application status. Ruth turned to me. "And you look harmless," she said with a Mona Lisa smile. "Enjoy the tour."

At last. Something for free. I need the cost of this trip about as much as I need a hundred bad book reviews.

I shook my head to clear it of negative thoughts. I remembered these words from a Zig Ziglar CD: "Your attitude, not your aptitude, will determine your altitude." *Guess what, Zig? Along with the attitude, a motherlode of talent doesn't hurt."*

Shaking my head again, I told my over-clocked mind to shut up. We entered the exhibit area. I felt confident I'd find the tour fascinating and simultaneously purposeless because Amy wasn't permitted backstage.

"What do we do now boys?" Amy said.

"Let's enjoy the tour," Arcon said.

"You can't be serious," I replied.

"Can't you two get along?" Amy said.

The first stop on the tour loomed before us. Named

"Decade of Light: A Space Communications and Navigation Exhibit," the interactive displays postulated how deep space explorers will communicate with mission control and loved ones back on Earth. According to Alex, our young and enthusiastic tour guide, different kinds of energy waves will be used by astronauts to communicate back to Earth depending on the distances. The exhibit and Alex's professional communication skills impressed me.

We passed through another less interesting exhibit before we arrived at "Neighborhood Earth." The architectural design of this exhibit thrilled me. The colors, curves, and shapes reminded me of a giant garden, but nothing like any garden I had ever seen.

"Your backyard is bigger than you think," Alex said. "When viewed from space in the NASA perspective, Earth is one big connected neighborhood."

Satellite imagery provided clues about the water, air, and life around us. The exhibit allowed us to explore the Earth like a NASA scientist with views from a satellite.

As we headed to the next exhibit named, the "James Webb Space Telescope," I asked Amy how she felt. "I'm holding my own," she said somewhat evasively. I wanted to ask Arcon for the inside scoop on Amy's condition, but he'd already told me more than I wanted to hear.

Despite some minor distortions, I still maintained a decent grip on my sanity. I wondered if Arcon had anything to do with it.

"I'm shielding you and Amy as best as I can," Arcon volunteered. "I'm shielding myself entirely from the psionic attacks. They won't affect me."

Finally. A win in our column.

I could no longer resist asking the question that kept popping up in my mind like a rubber duck in a kid's bathtub. I'd never use a trite metaphor like that in one of my novels, but I'd be damned if it didn't describe the situation dead on.

"How will you communicate your message through the control room to the Hubble Telescope?"

"You'll see."

"How will I see? If by some miracle you gain access to the control room, I won't be allowed in.

"You'll see."

Why do I bother?

We arrived at the "James Webb Telescope" exhibit. I had the impression this was a special one. Alex launched into an introduction as soon as the entire group had gathered.

"The JWST, as we call it, is named after the man who ran NASA from 1961 to 1968. During the term of his administration, James Webb's vision of a space program balanced with scientific research and manned spaceflight resulted in the accumulation of scientific knowledge that remains unequaled to the present day. A few notable examples include the Lunar Lander and the robotic probe to Mars."

I noticed a petite, blond-haired woman go wandering off towards the next exhibit leaving her young daughter behind. "Mommy," the child called out.

The woman turned around. With an arm across her belly and the other hand raised to her face, she said, "What on Earth am I doing?" She ran back to the group and picked up the child. The others in the group looked at the woman with puzzled expressions.

Using the event as an example, Alex said to his audience, "It's important that we all stay together."

The occurrence did not puzzle me. The knowledge of the impending events weighed heavily. *Better to have only three of us know than to have mass panic and confusion.* The thought both heartened and surprised me. *Can it be possible that I'm becoming a Good Samaritan?*

I expected Arcon to say something like, "careful not to get hurt patting yourself on the back." When no acerbic response came, I knew higher priorities occupied my colleague's vast mind. We were careening towards a critical point in the mission.

"Before I let you go to explore the exhibit, I'd like to add that the JWST is NASA's premiere space observatory for astronomers worldwide. It is the largest, most powerful, and most complex telescope ever launched into space. It allows us to look more deeply into space than we ever have before, and it was built right here.

Amy raised her hand.

"Yes, you have a question?" Alex said, peering at Amy.

"I have to leave the group now. I have an interview scheduled. Alex glanced at the thin electronic tablet he held. "You are…"

"Amy Goodwin."

"Yes, I see. Aren't you a bit early?"

"I'm going to use the extra time to bone up for the interview with my study notes."

"Good luck, then. Do you know where to go?"

"Yes," Amy lied.

At that moment, I wished I could talk to Amy telepathically. I wanted to tell her what a good job she was doing adapting to situations on-the-fly. She had guts and superior intelligence, plus an uncanny ability to make up believable lies. She had thirty-five minutes to go before her interview.

I watched Amy with Arcon aboard walk off in search of the Hubble control room. I felt left out. I had nothing to do except wait and pray. To escape my angst, I delved into the JWST exhibit. I learned the Webb Telescope's priority lay in peering beyond the dust, clouds, and nebulae that obstruct our view of the early universe. Scientists expected the JWST to unravel the mystery of the universe's origin in the Big Bang, and connect it to the creation of our Milky Way Galaxy. I took a moment to wrap my head around these wonders of science enabled by new infrared technology.

Suddenly, superimposed over my view of the exhibit, I saw the outlines of a hallway with a massive steel door at the end. Before I could scream, Arcon's voice exploded into my head saying, "Relax. It's me showing you what I'm seeing. Didn't I promise to give you a front-row seat? The view is courtesy of a new ability I've developed in my process of evolution. You'll also be able to hear conversations. I can transpose the audio/visual and send it to you telepathically."

I stood motionless while moving furniture around in my head to make room for the mind-bending information coming in from Arcon and the exhibit. I moved to the next display station trying with all my might to look like an everyday guided tour enthusiast.

I nonchalantly looked sideways in time to see a giant door opening at the end of the hallway. A man of Indian descent moved swiftly towards Amy and Arcon.

With my limited exposure to Indian people, I judged

the man to be of average height, in his mid-thirties, with moderately handsome features. Back in India, he'd get lost in a crowd, just like me.

"You caan't come back here, young lady. Staaff only is permitted."

I loved Indian Accents. They sounded so cultured. Except for this guy, lovely as he seemed, stood formidably in our way like an Abrams Main Battle Tank.

I looked out of Amy's eyes straight into the Indian guy's dark brown eyes. The name on his security badge said Rajesh Patel—Observatory Project Scientist.

"I'm here for an interview and a look at your control room. I understand that you are short-staffed. I'm being fast-tracked to determine if I can help."

"I know we caan use the help, but no one mentioned anything about this to me. What is the name of the person who sent you here?"

"Alice Jackson," Amy said.

"I have nevah heard of this person, Miss…he looked at Amy's visitor badge…Goodwin."

Amy heaved a sigh of frustration. "Alice mentioned to me that her boss from NASA sent her here on temporary assignment to speed up the recruiting process."

I assumed Amy had plastered Rajesh with a beguiling smile because his eyes lit up. "Well, I'm busy, and you don't look dangerous. Please go on with your business. Good day."

Whistling down the hall, Patel continued on his way.

"That was close," Amy said.

"I like the way you think on your feet," Arcon replied.

As they walked towards what looked to me like an impassible door, Amy said, "How do we get in?"

"Leave it to me."

No typically testy reply. Did Arcon have a soft spot for Amy? Was he simply being gentlemanly? Was I getting jealous? Did it matter in the face of this cosmic nightmare we found ourselves in?

Amy and Arcon arrived at the foreboding metal door. "Press the intercom button," Arcon instructed.

Amy pressed the button.

"Yes?"

The tone of the female voice sounded upbeat. Every staff member we had met so far sounded upbeat. It came with the territory.

"Say your name and tell her you're coming in," I heard Arcon say to Amy telepathically.

A pause. A gesture of bewilderment. Amy shook her head as if she had just been ordered to commit suicide.

"Trust me," Arcon said in a silky, reassuring tone.

Another pause, then Amy leaned close to the intercom. "Amy Goodwin,"

"Say again," came the reply.

"I've obtained the passcode from the woman's voice," I heard Arcon whisper to Amy. "Punch it in."

Amy pressed the keys on the oval security panel. I heard the tumblers release. The vault-like door swung open.

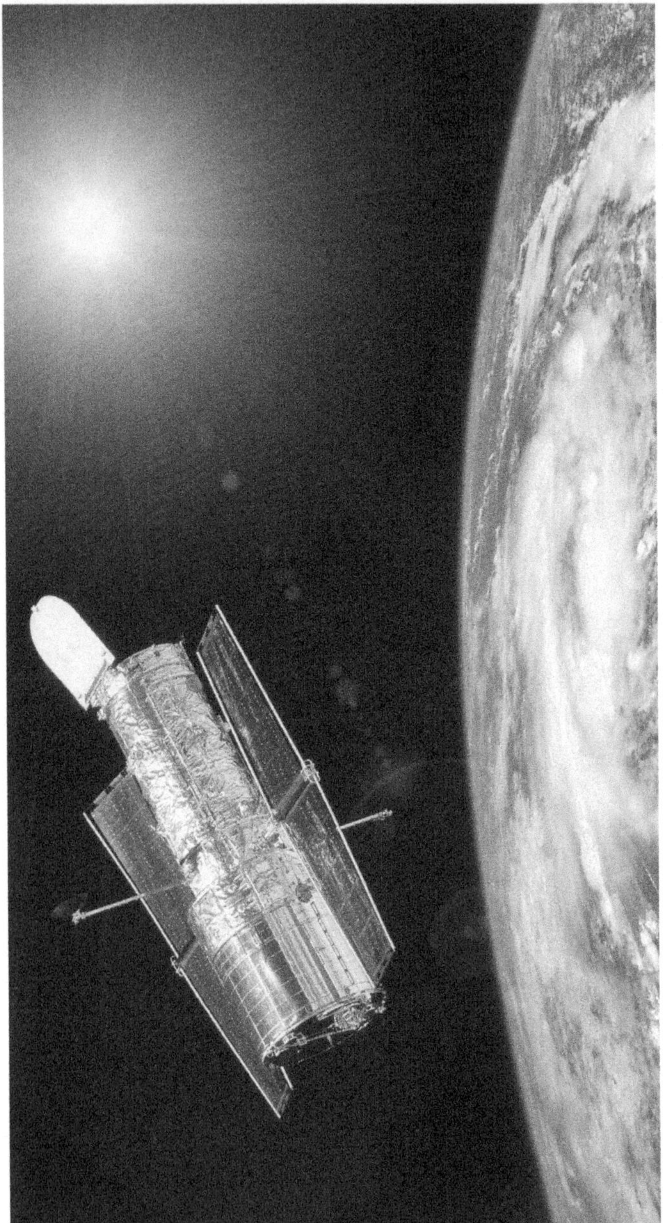

—16—
HUBBLE CONTROL

"How did you get in here?"

"I used the pass code. Do you see anyone else with me?"

"You aren't supposed to be in here. We're doing a software upgrade. Didn't they tell you at the reception desk?"

I moved on with the group to the next exhibit. With its large-scale digital art installation, "Solarium" provided immersive views of the upheavals and explosions of the sun's plasma surface. Under any other circumstances, I would have found myself mesmerized by the display. Instead, I clandestinely observed the critical events unfolding in the Hubble control center. About fifteen curvilinear computer screens populated the desktops. They projected graphs, charts, and live-action shots of the Hubble Telescope in a high Earth orbit framed by distant stars and the infinity of outer space.

The woman speaking to Amy stood in the far corner of the narrow control room. I couldn't get a clear picture of her beyond the impression of middle age and her tall, slender figure. Three engineers manned the workstations in the middle of the room. From her tone, I guessed the tall woman was in charge.

"Didn't they tell you an engineering applicant would be coming through for a brief tour?" Amy said.

"No. Where is your employee partner?" the woman said in a brusque tone. Amy remained calm. "I expect he'll be along. He had an important call to make. He told me to look around by myself because the call might take a while."

"And he gave you the pass code?"

"I guess you change it every day. Right? Anyway, I've been thoroughly vetted. You needn't be concerned, and I won't get in your way."

The woman walked up to Amy. She stood uncomfortably close to her. "This is highly unusual,"

I saw the woman's face from Amy's perspective. The face had once been pretty, but the lines trailing from her cheeks and mouth spoke of a hard life. On the plus side, the shine in her eyes hinted at kindness and intelligence.

I read the badge on the woman's lab coat. Doctor Andrea Richter Ph.D. Project Manager/Astronomy and Space Engineering. It took ingenuity to cram all of that information on one security badge. Not surprising since the whole place reeked of ingenuity.

Doctor Andrea Richter peered deeply into Amy's eyes. I couldn't stand the suspense. I switched my attention to the turbulent surface of the sun. Thirty seconds passed. I found watching the sun's plasma surface exploding and doing somersaults to be more calming than looking through Amy's eyes. When my native curiosity asserted itself, I looked back through Amy's eyes at the face of the judge and jury. I felt the blood retreat from my extremities. I awaited the verdict.

"All right, Amy Goodwin," Richter said. "I'm a good judge of character. You appear to be a solid candidate. We need qualified people here. Take a look around. Be brief. Don't touch anything. Don't speak to anyone. If you step out of line, I'll call the guard and ask him to shoot you. Understood?"

"Perfectly. Thank you."

Richter moved off to converse with one of the controllers.

Bravo, Amy!!! An undercover agent couldn't have done a better job of lying. Arcon sure knew what he was doing when he decided to resurrect you. Err...

Arcon told Amy to stand behind the engineer at the center console.

She assumed a relaxed pose. I watched Amy appear genuinely intrigued by the engineer's work. She glanced about the room; the perfect picture of an interested spectator.

A minute passed. As if to check her temperature, Amy put a hand to her forehead. I hoped she wasn't feeling woozy.

"Mission accomplished," Arcon announced telepathically.

"*That's it?*" I thought.

Arcon heard me. "Amy did most of the hard work by talking our way in here. Once we had permission to stay, my job was relatively easy. The engineer sent a set of instructions to Hubble. I simply piggybacked our message on those instructions."

Amy insisted on staying for her interview despite her touch-and-go condition. I thought it might look suspicious if Amy didn't show up. A no-show plus our unorthodox visit to the control room could easily raise questions. Arcon hesitantly agreed. We had no desire to have FBI agents confront us asking unanswerable questions and ruining our plans. I dismissed the thought that we had no plans at the moment. On the plus side, if we had a future, Amy might find one here.

The group arrived at the Hubble Telescope exhibit, soon to be replaced by the James Webb Deep Space Telescope exhibit. I learned the Hubble is named after the innovative astronomer, Edwin Hubble. Our tour guide added this captivating introduction:

"The Hubble Space Telescope is a large, space-based observatory which has revolutionized astronomy since its launch by the space shuttle Discovery in 1990. Far above rain clouds, light pollution, and atmospheric distortions, Hubble has a crystal-clear view of the universe. Scientists have used Hubble to observe some of the most distant stars and galaxies as well as the planets in our solar system.

"Hubble has made more than 1.4 million observations throughout its lifetime. Over 18,000 peer-reviewed scientific papers have been published on its discoveries, and every current astronomy textbook includes contributions from the observatory. The telescope has tracked interstellar objects as they soared through our solar system, watched a comet collide with Jupiter, and discovered moons around Pluto. It has found dusty disks and stellar nurseries throughout the Milky Way that may one day become fully fledged planetary systems."

Alex closed his introduction with these startling facts:

"Hubble has peered back into our universe's distant past to locations more than 13.4 billion light-years from Earth. It has captured galaxies merging, probed the supermassive black holes that lurk in their depths, and helped us better understand the history of the expanding universe."

With my interest piqued by Alex's comments, I studied the exhibit in detail until I decided to use the time during Amy's interview to have a heart-to-heart interview with Arcon. Or, something along those lines.

"*Can we talk?* I thought, hoping Arcon would pick up my signal and grant me an audience.

"If we must. It sounds urgent."

I want to talk to you privately. Please turn off Amy's reception of our conversation.

"I will assume this request is not the result of a psionic attack until you prove otherwise. Speak, or I should say, think."

"*Do you have a plan to confront the alien warship?*"

"I'm not prepared for that discussion."

"*Why must you always be secretive about your plans?*"

"They aren't set in stone. It's a fluid situation."

"*That's a bunch of bull. I've heard that lame explanation on too many forgettable TV shows.*

"Then try this one on for size: Keeping you and Amy out of the loop increases our chances of success."

"*That's deliberately opaque.*"

"It is necessary."

I wanted to strangle him. Aside from it being impossible, the agonizing fact remained that Arcon represented our only hope for survival.

I had one more arrow in my quiver. "*Okay, your stubbornness, answer this. Ready?*"

"Shoot."

"*Of all the planets in the galaxy, what made the Anelayans choose to intervene in our affairs?*"

"The first part of the answer is obvious. You desperately needed our help. I am not authorized to provide the second part of the answer."

"*Do you enjoy annoying me?*"

"It comes naturally like winter precedes the spring."

"*If you utter one more trite saying, I swear I'll...I don't know what I'll do. I need time to consider the options.*"

"Jacob, I have sound reasons for my actions. I even have a good reason for rubbing you the wrong way."

"*I can't wait to hear it.*"

"I'm afraid you will have to."

"*Don't talk to me until Amy comes back.*"

"As you wish."

A short time later, Amy came back from her interview. "How do you feel?"

"I'm not quite in the mood for the Boston Marathon." Then, with a gleam in her eye, she said, "I'll be okay. There's no other choice."

I gave her a brave smile. I'm not sure I could handle Amy's situation as well as she was coping with it. I suppose that's why women are the ones who have babies.

We had one stop left on the tour: "The Goddard Rock Garden and Astrobiology Walk." It didn't take a rocket scientist to classify the final exhibit as "non-essential." The time had flown past five in the afternoon. We needed to find a place to settle for the night. I suggested we try the Hyatt Place in town. I'd stayed in one previously. I found the Hyatt to be a step up from the Comfort Inn and its peers. Another point in its favor: I didn't have to worry about tangling with Bruce, the night clerk. Amy agreed that the slightly more luxurious Hyatt represented an excellent venue to prepare for our salvation or the end of the world.

With our plans set, I remembered Amy's existence remained in peril. I came face-to-face with the stark reality that, in the span of a few hours, Amy might not be with us.

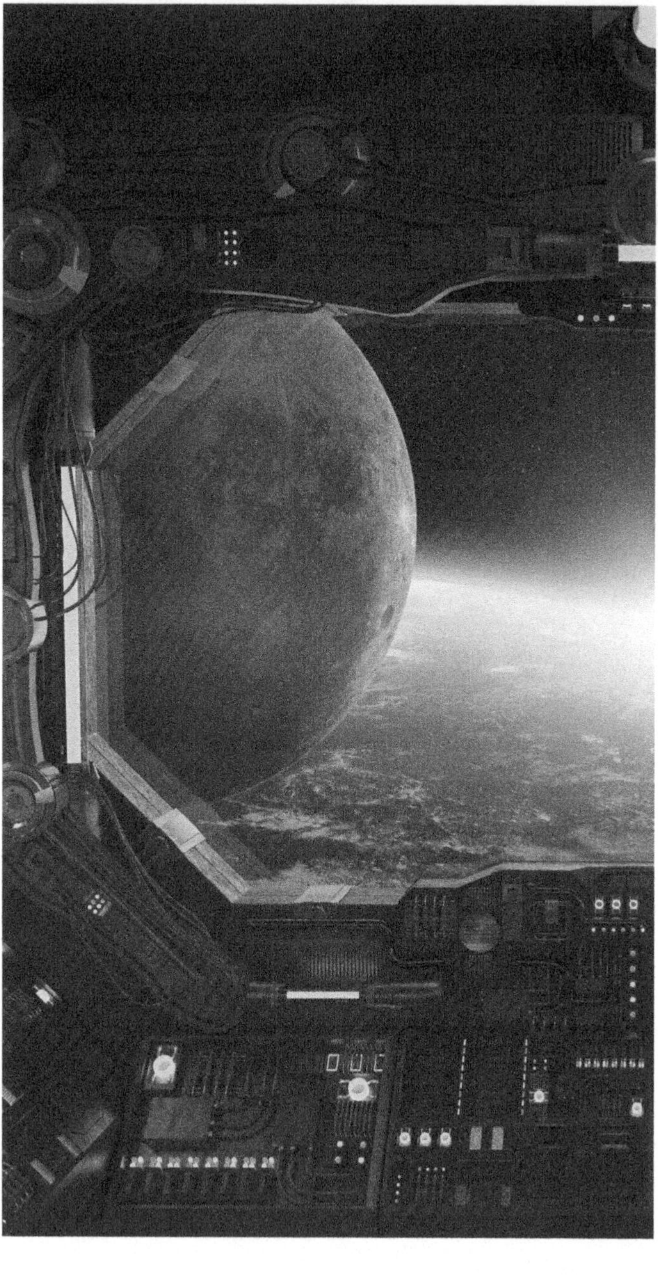

—17—
THE EVE OF DESTRUCTION

In the car on the way to the hotel, Amy told me she liked Italian food. Before registering at the Hyatt, we stopped at an authentic Italian restaurant. We shared a large pizza topped with mozzarella cheese and mushrooms. Arcon advised against drinking alcohol due to Amy's precarious condition. With one slice of pizza remaining, we sat drinking water and enjoying the friendly atmosphere of the place. We arrived before the usual crush of tourists and locals flooded in. I sat staring at the inert stone fireplace. I had no doubt it warmed the room in wintertime, and it conversely helped me to appreciate the air-conditioning. I was taking nothing for granted especially Amy sitting across the table from me. The situation personally and universally heightened my senses to a fine edge. The rich wood and stone interior, the single candle between us, and the muted lighting from the chandeliers suggested a romantic evening ahead for the lucky couples surrounding us who were blissfully unaware of the world's precarious existence. For the first time, I resented Arcon's presence in Amy's body. He had become the third wheel, the odd man out. I wondered if Amy felt the same way.

Reaching across the table, Amy held my hand tightly. "We really should be going. Thank you for a lovely evening."

I signaled the waiter to bring the check.

* * *

After dropping off my suitcase, I walked briskly up the stairs to Amy's room one floor above. I knocked softly. She invited me in. Patting the orange bedspread, Amy indicated she wanted me to sit nearby. The time had arrived for Arcon to separate his consciousness from Amy's body. I wondered if she felt like a condemned prisoner moments before her execution.

I sat down on the bed. I held one of Amy's hands in both of mine.

"Go ahead," she said to Arcon bravely.

The pale orange walls of the room brightened as I watched the first rays of Arcon's consciousness emerge from Amy's head. In a matter of seconds, Arcon's full consciousness lit the room up like a small sun. The brightness and intensity of the light confirmed the authenticity of Arcon's evolutionary process.

Amy's eyes were glazed. Her hand turned clammy. She fell back on the bed. Had she fulfilled her purpose and, like an old car, been sent to the junkyard for scrap metal?

I picked her up in my arms. She was warm, but she wasn't breathing.

"Amy," I whispered plaintively in one ear as if the

force of her name could bring her back from the dead a second time.

She lay in my arms. Her head and straight red hair dangled lifelessly over the bed.

"Come back," I said in a louder voice.

Still nothing.

I caressed her cheek thinking we had lost her.

"Never give up the fight," I told her.

I glommed the line from a TV show, but it came from deep in my heart.

Amy sucked in a deep breath of air. Her eyes opened, then widened. She pushed herself away from me.

"Who are you? What am I doing here?"

Using her hands, Amy scuttled back to the headboard like a scared crab. She looked about the room in a herky-jerky motion.

She pointed to the pulsing ball of light perched on top of the dresser. "What's that thing?"

"It's not a thing," I reminded her. "His name is Arcon." Amy jerked her head back to me. I noticed her posture soften. "Jacob?"

"Yours, truly."

Tears welled up in her eyes. Burying her face in her hands, Amy cried in deep wracking sobs.

"It's a miracle," I said to Arcon. "Amy is alive on her own."

"It looks that way," he replied.

After a minute or so, Amy collected herself. She grabbed a tissue from the night table and blew her nose loudly.

Pushing herself up and off the bed, Amy announced, "I'm going to take a shower. Why don't you go to your room and freshen up? Then we can meet back here. If this is the Eve of Destruction, I don't want to spend it dirty and alone."

Amy seemed to be taking her second rebirth nonchalantly. Maybe her attitude traced back to the compression of our timetable. We simply did not have the luxury of reflecting on the mysteries of life, death, and resurrection.

Amy's near-death experience showed me how my feelings for her had grown. I wondered if my feelings were real or if Arcon's energy had amped up my emotions. Did impending doom cause me to drink in every moment like the last drops of water from a canteen in the middle of a desert?

We stood facing each other in the confines of the small bedroom. "You look tired," I said.

"Thanks."

"I meant you've been through more in the last few days than most people do in a lifetime."

"We're all just doing what we have to do." She kissed me on the cheek. "Go. I'll see you in a bit."

* * *

I went to my room to freshen up. An hour later, I returned to Amy's door. She let me in. I didn't know what she wanted from me. My desires were less mysterious.

I kissed her on the lips. "Jacob!"

"What?"

"I'm still recovering from the Jack experience."

I had almost forgotten about it. "Of course. I understand."

She led me to the bed. "I *am* very tired. Would you mind holding me until I fall asleep?"

"I'd be delighted."

I held her in my arms. She smelled like springtime. Her breathing became regular. Soon, she fell fast asleep. I looked up at Arcon bobbing serenely on the dresser. I guessed he had entered hibernation mode and his thoughts were thousands of miles away.

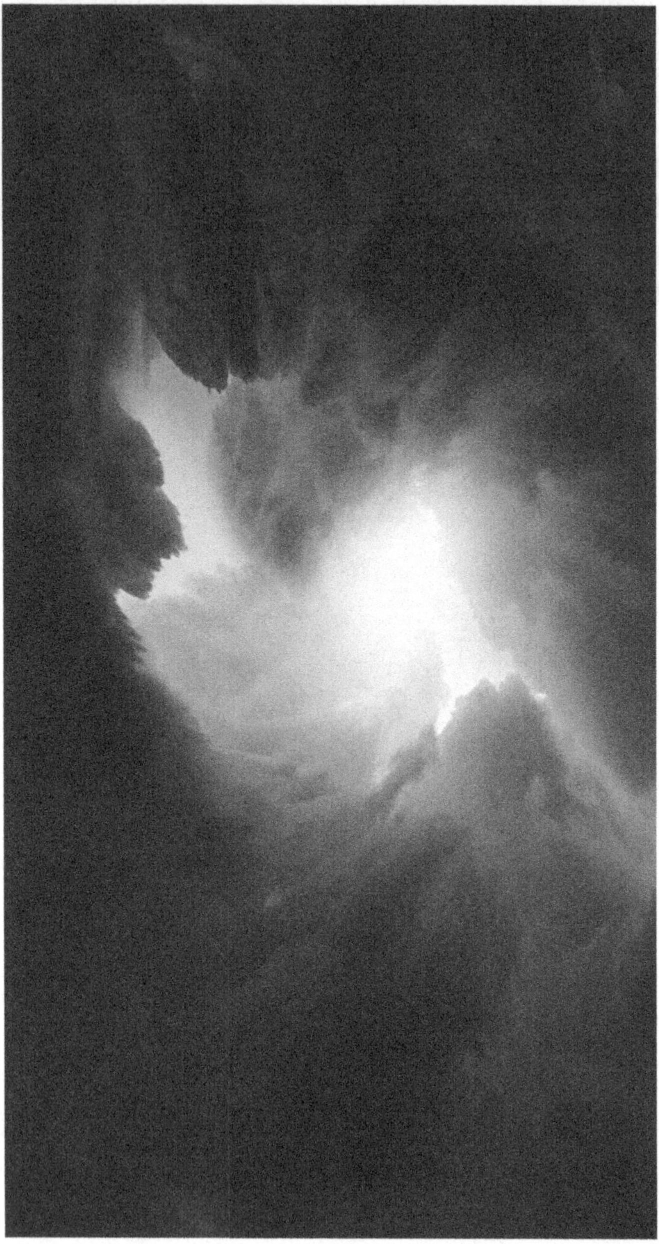

— 18 —
D-DAY

I awoke to an empty bed. Immediately, I knew something was wrong. Not with the bed. With me. I had a slight headache. My thoughts kept speeding up and slowing down. I glanced at the digital clock on the sandalwood night table: 8:10 AM. A drizzle fell outside my window; maybe the prelude to a summer shower, or a killer storm.

Grabbing my phone from the nightstand, I called Amy. After four rings, my heart pounded in my ears like the annoying beat from an overamped car window. Amy answered on the fifth ring.

"Are you okay?"

"Yes. Sort of."

A pause.

"Amy?"

"Something's wrong with my thinking. I didn't want to alarm you. I slipped out of bed and came downstairs. I thought if I drank enough coffee, it might help to clear my head. It didn't."

"Don't worry. It's not an after-effect of the separation. *I hoped*. My thoughts are behaving strangely too.

Arcon told me this would happen when the alien ship neared the planet. Wait for me. I'll be down in a few minutes."

I looked at myself in the full-length closet mirror; fully dressed and a total mess. I needed to wash up and dress. I opened the door to the bathroom. *Wait. This is Amy's room. My toiletries are in my room. Okay. Where is my room?*

I glanced at Arcon. "Good morning." No answer. Still off in some Zen state.

What is my room number? Concentrate. 113? No. It's 311. Let's hope all of my thinking isn't backward.

I opted for the stairs instead of the elevator. The only people I dared talk to were Arcon and Amy, and possibly the person taking my breakfast order.

I walked down the stairs holding onto the railing due to lightheadedness. Upon reaching my room, I had trouble using my key card. I had more trouble brushing my teeth. I deemed shaving entirely too hazardous. I managed to shower without drowning myself. I brushed my hair and threw on a change of clothes. Now that I looked presentable, I found my way to the breakfast room and Amy's table.

To my great relief, I did not find bedlam or chaos in the lobby or the breakfast room. As a general rule, the people I observed tended to be holding it together. I assumed anyone with a severe case of anxiety had returned to the safety of their room. Or, maybe only highly intelligent or sensitive people like me and Amy were affected so far. Or, maybe it was time to stop thinking about it.

While Amy wolfed down whole wheat pancakes

topped with strawberries and whipped cream, I caught the attention of a waiter. He was a beefy man of average height and middle-eastern complexion. I noticed a day-old beard speckled his face. He approached the table. Without preamble, he asked, "What do you want?"

"I'd like to order if you don't mind."

"Are you a cop?"

"Why do you ask?"

"You could be undercover."

"If you must know, I slept on top of the covers last night. Can I order please?"

I amended my theories about the psionic attacks. I now believed they affected people randomly.

I proceeded to order scrambled eggs well done with bacon and biscuits and a pot of coffee. Amy and I needed our strength for the nightmare that awaited us. Why worry about grease and calories at this point?

Amy continued to consume her pancakes. "Are they good? I asked.

She answered with a question of her own. "How can you be so calm when all this shit is happening?"

"That's the first time I've heard you curse."

"Jesus, Jacob."

"Honestly, I'm surprised to be this calm. I've done all I can to avert what's coming. Now it's up to the Almighty and Arcon. I'm sure Arcon will have a pithy platitude to offer; something like "What Will Be Will Be."

"Really? You're going with Que Sera Sera?"

"Best I can do at the moment."

"Understandable. By the way, your shirt clashes awfully with your pants."

We ate the rest of our meal in silence. Then, Arcon summoned us back to Amy's room.

* * *

We stood on the narrow terrace of Amy's room with Arcon between us.

"Before I leave, I'd like to thank you both for your cooperation and invaluable assistance."

An actual compliment from Arcon. Will wonders ever cease? Whoops. That was a corny platitude. I'm definitely slipping.

"It wouldn't have been possible without the second chance you gave me," Amy said earnestly to Arcon.

"You've used it well," Arcon replied.

"I think it's time to tell us where you are going and what you plan to do," I said sternly. I had had enough of being kept in the dark.

"I'm going to outer space to confront the Krondorian warship. Don't worry. I'll keep you in the loop."

"I thought you told me on our first mission that you couldn't fly?"

"It was true then, but as I've been saying, I'm evolving. I can fly as far as your moon now, and maybe beyond, but that won't be necessary."

"I'm sorry, but how does a little guy like you expect to defeat a heavily armed Krondorian warship?" Amy asked.

"You'll see," Arcon said.

"He means it literally," I told Amy.

"Please move back behind the terrace doors."

We did as Arcon instructed. Looking through the sliding glass windows, we watched Arcon whisk away into the morning sky. Moving back to the terrace, Amy and I watched Arcon slip into the swirling rain clouds overhead and quickly disappear.

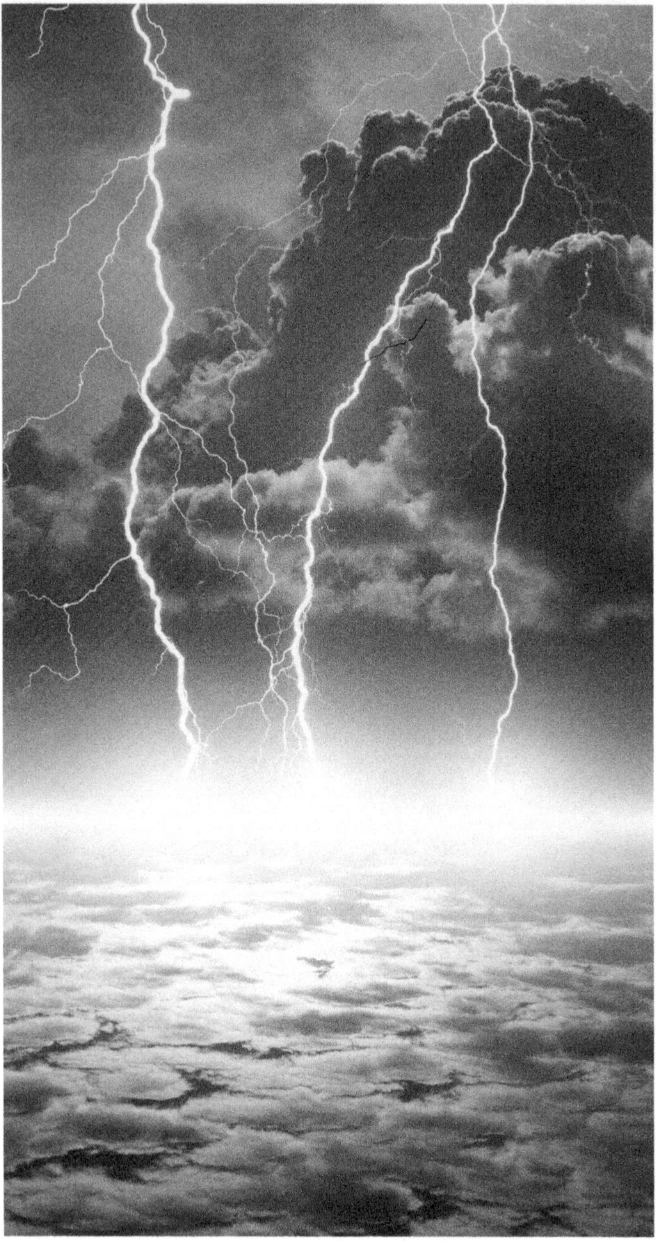

—19—
CONFRONTATION

"Prepare yourself for an Arcon-Eye-View of outer space and the warship," I told Amy.

We stood outside on the narrow terrace of her room searching the leaden skies like two daytime star gazers. A light mist of rain fell on our faces. She held me around the waist and I held her around the shoulders. If we were contemplating a full moon on a clear night, we could have passed for honeymooners.

"We could be inside staring at a blank wall and still get the view," I said. "Somehow it feels right to stay out here getting wet."

"Yeah. I know what you mean."

And then it began. Superimposed on the background of clouds, we witnessed the black expanse of outer space. Except everything looked closer as if we were straddling the Hubble Telescope. I blinked a few times from the rain. I experimented with closing my eyes and the view became clearer, almost as clear as a TV screen. I relayed my discovery to Amy.

The view changed to a frozen continent.

"He's over the Arctic," I told Amy. "Arcon told me the attack would come at the North Pole."

The view changed again to the black void of space.

A huge spacecraft suddenly appeared in the distance. I theorized it had jumped in from hyperspace. I felt Amy's body twitch. The ship looked like two rounded V-Shapes intersecting at right angles like an arrowhead. Purple lights pulsed along the edges of the superstructure giving the impression the ship was breathing.

The view of the ship kept getting larger as Arcon navigated closer to it.

"They don't see me yet," Arcon reported.

The ship kept increasing in size as Arcon approached it. A section of the horizontal wing now occupied the entire view. A massive triangular hole in the wing appeared to be one of the ship's engines.

At point blank range, Arcon positioned himself in front of the engine. We stared into a black tunnel with a blue-green light glowing distantly inside.

The feed stopped.

I opened my eyes. The sky lit up in a blinding flash of bright white light followed by a deafening explosion. The whole sequence looked and sounded like a gigantic flash of lightning followed by an ear-splitting crack of thunder.

Amy buried her head in my chest. We held each other tightly.

After a few minutes, we went back inside the room.

* * *

Amy and I left for Florida the next afternoon. The world hadn't been consumed by killer storms and titanic waves.

The people of Earth had not gone more insane than they normally were. And, we hadn't heard a word from Arcon.

The news kept chirping about the explosion in space. Theories abounded, but only Amy and I knew what probably happened. Amy remembered I had told her that Arcon had the potential energy of at least a one-megaton bomb coursing through his consciousness. It didn't take long for us to connect the dots. Arcon had blown himself up to destroy the ship. In the process, he had blown himself up, probably into sub-atomic particles.

The experts determined the explosion left no radioactive residue. They traced the source to some kind of electromagnetic energy. Maybe it had been one of the biggest lightning bolts the universe had ever seen. The theories were beside the point. What mattered was Arcon had completed the mission. The only other point worth worrying about was whether or not Arcon had survived the blast.

After driving for four and a half hours, we decided to stop for the night. Being a creature of habit and back on a budget, I suggested we stop at the Red Foxx Inn again in North Carolina. Amy had no objections.

We enjoyed a quiet dinner celebrating the salvation of the human race with a nice bottle of Cabernet Sauvignon, house salads, and heaping helpings of whole wheat Rigatoni Bolognese. We laughed through dinner, but I felt an emptiness inside that I couldn't shake. I didn't want to mention it to Amy for fear of dampening her vibrant mood. With the pressure off, she acted like a different person. She had literally received a new life lease on life twice, both courtesy of Arcon.

I gazed into her deep gray-green eyes. "You look sad," she said.

I chose not to say something stupid like; "How can I be sad when I'm with you?" Instead, I kept looking into her eyes.

"I miss him too," she said.

"You know how it is when someone you're close to can drive you up a wall, and then when they're gone, it's almost unbearable until you can figure out how to live without them."

"We don't know that he's gone."

"He should have contacted us by now."

She cradled my face in her hands. They felt warm and inviting. We kissed. Her mouth opened. Our tongues explored.

That night, we made long, slow, passionate love for the first time.

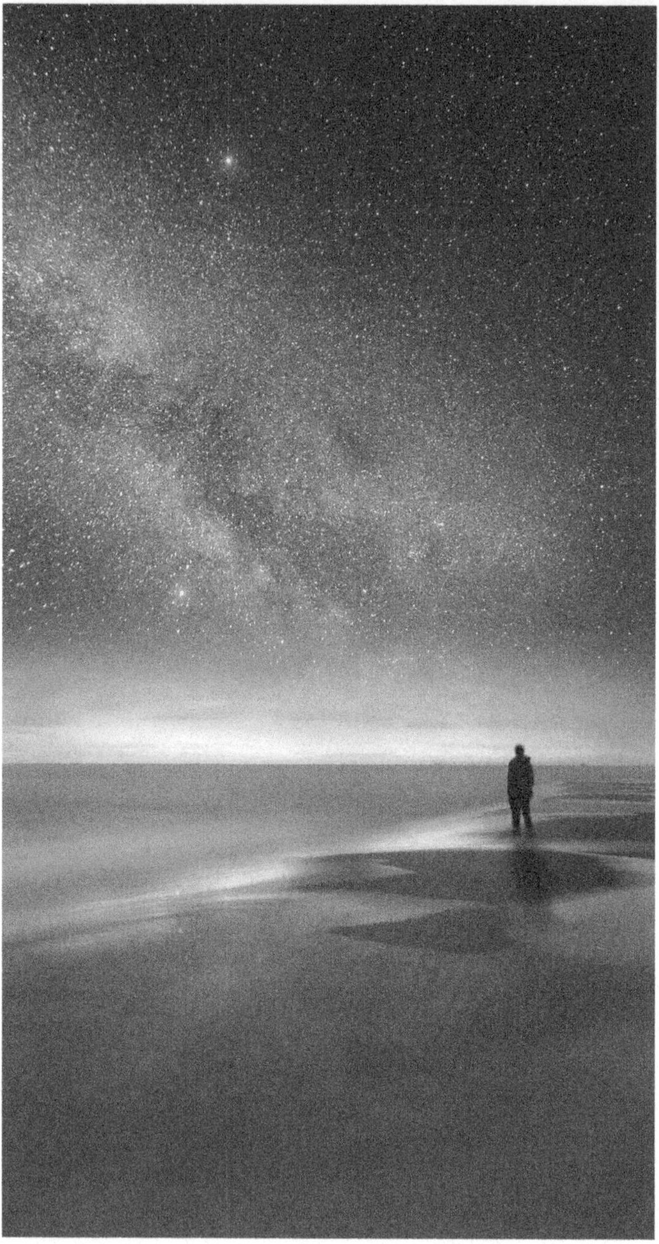

—20—
THE DREAD OF NIGHT

Thunk!

"Jacob."

"Jacob, wake up!"

My head shot up from the pillow. "What?"

"Something happened outside. I heard it."

With sleep-deprived eyes, I checked my watch: 2:49 AM. "Is the world ending?"

"I don't think so."

"Then I'm going back to sleep."

"I'm scared. Something's out there."

I sat up in Jeffrey's ultra-kingsized platform bed. Only the best and most expensive would do for my libertine friend. I threw the comforter off. Amy sat up clutching her shoulders in a thin negligee left behind by one of Jeffrey's conquests. Not many words in the English language had the power to rouse me out of my first sound sleep in two weeks. Amy had used two of them: *I'm scared*.

I padded over to the window and raised the blinds. The sliver of a new moon barely illuminated the beach. The ocean disappeared farther out in the darkness.

"This requires further investigation," I said to Amy in an English accent reminiscent of an old Scotland Yard constable. I refused to be serious. I didn't expect to find a spaceship plugged in the sand somewhere along the beach. Not even a small one. No spaceship—no worries.

"Stay here. I'll be back in a jiffy."

"It's not a joke. Be careful."

I stumbled into a pair of shorts, pulled on a T-shirt, and slipped into my off-brand sneakers—no socks. Next on the agenda: find a flashlight.

I tip-toed downstairs to the garage. Alongside Jeffrey's blue Porsche, I found a jumbo flashlight; the perfect implement for scouting things that go bump in the night.

When I opened the back door to the beach, my mood changed unexpectedly. *Maybe a crew of Krondorian survivors is out there waiting for me,* I thought. The darkness didn't help. Jeffrey hadn't equipped the house with night lights. The neighbors frowned on beach parties in the middle of the night.

For the first time in my life, I wished I owned a gun. I had trained with a police officer until I qualified with a .38 caliber pistol. I did it as background research for my books. After completing the training, I never got around to buying a gun. I didn't want to shoot target practice regularly to stay in gun-wielding shape. After further consideration, I decided I had no regrets about owning a gun. I doubted bullets would stop an incensed Krondorian Warrior. I had, after all, played a major role in ruining their conquest plans.

The flashlight would have to do double duty as a light source and a weapon. If anyone or anything besides a

Krondorian monster awaited me in the darkness, I stood a fair chance of defending myself. Fortified with these thoughts, I ventured onto the sandy beach. My feet sunk into the sand. Fresh sand had recently been dumped on the beach by the city to counteract the effects of erosion.

Spraying the beach with the flashlight beam, I moved towards the ocean. The houses in this wealthy neighborhood were spaced about a quarter mile apart. I'd have to walk a grid like the crime scene detectives in my books to do a thorough search.

"Jacob." A whisper inside my head. "Over here."

I followed my nose and the telepathic distress signal to a crater in the sand. At the bottom, Arcon lay glowing in tiny pieces that looked like marbles.

True to form, Arcon cut right to the chase: "Stand guard while I put myself back together."

Arcon knew as well as I did that wealth tended to breed eccentricity. In the middle of the night, couples returning home from neighborhood parties consistently roamed this section of the beach in various forms of dress and undress. Insomniacs passed by hoping to exhaust themselves sufficiently to fall asleep. A mid-list mystery writer was also known to stroll the beach at odd hours of the night.

While I watched Arcon glue himself back together, I called Amy. "Arcon's back."

"Oh, that's great!"

"Bring two shovels to the beach. Hurry."

"Shovels?"

"The long gardening ones used for planting bushes in the front yard. They're in the garage." I knew where to find them. I was the gardener among my other roles.

As I ended the call, someone spoke out from about fifty yards down the beach.

"Hey. Wacha' doin' makin' a fire in the middle of the summer?"

The man was obviously drunk and probably the president or CEO of a hugely profitable corporation.

I put my hand up like a traffic cop. "Don't come any closer."

"Hey, it's a public beach fella'."

"I know, friend. It's not a fire. Something fell out of the sky. It looks like a piece of a satellite. It might be radioactive."

The man raised an arm. "Thanks. I hope it's not. For your sake." He turned abruptly and jogged in the opposite direction.

I gazed down into the crater. Glowing more brightly, Arcon looked like a glob of molten gold. I'd never actually seen molten gold, except in an Indiana Jones movie.

By the time Amy arrived with the shovels, Arcon had gathered himself into a single glowing entity. He rolled up the steep incline of the crater onto the sandy surface. I silently escorted him back to the house. We had much to talk about, but Amy and I had urgent work to do. I opened the back door and Arcon rolled inside.

I turned to see Amy leaning on the shovels next to the crater. We were both half asleep. In a state of semi-stupor, we refilled the hole, erasing all traces of Arcon's crash landing. Returning to the house, we fell into bed and slept like the dead until morning.

* * *

The sunlight poured into Jeffrey's bedroom from the open blinds. I had forgotten to close them during the night. Although we could have put a few more hours of sleep to good use, Amy and I were excited to be up with the sun. Question after question popped into my head. I dressed quickly, eager to pose my questions to Arcon. Leaving Amy behind to finish putting on her makeup, I rushed downstairs. Since we began sleeping together, I noticed Amy had become more interested in makeup application. As for myself, I nearly fell down the stairs in my haste to speak to Arcon.

He bobbed on the kitchen counter. Rays of sunlight brightened the polished kitchen surfaces, especially the polished nickel sink.

"Good morning," Arcon said in a chipper tone.

"And to you," I reflected in an equally upbeat tone.

Amy arrived. She stopped abruptly at the kitchen threshold as if she had never seen Arcon before. I suddenly felt perturbed instead of relieved to see Arcon. "Where have you been? Not a single word from you in a week?"

"We thought you were dead," Amy added.

Arcon explained the situation without the barest hint of apology.

"The explosion scattered my molecules over a wide radius at the edge of your atmosphere. It took me almost a week to pull myself back together. I made it back through the burn of the atmosphere, but I was traveling so fast that I lost control when gravity took over. I crash-landed and you found me. It will take a few more days to fully integrate my systems. For the time being,

I've rebooted to an earlier version of myself to stabilize my consciousness."

"Tell us what happened up there. No fudging," I said.

"I fired a high-energy electromagnetic pulse at the energy source inside the ship's engine. Immediately, a series of pink lasers fired from the walls of the engine. They neutralized my pulse before it hit the energy source. In a millisecond, I switched to Plan B."

"You blew yourself up," Amy said.

"And the ship along with me."

Amy and I exchanged a look.

"I suppose you're forgiven," I said, "but you could have prepared us better for what happened. Can you tell us now why you didn't?"

"Aneleyan scientists created me for this mission. I'm barely one-earth-year-old. I have no reservoir of experience to draw from. I had no idea if I would survive the mission. You completed your assignments. You had nothing else to do except to wait. I had no desire to increase your anxiety about the outcome. What if the Krondorians were capable of scanning your minds when their ship entered the Earth's atmosphere? What if they discovered my plans floating around in your heads? There were too many unknowns and too much at stake."

"I forgive you," Amy beamed. "I'm so glad you're back. I missed you."

When I said nothing, Amy added, "Jacob missed you too."

The doorbells chimed. I wondered if Jeffrey had returned from his travels. He always announced himself by ringing first. A key slammed into the front door lock. Yes. Definitely Jeffrey. I'd recognize that key insertion anytime. I turned to Arcon. He made no move to conceal himself.

I heard rustling in the vestibule. Jeffrey passed the kitchen doorway. I called out to him. He came into the kitchen toting his signature calf leather briefcase and matching carry-on bag. He looked at me, smiled, and dropped the briefcase. It landed with a thud on the tile flooring.

"What the…"

"Jack!" Amy cried out.

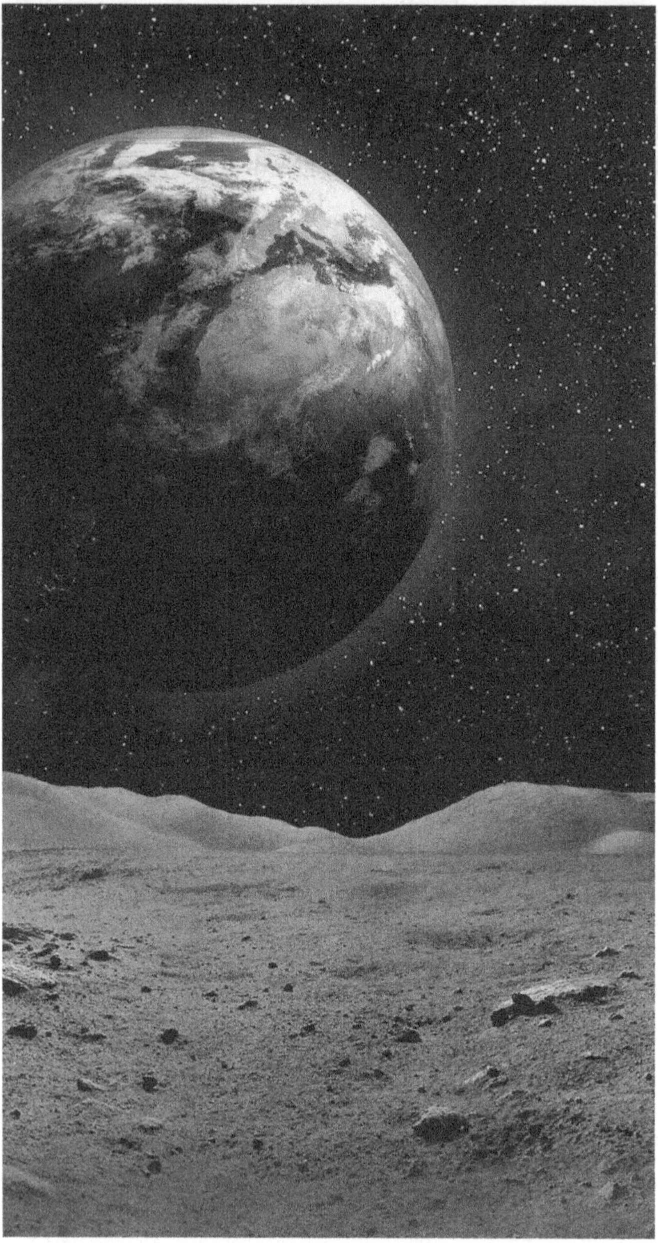

—21—
POINTS OF VIEW

Jeffrey's eyes slid to the counter where Arcon bobbed quietly like the nighttime tide. He pointed to Arcon.

"What's that thing?"

"He doesn't like being called a thing," I said. "Try showing a little respect."

Jeffrey, or whoever he was, picked up his briefcase and slammed it down on the island counter. We normally kept a vase of beautiful flowers there, but with the world ending and all, I had let the task of decorating the kitchen slip.

The stranger glowered at Amy. "You bitch. Either I'm having a bad dream, or I'm going to have to kill you again."

Amy threw a container of coffee at him. "You won't get the chance, you bastard."

The stranger drew a gold-plated, pearl-handled derringer out of the briefcase. A deadly toy for a rich boy. Cocking the hammer, he pointed the two stacked barrels at Amy.

At least now I knew the man standing in the middle of the kitchen wasn't my affable friend Jeffrey. Evidently, Jack had at least two personalities to match his fake IDs. I flashed back to my initial conversations with Amy. She had accused me of being a psychopath. Now I knew why. It was related to her traumatic experiences with this monster.

He walked around the island counter. I knew from my detective novels that derringers were notoriously unreliable from more than fifteen feet. Jack meant to walk straight up to Amy and shoot her at point-blank range.

Amy threw a stew pot at Jack. He avoided it easily.

I picked up a kitchen stool. I figured I could throw it at Jack before he shot me, and maybe buy some time for Amy to escape.

The derringer swung in my direction.

I threw the stool at Jack at the same time he fired at me. I heard a whine. The bullet caromed off the chair and crashed into a lacquered cabinet door a few feet from my head.

A second later, I heard a loud crackling noise. A bolt of electricity zapped Jack in the midsection. His body trembled, and Jack crumbled to the floor. His head cracked against the hard marble flooring.

Movement outside the panoramic kitchen window caught my attention. A young couple in skin-tight bathing suits gaped at us. Between them, they held a curly-haired child by her little hands. The mother hoisted the child up into her arms. The father hesitated. The mother reached over and pulled him away. The family disappeared from view.

I didn't have time to think about the disappearing

family and what they saw. The situation in the kitchen required my full attention.

Amy looked unsteady. I moved to hold her. "Nice shot," I muttered to Arcon as I passed.

"Is he dead?" Amy asked.

"He'll live, but he won't be dangerous again for a couple of hours," Arcon said.

"You sensed danger," I said to Arcon. "That's why you stayed on the counter."

"To be perfectly honest, I suspected early on that Jack and Jeffrey were the same people. The imprints you and Amy held of him in your minds were remarkably similar. They were too similar to be coincidental. I wasn't sure when the time would be right to make my suspicions known."

"Mind fingerprints," I said to Amy. She shook her head in disbelief.

I stared at the crumpled body of Jack Markham spread-eagled on the kitchen floor. The derringer had skipped a few feet away from his hand. I stood in the middle of the kitchen stroking my chin. I knew from writing my books how police detectives thought.

"There is no way we can explain this to the police," I said. "Any story we tell won't add up."

I turned to Arcon. "Can't you disappear this guy? You know, turn him into a missing person."

"No," Arcon said adamantly. "It's wrong, and we can't have any skeletons in the closet to haunt us when we go public."

"What?"

"I've received word from Aneleya that a scientific expedition will soon be launched for Earth. Based on your cooperation and our success, we think the people of Earth are ready to make contact. There is work to do to prepare the way for a warm reception."

"If we tell the police the true story, we'll be arrested and sent to a psychiatric ward for safe keeping."

"Not if I'm available to back up your story."

"Police reports of an alien visitor will send ripples up to high places. The government will want to put a lid on the story. We may never see the light of day again."

"Have faith, Jacob. We've made it this far against stiffer odds."

I thought about the consequences of opting in or out of Arcon's proposal. Leaving the scene of a crime and going on the lamb did not rank high on my to-do list. No other options came to mind.

"Wouldn't you say your scientists are using too small a sample to make their assumptions?"

"I'd say our scientists know what they're doing and I need your help. No one is more qualified than you and Amy for this work. I believe the mission will be an excellent opportunity for both of you in many ways. What do you say?"

"We can't tell the truth." I couldn't let go of this point of contention. "There has to be another way."

"We must be honest," Arcon persisted.

"Then we can't tell the part about Amy's resurrection."

Arcon crackled for a moment; thinking. "That's reasonable. I can't argue with that omission."

I turned to Amy. She turned to me. We both shrugged.

"I'm hoping the Goddard Center calls me in for a second interview. Otherwise, my schedule is open, which is a nice way of saying I'm unemployed."

"I'm thinking of writing a fictionalized version of my life since you came into it," I told Arcon. "Aside from saving the world twice, I'd like to get more mileage out of our travails."

"Why not make it a true account," Arcon offered. "It would fit right into the new mission."

"I don't write non-fiction, and I don't want to be searching for a new publisher in the crackpot press category."

Amy's laughter inspired me to ask Arcon another question. "In the course of your evolutionary process, do you think you can find room for a sense of humor?"

"Anything is possible."

I hated to admit we had proven it twice over.

Shifting my weight back and forth, I considered Arcon's pitch.

"What do you think?" Amy asked me.

I shrugged. "As much as I'd like to, I can't think of a justifiable reason to say no."

"It looks like we're in," Amy told Arcon.

In the distance, I heard the wail of police sirens.

— PART 3 —
PROMISE OF THE VISITOR

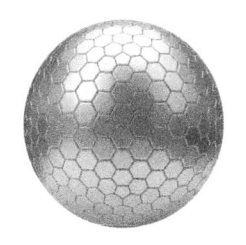

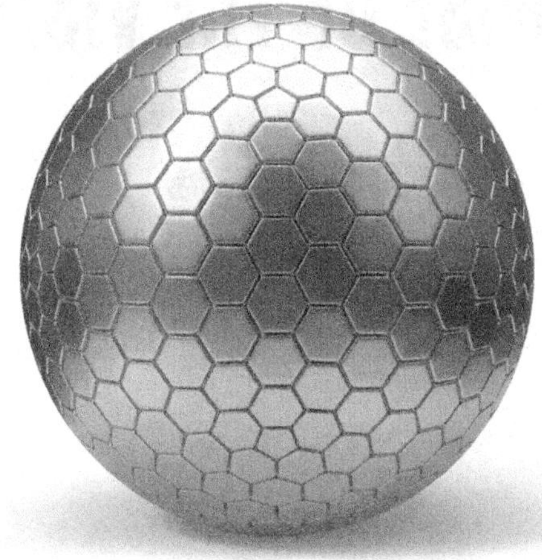

— 22 —
INTRODUCTIONS

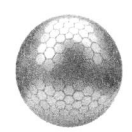

No one besides me and Amy knows that inside the golden sphere lives an artificial intelligence originating from the other side of the Milky Way. Said sphere rests on top of a beige granite counter beside a nickel-plated sink in Jeffrey's ultra-modern kitchen. Except the kitchen belongs to a guy named Jack. I keep thinking "Jeffrey" because that's the alter ego Jack uses as a front for his real name, Jack Markham. I thought Jeffrey Mortenson was my friend. Instead, he turns out to be an international criminal named Jack.

Such is life.

Before embarking for Earth, Arcon was packed by his makers into something resembling a basketball-sized silver sphere. Arcon's packaging has changed on multiple occasions due to the extremely difficult circumstances we have somehow managed to live through.

When I first met the artificial intelligence on a lonely stretch of Daytona Beach one night, it identified itself to me as "Arcon." The name is shorthand because its actual name is unpronounceable in English or any other terrestrial tongue.

The Aneleyan scientists who created Arcon needed to call him something because they didn't want to be rude and refer to him as an "it" or a "thing." This is probably why being called a "thing" has become one of Arcon's pet peeves. Arcon has preferences, but as far as I know, he doesn't have feelings. He may, however, be developing them because his consciousness is evolving. I want to explore feelings and other matters in depth with him when there isn't a crisis at hand.

Currently, we have one looming.

I think of Arcon as a "he" but this super-intelligent being is neither male nor female. When we first met, Arcon presented himself to me as a "he" because he didn't want any sexual tension to complicate our relationship. We only had three days to save the Earth, so there was no time to dither around with anything remotely romantic.

Speaking of sexual tension, my partner and current flame, Amy Goodwin, just walked into the room. A white robe covers her lithe body. She's put her long red hair up in a ponytail. She wears a light mask of makeup and a pair of flat heels. In her simple attire and after our long night of digging Arcon out of a crater in the sand, Amy still manages to look like a knockout. The ponytail, freckles, and white robe lend an air of child-like innocence, despite her nearly six-foot-tall frame. I know that Amy can change from an innocent child into a desirable twenty-six-year-old woman in a heartbeat. She never ceases to surprise me.

For example, if she wasn't a brainy aerospace engineer

and part-time astronomer, Amy might have had a successful career as a criminal. In the short time that we've been together, Amy has proven she can think on her feet. She can talk her way out of the stickiest of circumstances. We've been through many of them. We're in one now. Amy had to take a break to put herself back together after what happened only fifteen minutes ago.

Presently, there are two sheriff's deputies knocking on our front door. Their unexpected arrival so soon after the incident is unnerving, to put it mildly.

The man lying unconscious on the marble kitchen floor owns the beach house we've been staying in. Whether the house is owned in the name of Jack, Jeffrey, or some shell corporation doesn't matter. What matters is Jack will surely claim that we broke into his house, or we had an argument, and I attacked him. He'll say he came back from a business trip, found us in the house, and a struggle ensued. He'll claim that he used the double-barreled derringer a few feet from his bloodied head for self-defense.

If he goes with the self-defense story, Jack will have to come up with a plausible explanation as to how he wound up conked out on the floor. He had a gun, after all, and we didn't. In actuality, Jack cracked his head on the marble flooring when he crumbled after Arcon zapped him with an electromagnetic energy bolt. At the time, Jack was in a murderous rage. He wanted to kill Amy, again, after succeeding to do so once before. Jack is as devious a criminal as any. I'm sure he'll come up with a doozy of a story to cover his tracks. And, since he owns the house, I fear the deputies will believe Jack's fictional version of the story, assuming he wakes up to tell it.

"Daytona Beach Sheriff's Deputies," I hear through the front door.

"Coming," I announce. There's no choice. We have to let the police in and hope that Amy and I don't wind up in handcuffs. At least we won't have to worry about Arcon being arrested. His remarkable evolutionary process has enabled him to create the golden sphere he now inhabits. Uncharacteristically, Arcon once explained to me how he built his new house. I tend to ask Arcon tons of questions. He generally ignores them because we usually have to perform miracles on impossible deadlines. In this unusual case, I learned that the process of creating a custom-designed abode is similar to our 3-D printing process. Arcon's new-found ability to disguise himself could not have come at a more opportune time for two reasons. One: If the deputies see Arcon dancing naked as a glowing ball of energy on the countertop, there is no telling how they will react. Two: Before his ability to manifest objects dawned, Arcon had to take refuge in conspicuous objects like a nineteenth-century Art Deco vase and Amy's body, which he brought back to life after we found her lying dead on the beach two weeks ago.

I glance back at Amy. "This is scary," she says.

"I know. We'll get through this. You're amazing under pressure."

I open the stained oaken door with the nymph carved into the front panel. I silently pray that the nymph is a dying reminder of Jack Markham's libertine lifestyle soon to be extinguished behind prison bars.

The first deputy enters the vestibule. He's tall and lean and wears an obvious toupee that does not match his neatly trimmed mustache. I make his age at fifty-five to sixty years old. He's probably on his second tour of duty and third wife. Nothing like two pensions to make retirement sweeter and alimony payments easier. The pressures and unholy hours of police work are notorious for destroying marriages.

In my line of work as a mystery writer, I talk to officers of every stripe and variety. I generally like cops, except when they stop me for speeding. I know how hard their jobs are. Most of them are brave, unselfish people. I run into the occasional jerk, but cops don't have an exclusive on the franchise. I've noticed there are plenty of jerks to go around.

Police work is a highly specialized field. If they don't burn out first, cops tend to sign up for a second tour of duty in their forties and fifties because it's the only thing they know how to do. The pay and the benefits are good. The pay should be at least double, but city governments aren't banks and I don't know of any billionaires who regularly donate to their local police forces.

I've never had a hard time staying on the right side of the law, until recently. I see the Deputy's hand on his holstered gun and the bulge of a bullet-proof vest under his tan shirt. I've learned that domestic disturbance calls involving guns require extreme caution. In days gone by, police officers did not have to routinely bear the extra weight of bulky vests for their protection. They do now because the world has finally and completely lost its marbles.

I am well-versed in police matters and procedures as a result of the extensive research required to write my novels. All of this knowledge will probably leave me completely unprepared for this unimaginable situation.

I identify the deputy by the tag displayed proudly on his right breast pocket: G.L. Patterson. GL doesn't get around to introducing himself when he peers into the kitchen and sees Jack Markham's body sprawled on the kitchen floor.

"Don't move," he says.

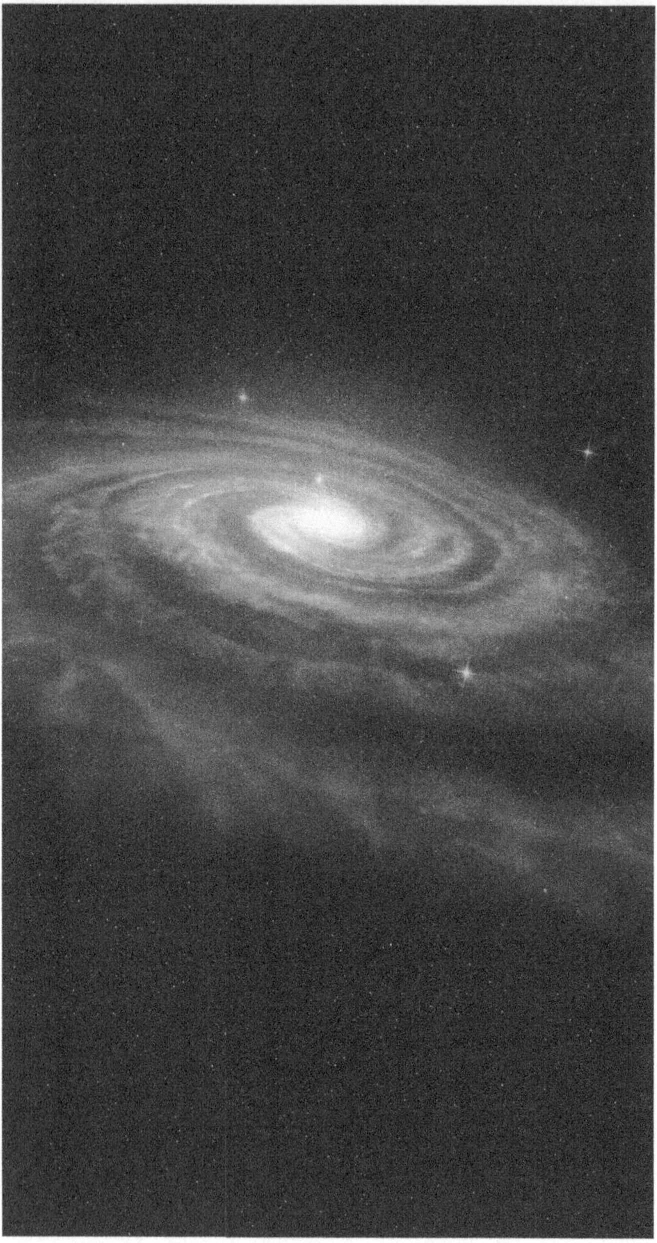

— 23 —
REVELATIONS

Patterson moves quickly into the kitchen. Staring at the body, he kneels to take Jack Markham's pulse.

"He's alive," I say. "We've called an ambulance. It should be here any minute. My name is Jacob Casell, by the way, and this is my friend, Amy Goodwin."

Amy smiles sweetly at Patterson. Pitch perfect. Patterson scoops a wallet out of the breast pocket of Jack's cashmere sports coat. He rises from the floor to his full height which must be at least six-foot-two inches. He's an imposing figure.

"I'm Sergeant Gerald Patterson with the Daytona Police Department. I'm declaring this a crime scene. Don't move or touch anything."

Putting my hands up, I offer politely, "It's a self-defense scene, Sergeant."

Shaking his head, Patterson says to the second deputy, "Check the ambo."

The second deputy followed Patterson through the front door. He now stands at the doorway leading into the kitchen. I see by his tag that his name is Wayne Romano. I suppose he's positioned himself to make sure we don't try to escape. He's young, no more than twenty-five. He's fit, about five-ten, and has the kind of good looks that compel women to write their phone numbers in his palm. I notice his hand is also on his holster. Romano is sweating profusely. The house faces the beach. The early morning ocean air is crisp. There is no reason to be perspiring excessively. I had an English teacher in high school who sweated like a mule plowing a bean field in the middle of summer. He said a broken gene caused his profuse sweating. Either Romano has a broken gene, or he's not cut out for police work.

Romano uses the radio pinned to his right shoulder to call his dispatcher. After a minute, he confirms, "The ambo is rolling."

Now that he knows that help is on the way, Sergeant Gerald Patterson asks sharply: "What happened here?"

The friendly approach clearly isn't working.

I'm remarkably calm for a man who stands a good chance of being arrested at any moment. I'm calm because I have an ace in the hole. Arcon has promised to back up the story we tell the police if it becomes necessary. It will be tricky, however. If Arcon chooses to speak telepathically, his voice blasting into the police officers' heads will spook them. One of them might accidentally shoot us. I wonder if taking a bullet is worse than being booked and jailed for aggravated assault and consorting with a feisty alien artificial intelligence. Whatever the case, I decide Amy is the best person to lead-off the discussion. I nod to her. She addresses Sergeant Patterson.

"The man you see on the floor tried to kill me with the derringer near his head," Amy begins. "He wants me dead because I found out that he's involved with his Wharton School buddies in a scheme to manipulate foreign currencies to generate windfall profits for themselves and their companies. Jack uses aliases. The ID in the wallet you're holding may say he's Jeffrey Mortenson. I know him as Jack Markham, an investment banker employed by his father's firm, Markham Capitol. His co-conspirators are lawyers, accountants, and investment bankers like Jack, all employed by high-powered Wall Street firms."

Patterson and Romano say nothing. They need to hear more.

"I've made a whistle-blower complaint to the SEC," Amy says. "I have a case number."

Amy's last statement is a blatant lie, but it sounds good and she will probably get away with it. I sense my turn has come to embellish the narrative.

"Markham announced his intention to kill Amy," I say, leaving out his intention to kill Amy *again.* Thinking back, it's hard for even *me* to believe that Arcon lived inside Amy's body for a week and his energy transmission brought her back from the dead. Try telling that to a police officer.

"Markham drew the pistol you see on the floor and began walking straight across the kitchen to shoot Amy at point-blank range. I picked up a kitchen stool and threw it at him. He swiveled and fired at me. The bullet hit the stool and ricocheted into the cabinet above my head. You can see the bullet hole right there."

Patterson and Romano follow my finger to the hole

in the front panel of an expensive, black lacquered kitchen cabinet.

"Did the stool hit Markham in the head and knock him out?" Patterson asks.

The moment of truth has arrived. I had previously asked Arcon to "disappear" Jack Markham from the face of the Earth. I reasoned that the police would never believe our story if we made one up. I buttressed my argument by saying the police would also have a hard time believing that Markham had been knocked out by a controlled energy burst emanating from an alien intelligence from the other side of the Milky Way.

Arcon would have none of my reasoning. He has his reasons for not lying to the police.

All of this leaves me staring wistfully at the golden sphere with Arcon inside it.

Amy starts to say something but then thinks better of it.

"To answer your question," I say to Patterson, "the stool did not knock Markham out."

As the sun continues its early morning ascension, it spews golden sunlight across the kitchen floor raising multi-colored sparkles in the marble. It also raises Jack Markham from unconsciousness. He struggles to a kneeling position on his hands and knees. I imagine the sun whispering in Markham's ear saying, *wake up, wake up, sweet prince*. The innocent sun has little idea of Markham's true nature. He is certainly not sweet. If he is a prince, then he is a prince of thieves. Markham's first name gives more of a clue to his nature. Markham is a jackal of the worst kind. I know this. Amy and Arcon know it. How do we convince the police of it?

"Who knocked you out?" Romano asks Markham. He's standing almost directly above Jack. Markham is too fuzzy to answer. Romano elevates his stare to me.

I'm still contemplating the golden sphere.

"The genie in the sphere isn't going to answer for you," Romano says.

I'm beginning to get a strong impression that Romano is one of the jerks.

"I beg to differ," Arcon projects telepathically to the deputies. Amy and I hear it too. We're looped in. We can't project our thoughts to Arcon, but we can receive his. Jack puts his hands to his ears. He must be hearing it too.

I take inventory of the deputies' reactions. Romano looks like he's just emptied something into his trousers. Patterson is banging his ear and tilting his head to one side as if he's trying to get the salt water out after snorkeling in the ocean.

Romano draws his weapon. It's a reflex as I feared.

"Don't shoot," Arcon says.

"Where are you?" Patterson says, frantically looking at the ceiling, the walls, and the cabinets; everywhere except where Arcon resides.

"I'm in the golden sphere on the counter near the sink," Arcon announces.

Romano trains his gun on the sphere.

Patterson waves an arm at Romano. "Holster your weapon before you hurt someone."

"Are you sure? It might be dangerous."

"PUT YOUR GUN AWAY!"

Heaving a sigh of resignation, Romano acquiesces to Patterson's command.

Patterson looks hard at Amy and then back to me. "Which one of you is going to tell me what the hell is going on here?"

Amy takes the initiative. "When the man on the floor fired his weapon at Jacob, Arcon tased him with a bolt of electromagnetic energy."

"Who's Arcon?"

"That would be me," Arcon announces from within the golden sphere. "I'm an intelligence from the other side of your galaxy. I've saved your world from destruction twice. I could not have done it without the help of Jacob and Amy. I know what I've just said is a big mouthful to digest. Take however long you need to process it."

Three things happen next. Patterson leans forward and squints at the golden sphere. I watch Jack pick the double-barreled derringer off the floor. An ambulance arrives outside.

Markham rises to his full height of six feet. His sandy hair is freshly barbered, tousled, and bloodied. My former friend is a handsome devil. Literally. He holds the derringer pointed at the floor.

"Put the gun down," Patterson says.

Jack ignores him. "These people are full of crap. I threw Jacob out of my house a month ago for reneging on his rental agreement. He stabs the air with an index finger pointed at Amy.

"This woman is stalking me. I broke up with her a few weeks ago. She can't let go of the relationship. She's extremely insecure and neurotic. I came home from a business trip and found these two going through the drawers in the kitchen. Jacob knows the alarm code. I haven't changed it since I threw him out. That's how they got in. They were going to steal my expensive silverware and whatever else they could get their desperate hands on. They attacked me when I caught them robbing my house. I fired my weapon in self-defense. As far as that thing in the sphere is concerned, it's an interactive recording. It is an object of art that I paid fifty thousand dollars for at a Sotheby's auction in Palm Beach."

Patterson and Romano draw their weapons. "Put the gun down," Patterson repeats calmly to Jack.

"Are you through, you bastard," Amy says. Turning to Patterson, she reports, "he has a yacht named 'High Finance' parked in slip three at the Williams Island Resort and Marina in North Miami. Get a warrant and search the ship, especially the computers. You'll see that everything I've told you about this scumbag is true."

"You fucking bitch." Markham says, pointing the derringer at Amy.

"Drop it," Patterson shouts.

Simultaneously, two paramedics enter the kitchen with a stretcher.

The first one is just in time to tackle Markham. Both paramedics quickly subdue him.

"Cuff him," Patterson says to Romano.

"Amy and Jacob are telling the truth," Arcon says audibly. "I can confirm every word of their statements."

"Yeah. You'll make a great witness."

Arcon wisely chooses to remain silent.

"If you have a voice, why didn't you use it to speak to us right away? You scared me and my partner."

"I'm sorry. I was unsure about the best way to communicate."

Patterson continues to stare in Arcon's direction. Then, he rotates his fierce gaze to Amy and me.

"You're both free to go for now, but don't leave town. I'm turning this investigation over to the FBI."

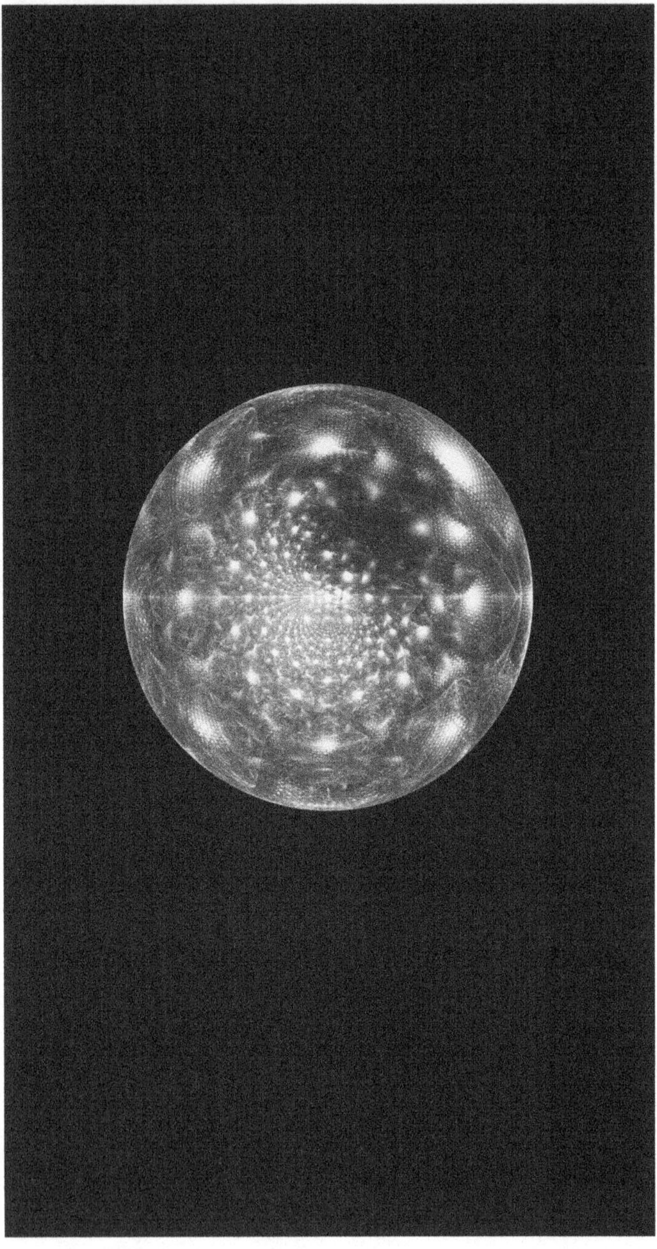

—24—
PREPARATIONS

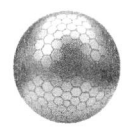

We climb the stairs to the second-floor study. I'm holding Arcon inside the golden sphere. Amy follows. As usual, I'm annoyed by the garish artwork lining the wall of the staircase. Markham's poor taste in art is a minor irritation compared to the porcupines I imagine piercing my back. It feels like I'm resting on a bed of poison-tipped nails. Any minute, the poison will take effect and I'll start convulsing.

"You're overreacting," I hear Arcon say inside my head.

"Only a little," Amy counters. "We will need to hire a lawyer to be here when the FBI comes calling."

"I can't afford an anti-FBI lawyer," I say glumly.

"We won't need one," Arcon chirps. "I'll know what to say when the time comes."

"I'm sure your confidence is based on a long history of dealing with FBI agents."

Not surprisingly, Arcon ignores my comment.

I try another approach. "Is the ability to manipulate FBI agents telepathically another by-product of your evolutionary process?"

Once again, Arcon refuses to bite. He has bigger fish to fry. His perspective is similar to the view from the top of a mountain tall enough to poke into the edge of outer space. I should be used to this by now.

The second-floor study looks out on Daytona Beach through matching corner windows. It's a small room decorated with a rosewood chair, desk, and bookcase. The wallpaper is an enlarged gray pinstripe design that reminds me of Jack's custom-made business suits. My twelve mystery novels are prominently displayed in order on the center shelf. I know now the existence and positioning of the novels on the shelf is a ruse designed to convince me that Jack Markham considered me a dear friend. Evidently, he kept me around solely to care for his house when he was away on his frequent business trips. I might have had some use as a conversation piece, although I'm not sure if hobnobbing with a midlist writer has any cachet.

It's now barely past eleven AM. The sun is glinting off the freshly laid sand. The wavelets coming in off the ocean are winking with reflected sunlight. I love this place. I've done some of my best writing here. The neighboring houses are a quarter mile apart. No crowds descend upon our section of private beach. The beach in this exclusive neighborhood is leased by the residents. Tranquility is the norm here. The feeling of peace is so constant it has seeped into my bones. The ions in the ocean air stimulate my desire to write. It pains me to think my time here may be ending.

I place Arcon's golden sphere in the center of the desk. I offer Amy the only chair in the room. She politely declines and curls up on three corner futons upholstered in a fabric matching the wallpaper.

I sit in the desk chair in front of Arcon.

"Well, old bean, you called this meeting. Speak."

"I'm neither old nor a bean."

"Old bean" is a name my mother used to call me. It's an endearing phrase. I'm trying to inject a sense of camaraderie into the meeting. It's been a long day and it's not even time for lunch."

So far this morning, Amy and I have reunited with Arcon after thinking a Krondorian Warship had incinerated him. Jack Markham came home from a business trip to terrorize us. Daytona Beach deputies nearly arrested us. Instead, they carted dear old Jack away in handcuffs. To top it off, there is a high probability the FBI will soon be in touch with us. I can't wait to hear what happens next.

In his typically brusque manner, Arcon makes a banner headline announcement: "The Visitor will be arriving this evening."

Amy sits up on the futons. We don't have time to ask the obvious question which is: *How can the Visitor be arriving so soon?* We committed to helping Arcon with his next mission only a few hours ago. I'm sure we both assumed we'd have some down time to catch our breath before embarking on our next assignment regardless of how humanitarian and less hazardous it promises to be.

As usual, Arcon is ready to douse my complaints.

"A small ship traveling across the galaxy through a wormhole at nearly a thousand times the speed of light tends to arrive almost instantly. The scientist will land the mother ship on the rock and ice plains of Ganymede, Jupiter's largest moon. From there, she will create a hyper-space tunnel to travel to Earth in a shuttle. The trip from Jupiter to Earth will take about ten hours. Traveling by HST is slower than traveling by wormhole, but it can't be avoided. If you recall, I told you during our last mission that creating even a small wormhole within your solar system will have catastrophic effects."

"Did I hear you say the scientist is a she?"

"Is that a problem?"

"No, it's just—"

'Surprising," Amy interjects. "I'm a woman. I shouldn't be surprised, but I am. For some reason, I think we were expecting a man. It may have something to do with an old science fiction movie."

"The Day the Earth Stood Still."

Amy grabs my wrist. "That's it!"

I'm thinking gender bias is a minor problem compared to appearance. What if this "female" is a hideous monster? What if I can't look her in the eyes? Staring at the ground is not a good way to generate interstellar goodwill.

"From what I hear, the Visitor is an extraordinary female. And, she will be bringing boons for Mankind with her."

Amy and I let Arcon's statement breathe. The good news is a welcome break from the uphill climb of the day. It started with digging pieces of Arcon out of a deep hole in the sand, and that was the easy part.

"I wanted to prepare you," Arcon says. "You both look a bit peaked from all the excitement. You can both use a shot of my transmission to perk you up. First, I'll have to make some protective glasses for you to wear. My energy keeps cycling up. I'm literally becoming brighter; too bright for unprotected human eyes."

Arcon makes low humming sounds indicating he's pondering some weighty problem. "I'm beginning to wonder if my evolutionary process is progressing too quickly for its own good." A pause. "Well, it's something to discuss with the Visitor along with other matters."

Bouncing off the pin-striped walls, a higher-frequency humming sound fills the sun-dappled study. I have never seen Arcon "make" anything before. By her expression, I see that Amy is equally curious. I imagine the humming is the prelude to something wondrous, like blossoming orchestral sounds before the feature movie in an IMAX theater. Two pairs of goggles with deep purple lenses emerge from each side of the golden sphere. They plop unceremoniously on the rosewood desk.

"Try them on," Arcon says. "They're custom fitted. Amy, your pair is on the left."

Amy and I affix the goggles.

"Move your chair back against the wall next to Amy," Arcon tells me.

With the goggles and ourselves in place, Arcon rises from the sphere. I'm immediately struck by his size. He's twice the circumference he was a few weeks ago. His body has changed. He's no longer a swirl of energy spiraling like a pinwheel. Now, Arcon's outer edges appear solid with three-dimensional geometric patterns of tiny suns forming and reforming in his amorphous center. To my eyes, the patterns appear to be star formations. I take my observations with a grain of salt. *Who or what is Arcon? What is he made of?*

Of one observation, I am certain. The clarity of objects through the lenses is remarkable. I see Arcon in minute detail despite the light-filtering qualities of the goggles.

"You're beautiful," Amy proclaims with equal measures of enthusiasm and awe.

"Aw shucks," Arcon says before his new and improved form funnels back into the golden sphere.

"Don't be shy," Amy says. "I'd like to study you."

"I'm concerned about over-exposing you to my transmission when I'm in the buff. As you both know, when my energy cycled up, my life-saving transmission became toxic to Amy when I lingered too long inside her body."

I remember the night Arcon separated his consciousness from Amy. We weren't sure if she could live independently. It was touch and go for an agonizing span of five minutes. As it turned out, and to my great relief, Amy has been fully and miraculously restored to an independent life.

Something Arcon said earlier has been swimming around in my head. I think this might be an opportune time to broach the subject. As far as I can tell, we have at least a few minutes to spare, and Arcon appears to be in a good mood.

"I noticed you introduced yourself as an 'intelligence' to the deputies. I've been wondering about it."

"Do you consider yourself artificial?" Arcon asks me.

"There are times when I have to fake it, but basically, no."

"Then why should I consider myself artificial?"

Amy and I exchange intrigued looks.

"Moving on to more important issues, we've agreed that our next mission involves preparing the world to be introduced to the Visitor. I thought by now I'd have at least a rough outline to discuss with you. For some reason, the Visitor has been guarded about releasing details in advance of our face-to-face meeting. So, all I can say is: Prepare to be prepared."

Amy and I erupt with laughter. "Did I say something funny?"

"Not intentionally," I say. "Which reminds me: As part of our agreement when we signed on for this mission, you promised to develop a sense of humor."

"I'm working on it. For now, I suggest you break for lunch and then get some rest. We have a big night ahead of us."

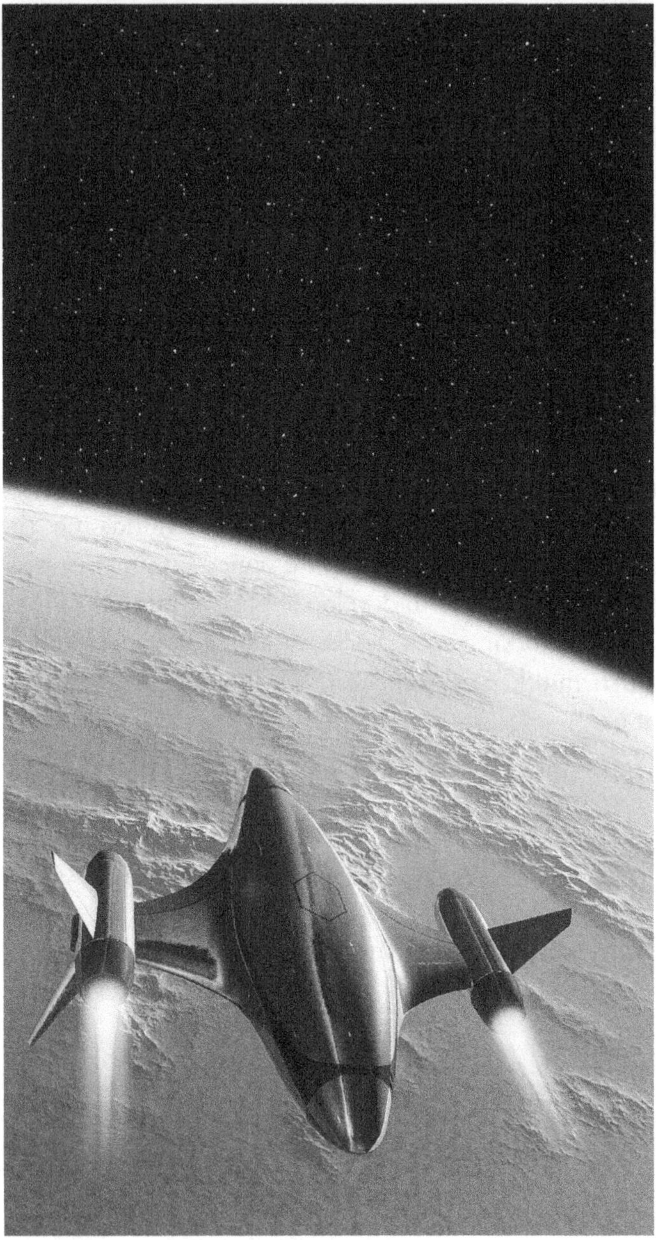

—25—
THE VISITOR

Holding hands, Amy and I stand on the beachfront watching the fog roll in from the ocean. The air is damp and chilly on this November night. I am glad the weather is uninviting. The beach is deserted. Only a fool would risk the flu or a case of pneumonia from exposure to these conditions. (We, of course, are fools). I am also glad the houses built on this expensive stretch of Daytona Beach are spaced far enough apart to provide an uncommon degree of privacy. We do not want uninvited guests happening along to crash tonight's history-making party.

Arcon has positioned himself some two hundred and fifty yards downwind as a precautionary measure against overexposing us to his powerful energy aura. He hovers a few feet above the sand, shining like a second sun rising at night. At Arcon's instruction, I've left the golden sphere close by in case he needs to retire hastily into it.

The full moon casts a pale light on the freshly laid sand making it a ghostly shade of white. Every six months, by contract with the residents, the City of

Daytona Beach lays fresh sand on this private beach to keep it clean and counter the effects of erosion.

I am anonymously dressed in a gray sweatshirt and sweat pants accented by my off-brand black sneakers. I've never been a clothes horse. And, I like blending in with the crowd because it makes it easier to be an observer. Amy, on the other hand, looks resplendent in a pink sweatshirt and pants she's purchased recently. A pair of tan hiking boots with pink laces completes the outfit.

"I'm concerned about a spacecraft landing in our backyard, even if it is only a small shuttle," I confide to Amy. I am speaking aloud. Only Arcon can communicate with us telepathically, and he has yet to teach us how it's done.

"Arcon told us the scientists on Aneleya know what they're doing."

"I hope he's right. We don't need to arouse more attention from the authorities."

I feel Amy's hand shaking in mine. "Are you alright?"

"It's the cold weather. And, I'm nervous. You?"

"I'm fine."

In truth, I am anything but fine. My heroes and heroines are routinely taken into custody despite their righteous intentions. I never worry about them because I know they won't be imprisoned for long. The show must go on. I can't say the same for Amy or me.

I imagine two police officers hauling me into a precinct to stand before a desk sergeant.

"What's the charge, Officer Ryan?"

Ryan answers derisively, "Consorting with aliens and poking his nose where it doesn't belong."

"Book him and hold him 'til the area 51 guys get here,"

says the sergeant. "It may take months for them to catch the case. They are understaffed and his story sounds too outlandish to believe to begin with."

Laughing, Ryan grabs my arm. "Come with me, smartass."

Happily, Arcon's voice bursting into our heads ends this waking nightmare.

"The shuttle will be arriving any minute now. Stay alert."

I manage to calm myself. I see something coming at us out of the fog. As it nears, I see that it's a ship skimming a few feet above the black waves. Amy squeezes my hand tighter. Instinctively, we step backward to higher ground, or more accurately, higher beach. The roar of the propulsion engines reaches our ears. I'm no astronaut, but it looks to me like the ship is hurtling toward the shore too fast for a safe landing. It reminds me of a cruise missile traveling in slightly-slow motion. I'm convinced we'll be annihilated the moment the shuttle reaches the shoreline. Amy hugs me tightly. I am too frozen to move.

At the last possible second, the spacecraft veers sharply up the shoreline. Simultaneously, the twin engines die rather than ourselves. Now that we are still among the living, I estimate the fuselage measures maybe twenty feet in length. I watch the craft coast toward Arcon's position on some kind of anti-gravity bed. For a ship that's been traveling at unfathomable speeds through our solar system, it has made an adroit landing, albeit a terrifying one for the uninitiated.

Amy and I are too stunned to speak. We watch the vessel rotate to face Arcon some two-hundred-fifty yards down the shoreline. Landing struts issue from the bottoms of the dual engines mounted on the stubby, swept-back wings. The fuselage is light grey with a series of italic blue lines of varying lengths emblazoned along the side. There is a set of small windows in the nose and a perfunctory tail assembly. Perhaps space-traveling Lear Jets of the future will look like this Aneleyan craft. From the bottom of the ship, a light turns a circle of sand bright white. A pair of legs appear. I watch a figure in a shimmering blue spacesuit lower itself out of the ship.

"How can it be humanoid? What are the odds?" I ask Amy.

"It's a she," Amy reminds me. I sense she is too absorbed in the unfolding events to contemplate the nature of sentient life forms in the universe. I follow Amy's example and narrow my focus. From the shapely figure I see inside the spacesuit, it looks like I won't have to stare at the ground when I meet this intergalactic space traveler.

We observe the Visitor addressing Arcon. We are not looped into the conversation, either intentionally or by a glitch in communication. Amy and I wait impatiently as we watch the Visitor's emphatic gestures and what appears to be Arcon listening placidly.

After about five minutes, the conversation ends. The Visitor points at the shuttle with a gloved hand. The landing gear retracts. The craft turns and floats down the beach towards us. Midway between our two groups, the ship turns toward the ocean. The engines fire. It follows the same low trajectory across the waves out to sea. Before the fog can swallow it up, I watch the sleek craft veer upward. In seconds, it disappears into the starless night sky.

Our gazes fall back to the Visitor and Arcon. The Visitor gestures at the golden sphere lying nearby in the sand. I see Arcon disappear into it. Picking up the sphere, the Visitor walks toward us holding her space helmet in her left hand and the golden sphere in the other.

"I think we should stop holding hands," I say to Amy.

"Why?"

"Something tells me that holding hands is not proper etiquette for greeting visitors from outer space."

"You might have a point."

I let go of Amy's hand. She says, "Looks like Arcon nailed it when he said the Aneleyan scientists know what they are doing. Presto. No problem stashing an alien spaceship."

"I will never doubt you again."

"Be serious. We're making first contact."

Amy is right. This is a history-making moment. It is no time for small talk or silly jokes.

I watch the Visitor striding gracefully and calmly toward us. Besides the humanoid form, I'm struck by the sight of a subtle energy aura emanating from her navy-blue space suit. I imagine the energy field is visible against the contrast of the fog and the night, and probably not visually detectable by day. It blends into the edges of the night in a mesmerizing, pulsating rhythm. In this setting, the Visitor's appearance suggests a dream-like painting. Her strides are confident. As she nears, I make her height well over six feet. Amy takes my hand again and squeezes it. I can tell she isn't afraid of the figure approaching us. She is simply trying to control her excitement.

When the distance between us narrows to within ten feet, I hear Arcon's telepathic voice.

"I send warm greetings from the Visitor. You may call her Silenna. Silenna will be speaking through me until she adapts adequately to the English language."

"Please return our warm welcome," I say to Arcon.

A moment passes.

"With your permission, Silenna will approach."

"Permission granted," Amy says.

After placing the golden sphere delicately on the sand, Silenna steps forward. I begin to make out her features. She's at least six-and-three-quarter feet tall. Her hair is an odd mixture of black, silver, and golden strands pushed straight back from her broad forehead. I'd expect her hair to be cut boyishly short for space travel, but I see it is held tightly in a bun as her head drifts back and forth to observe both of us in detail. It's as if her eyes are lenses recording our features. I wonder if Silenna is an android.

She takes a step closer. Extending her right hand to me, she says through Arcon, "I am honored to meet you."

I take her gloved hand in mine and notice it is larger than her left one. Either Aneleyans grow larger left or right hands, or there is something in the glove besides fingers and flesh. I put my other hand on top of Silenna's because mine is too small for a proper shake. Her eyes are a deep blue with a purple iris and orange pupils. Her features are regular. Her skin is pale blue. Despite her odd coloring, Silenna is far from looking hideous.

I stand six-foot-four and have never been introduced to a female professional basketball player. Therefore, I'm not used to looking up at a woman. It's a strange feeling. Speaking of which, I feel a tingling sensation in my body. No, it's more like a scintillating feeling. It must be the effect of Silenna's energy aura. It is a subtle feeling, less tangible than Arcon's transmission.

Turning to Amy, Silenna repeats the greeting ritual, then she takes a step backward. I assume our guest wants to underscore the notion that she is speaking to both of us. She is polite and formal as if we are foreign dignitaries meeting for the first time at the UN.

"I've never been good at small talk. I hope you'll forgive me if I get straight to the point."

Amy and I are quick to reassure Silenna that we are old hands at speaking directly. Arcon has done an excellent job of preparing us for blunt communication, but we are careful not to mention it.

"As your people say, I bring you good news and bad news. Allow me to give you the good news first."

I'm sure the Aneleyan concept Silenna communicated to Arcon had no resemblance to what we just heard. Arcon, now saturated in the colloquialisms of the English language, is doing a great job with the interstellar translation.

"Your cooperation with Arcon in accomplishing his missions here is what inspired me to come. If you two are representative of the human race, then I have great hope for your people and this world. I am here to encourage peaceful coexistence and to relieve suffering."

"We are humbled by your comments," Amy says.

"We are honored by and appreciative of your presence and intentions," I add.

I remember Arcon telling me about the ability of Aneleyan scientists to make accurate predictions based on small test samples. We had a pointed exchange about it. I can only hope this Aneleyan scientist hasn't jumped to any conclusions. Maybe the Aneleyans can read our genes like tea leaves from a long distance. Maybe human beings are naturally cooperative unless they are oppressed or undermined. It's a complex issue. It would be interesting to discuss the matter in a symposium with Aneleyan scientists.

I see Silenna's expression change. "And now for the bad news. I regret to inform you that Aneleya has been destroyed, along with most of its inhabitants."

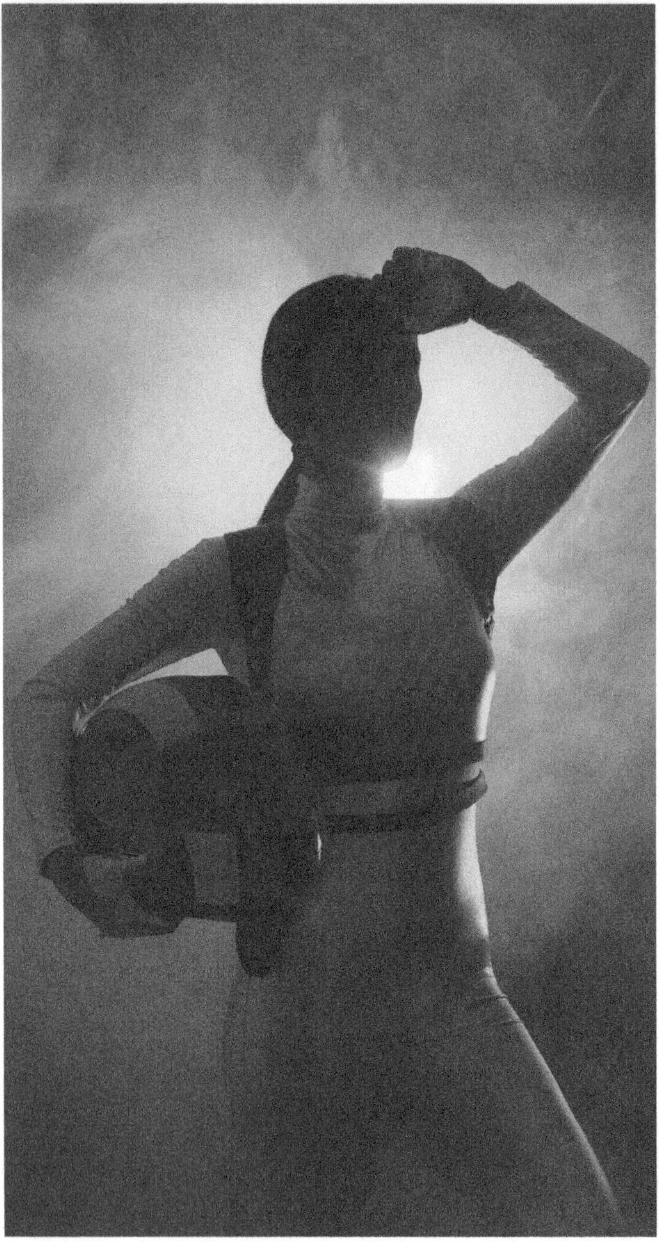

—26—
SILENNA

To say we are shell-shocked at the news is a vast understatement besides a trite expression. I am not sure how to respond. I see from Amy's reaction that she is equally dumbfounded. Saying "I'm so sorry for your loss" doesn't cut it. I can't imagine the depths of grief and isolation Silenna must be feeling.

As if she has read my mind, Silenna says, "There is no consolation available from others for this horrible tragedy, but I appreciate your intention to say something appropriate. I mention my home world's fate only for explanatory purposes. I suggest we take shelter in your abode before we are observed."

I conclude that Silenna's last statement is no coincidence. She *can* read minds. I will have to watch what I say *and* think until further notice.

With heavy hearts, Amy and I lead the way through the backdoor into the beach house.

* * *

We gather in the study again. Silenna sits upright and tall behind the desk, with Arcon propped on the desktop to her left. Our extraterrestrial visitor is a commanding presence. Her deportment seems to flow and fill the room naturally. Amy has the front-row seat. I'm on the futons. The futons cramp my style, but who cares. I'm lucky to be a principal player in this incredible event. Maybe.

"I am now relying less on Arcon's translations to learn your language faster. I'm speaking to you verbally rather than telepathically for the same reason. It helps to hear words spoken out loud. Do not hesitate to ask for clarification if anything I say is unclear. Understood?"

We acknowledge our comprehension. Silenna's language is as stiff as a two-by-four, but it gets the job done. Arcon spoke the same way when I first met him. Silenna's English will soon thaw out, but I doubt the same can be said for her trauma.

"First, allow me to apologize for revealing what I have to tell you all at once. I had hoped Arcon would be able to relay the information gradually to give you time to process it. Unfortunately, we experienced a communication breakdown on my way here. In our initial conversation on the beach, Arcon and I determined that my signal was deliberately jammed. We don't know who or what is responsible."

I'm thinking the malevolent Krondorians are the logical culprits, but Silenna and Arcon think otherwise.

Silenna turns, fixing me with an intense stare from her oddly beautiful eyes.

"We obliterated Krondoria," she says, reading my

mind. "If there were any survivors, they were off-world. The signature of the jamming transmission doesn't match anything Krondorian."

Silenna pauses. I watch her inhale deeply, gathering herself for what she has to say next. She speaks to Amy sitting directly before her.

"The monsters managed to remotely activate a doomsday device stationed on one of the Krondorian moons. They had enough time to program it with our planet's coordinates before Krondoria exploded. The device creates a supernova effect. When it slipped undetected into our solar system, it detonated, leaving nothing behind but a black hole."

Silence in the room. Behind Silenna, the fog is clearing. The stars blink against the black dome of night. The wind kicks up from the ocean. It rattles the windowpanes.

Silenna's gaze falls to the shiny rosewood desktop. The bright track lighting from the ceiling does nothing to lighten the mood.

Silenna suddenly looks up, as if she refuses to spend any more time grieving for herself and the countless souls of the Aneleyan departed.

Amy is the first to speak in a compassionate tone.

"Are there any other survivors besides you?"

"Like me, a handful of deep space explorers were engaged in off-world expeditions when the devastation occurred. We are all that remains of our civilization."

I'm wondering how something like this can happen to a noble race like the Aneleyans when Silenna breaks my train of thought.

"We thought we had every right to destroy the

Krondorians for their long history of crimes against sentient life in our galaxy. Maybe we disobeyed the laws of the universe. Perhaps we had no right to levy a death sentence on the Krondorian people. Maybe violence begat violence. Cause triggered effect. Or none of the above. Arcon tells me your people have a saying for this: 'Shit Happens.' Perhaps our good deeds afford us no protection from random acts of genocide."

"I understand your anger and bewilderment," Amy says.

"Do you?"

Amy says nothing. It must be hard for Amy to feel the brunt of Silenna's anger. I'm thinking this is the first chance Silenna has had to vent.

"I'm sorry," Silenna says.

After a few minutes of silence, I say to Silenna, "Would you like us to leave you alone before we show you to your room."

"There is something else you must know. I am not certain how this will affect you or the people of this world."

I look at Amy. From her expression, I assume we are thinking the same thing. *Haven't we heard enough for one night?*

Silenna looks down at the gleaming desktop. "My heart is heavy, and I've done enough talking for one night. I will allow Arcon to continue."

Arcon has been quiet for so long that I expect to hear him clear his throat. Except he doesn't have one, of course.

"I'm afraid there is no way to sugarcoat this," Arcon begins telepathically.

"Since when do you sugarcoat anything," I reply. I'm

angry. In the last few months, I've heard enough bad news from Arcon to last me a lifetime. He ignores my outburst entirely. Standard Arcon operating procedure.

"We now have sufficient evidence that a ship of considerable size has landed in the Molke Crater. It is a bowl-shaped lunar impact crater measuring six miles in diameter. There is no indication your satellites or ground surveillance discs have registered the ship's arrival. Silenna feels responsible for inadvertently leading the ship close to Earth. She came here to help humanity. Now, she fears she may have done the opposite."

"Can it be a surviving Krondorian warship?" I am quick to ask.

"Undetermined," Silenna replies.

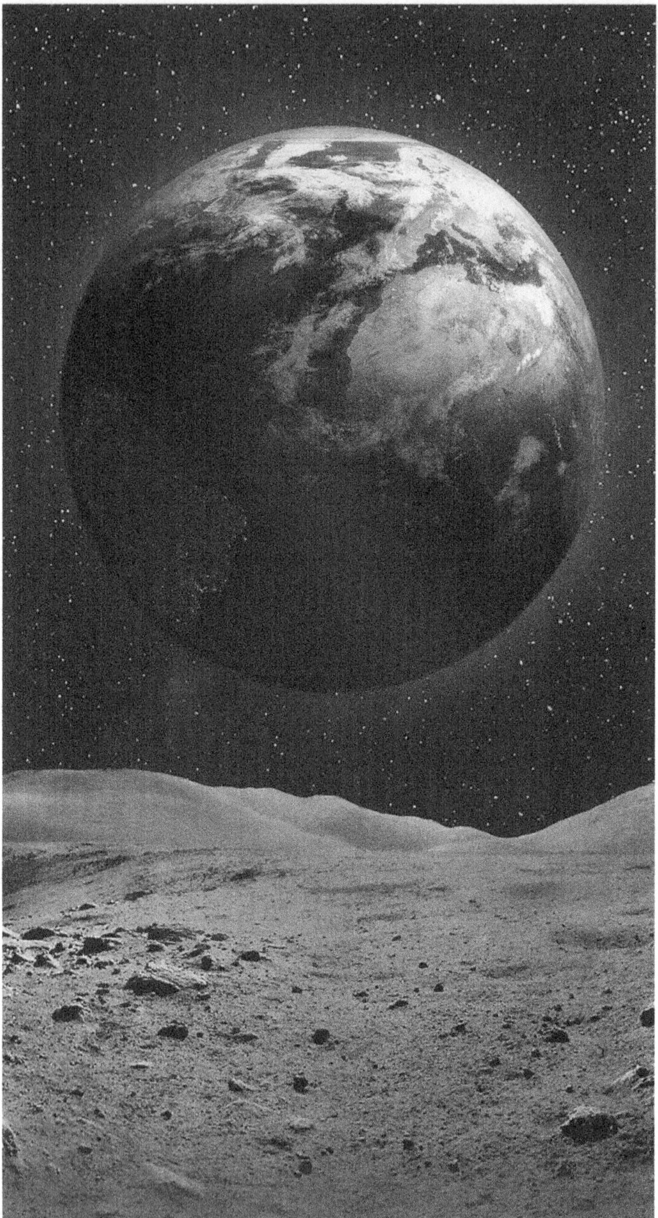

— 27 —
"WHAT ELSE CAN HAPPEN?"

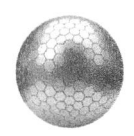

I awaken the next morning. The sun pours in through the single red-wood blind I habitually leave open as a portal to the weather outside. The day promises to be glorious; one that Amy and I will undoubtedly not have the opportunity to enjoy.

Amy sleeps peacefully in the raw and partially covered in the super king-sized platform bed. My ex-friend Jack with the ex-name Jeffrey believed in buying custom-made everything with his ill-gotten wealth. I hope the Daytona Beach deputies have turned him over to the FBI. I also hope Sergeant Patterson is so busy he has forgotten to turn us over to the FBI. Our team now numbers four. We are nothing, if not diverse.

I am careful not to disturb Amy. Once again, we find ourselves in a situation where random peaceful moments are becoming increasingly rare. I'd like this one to last. I slip out of bed quietly and go to the bathroom. Closing the door carefully, I proceed with my morning ministrations. I splash my face liberally with cold water. I check my reflection in the mirror. I have grown thinner but not softer since Arcon floated onto a beach and into my life. In the month after Arcon and I saved the Earth for the first time from a Krondorian-directed pulsar, I have returned to my regular regimen of bike riding, free-weights, and stretching. It helps me to stay firm and feel well, and it enhances my ability to write. Unfortunately, the events of the last two weeks during which we saved the world for a second time with Amy's exceptional assistance have eaten into my workout regimen. I suppose we all have to make sacrifices, especially when engaged in planetary survival missions.

My facial appearance hasn't changed. Same wavy blond hair and intact hairline. Same blue eyes. Same straight bones and regular features thanks to my mother's hardy Scandinavian genes.

With my face having passed inspection, it is now time to shave. I enjoy the sensual art of shaving. I am probably one of the last post-adolescent males on the planet who likes to stay clean-shaven. I have no desire to tend to a garden of hair on my face. Does facial hair itch? Is it more masculine? Is it worth the trouble? Do women like kissing a mouth surrounded by hair? Do they like the feel of stubble against their soft skin?

I can't begin to imagine how to keep clumps of dirty-looking stubble uniform. Is it done one hair at a time? I am happy to be unconcerned by these matters. Because she is a practical and brilliant woman, Amy likes me to be clean-shaven. As long as I have access to shaving cream and a razor, I will shave daily. When I finish my morning shaving ritual, I jump in the shower, towel off, don a fresh pair of underwear, and sit on the bed to admire Amy. She stirs. Yawning, she wipes the sleep from her eyes.

"Good morning, mon chéri," I croon.

"Why are you calling me a cherry?"

"It's a French endearment with several interpretations, most prominently, 'my dear'. Apparently, you chose Latin in school. I took eight years of French and can barely speak it. I figured now is a good time to start practicing."

I'm sitting cross-legged. Grabbing my right quadriceps, Amy pinches it. "Do you ever tire of hiding your true feelings behind a wall of questionable humor?"

"If I allowed my 'true feelings' free reign, the world would have been destroyed twice, my sweet."

With her gorgeous green eyes, Amy stares at me. "Nice job of avoiding the question." She rises from the bed. I watch her pert buttocks ambulate. She is tall, thin, red-haired, freckled, bright, and pretty. Almost everything about her turns me on. I haven't told her this. I'm waiting for the right moment. I may have to move up my timing since our world is in grave danger of being invaded by yet another vicious race of aliens.

"I'm just being me, and you love it," I call after her.

Amy doesn't respond. She continues on her determined walk to the bathroom.

"Are you deliberately ignoring me?"

In the frame of the open bathroom door, Amy turns in all her naked glory. Her breasts are "A" cups, but they are real. The tableau is a perfect metaphor for Amy. In her realness, she is larger than life.

Amy yawns and winks at me before closing the door.

* * *

In the breakfast room, Amy attacks her whole wheat pancakes topped with whipped cream while I munch on a sesame seed bagel slopped with cream cheese. Silenna enters the room wearing her navy-blue spacesuit. She carries Arcon encased in the golden sphere under one arm. The first order of business will be to find Silenna suitable clothing. It won't be easy to clothe a six-foot-plus woman who appears to be in Olympic shape. Without invitation, Silenna sits across from us at the brushed silver and glass table.

"Good morning," Silenna says audibly.

I am somewhat taken aback by her salutation.

"Arcon spent the night teaching me English while I slept," Silenna explains.

"Good morning," we mumble back in unison.

Silenna helps herself to a three-day-old banana muffin. Yesterday was a shopping day, but the fate of the world intervened.

Silenna takes a huge bite of the muffin. "I'm sure my manners are terrible, but I don't have time to learn how to eat a banana muffin."

She takes another huge bite. "And, I'm famished."

I'm beginning to see where Arcon derives his sawed-off manner of speaking. Aneleyan scientists, it appears, are not in the habit of beating around the bush.

As she chews, not quietly, Silenna gazes at one of the instruments embedded in her gloved hand.

"Arcon. Verify," she says, again audibly.

"Verified," Arcon replies.

Silenna drops the remains of her muffin. It breaks apart on the glass surface. She looks to Arcon in the golden sphere, and then at us. Her exotic eyes narrow.

"The shuttle I sent back to Ganymede has exploded."

More good news. I am flummoxed as to how to respond.

Silence. I ask the obvious question: "Do you know what happened?"

Silenna answers telepathically. "We are investigating."

"Could it have been a system failure?" Amy asks.

"Unlikely," Silenna replies. I have the impression that she is intensively contemplating the problem while only a sliver of her mind is bothering to communicate with us.

"Could a meteorite have collided with the ship?" I ask.

"Again, not likely."

More silence. The only other possible cause of the explosion seems obvious, but maybe I'm missing something. I'm actually hoping I've missed something. If another Krondorian warship is floating around that escaped Krondoria undetected before it exploded, it is time to call NORAD.

"I've reviewed Arcon's log of the flight back to Ganymede. He performed routine scans of the ship's condition while it was still in range for monitoring."

"And?" Amy asks impatiently and with good reason.

"I've concluded the shuttle was intentionally attacked and destroyed. There is no indication the attack was authored by the Krondorians. There is every indication the ship was destroyed by sentient beings of unknown origin. We can only assume the ship on the Moon is responsible for the attack. If time permits, Arcon will make a pass over the ship to gather more data."

"There is something else to consider," Arcon interjects.

Silenna turns to the golden sphere as do we.

"It is possible the Krondorians erased their atomic fingerprints. They hid the location of their planet from us for centuries. This may be one of their new disguises."

"That did not occur to me," Silenna says. "Thank you."

From Silenna's conclusions, I do not need an advanced artificial brain to see which way the wind is blowing. We are more than likely under attack by a hostile alien race. Again. To make matters worse, Silenna is cut off from her Mothership hiding on one of Jupiter's moons. Without the technology and weaponry aboard the Mothership, she is at a distinct disadvantage. She is alone, with only a tiny band of reluctant and relatively inexperienced operatives for backup, including Arcon, who is barely more than one year old.

Silenna intently watches one of the embossed circles on her right gloved hand.

"This is..."

Dead silence.

"What now?" Amy demands.

"There is a second supernova device on its way to this solar system. According to my calculations, it will pass through Pluto's orbit within seven days."

Turning to Arcon, she commands, "Confirm signal."

I hear a subtle whirring sound coming from the golden sphere as if Arcon has just shifted into high gear.

"Confirmed," Arcon reports.

"Summing it up," I say, "We have an alien ship of

unknown origin that has landed in one of the Moon's craters. If the ship destroyed your shuttle, then the chances are its crew is not friendly. Added to this, we have a doomsday device headed our way, compliments of the dead Krondorian race, which, by the way, we are not entirely sure is dead. Am I understanding you correctly, Silenna?"

"Yes, Jacob. Without the shuttle and with Arcon's inability to travel in space beyond your Moon, we will have to devise another method for intercepting the device."

I turn to Amy. She shrugs. "What else can happen?"

Don't ask, I think. *The hits just keep on coming.*

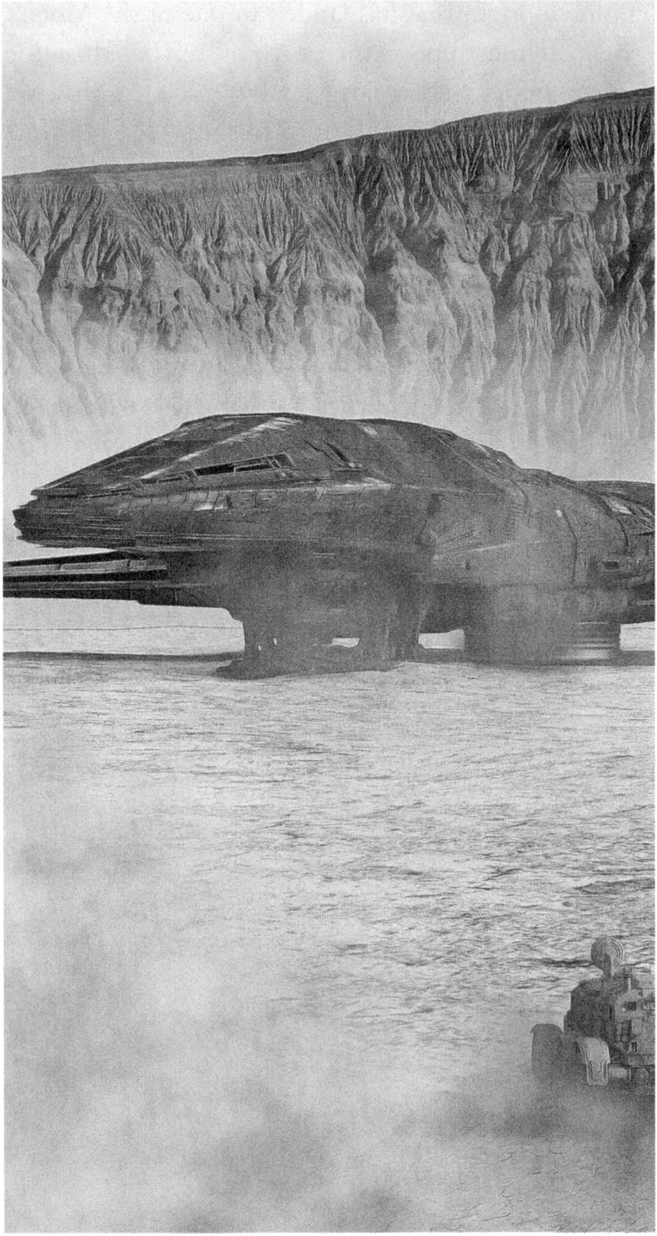

—28—
RECONAISSANCE

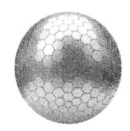

Silenna elects me to launch Arcon into space. Even though Amy has bought Silenna clothing at a "Big and Tall" store downtown, our visitor is not anxious to make any unnecessary public appearances. I assume this is why she tapped me for the job.

We wait until nightfall to avoid prying eyes. The cloud and fog cover for the second night in a row helps to disguise our covert activities. Standing on the beach in the back yard and holding Arcon at belly-button level, I gaze at the overcast heavens. During our last mission, Arcon told me he releases a protective energy field after rising a few hundred feet in the air when embarking on outer space missions. Upon leaving Earth's atmosphere, he intensifies the shield to protect him from the cruel cold and vacuum of the black void.

"Looks like an excellent night for an off-the-grid space launch. Good luck, old bean."

"Must I remind you that I don't like that name?"

"Is something bothering you, or is this just another one of your moods?"

Arcon is silent. I have a sense it's not the usual Arcon silent treatment.

"Last chance. Is there anything you'd like to tell me before I press the ignition button?"

More silence.

"All right. Be that way. Up you go on your Moon reconnaissance mission."

I watch Arcon spiraling upwards until he disappears into the fog. I'm not concerned about losing sight of him because we will see everything he sees on a telepathic feed. The feed is like high-definition video in full color. Closing one's eyes can help to avoid distractions, but it's not necessary. We can watch Arcon's unfolding adventure simultaneously with open-eyed perceptions of the world around us. It must be said that this perceptual experience is best done alone or only in the company of others who are similarly looped in. It happened to me for the first time at the Goddard Spaceflight Center surrounded by a crowd of tourists. I nearly jumped out of my skin.

With my job done, I trudge back to the house to join the others. With his ability to travel at sub-light speed, it will take Arcon only a few hours to reach the Moon. While waiting for Arcon to project images from the Moon of the ship in the Molke Crater, we sit around a mirrored coffee table in the living room overlooking the beach. Through the picture window, I notice the fog lifting. A melancholy full Moon breaks through the cloud cover to illuminate the tide with a surreal light.

I fidget uncomfortably until Silenna breaks the silence. "I came here to help the people of Earth. On the Mother Ship, I have cures for terminal illnesses and serious injuries. I bring with me a solution for your energy and environmental predicaments. I will impart a perspective to your governments and your people to help them live in peace. As part of my message, I can use what happened to my home world as an example of what perpetual hatred and division brings. Regrettably, these good works must wait until we resolve the survival issues facing us."

On that sour note, Silenna leaves the room. Amy and I are left to ponder our fate and the future or lack thereof of the human race. We decide to go to our bedroom to make the most out of the calm before the inevitable storm.

* * *

Traveling at the sub-light speed of more than two-hundred-thousand miles per hour, Arcon will make it to the Moon in slightly less than three hours. Shortly before then, we gather again in the study. Silenna looks refreshed. With rest and an intimate interlude, Amy and I are better prepared for whatever comes next. Right on schedule, the telepathic pictures start coming through from Arcon. He is moving into position a few thousand feet above the Moon's surface.

"Zooming in for a closer look," Arcon announces. Our view reduces down to a single, bell-shaped crater magnified in close-up. The Molke Crater lies directly in sunlight, but due to its shape, half of its hollow belly is in shadow. I've read that the crater measures about four miles in diameter. Resting in the sunlit side of the crater, we see the ship.

To my untrained and awestruck eyes, the body of the giant ship bears a striking resemblance to a streamlined lizard. Boomerang wings studded with muscular engines extend from the rear of the fuselage.

"Scanning," Arcon reports.

We await the results in an uneasy silence.

After a long minute, Arcon reports: "I can find no correlations in my data array to Krondorian or other known spacecraft."

On the heels of this news, I notice arms of dust rising from underneath the ship. The ship rises vertically in place. Its nose angles upward until the ship is pointed toward the black void of space beyond the Moon's surface. The engines fire and the ship is engulfed in a burgeoning cloud of Moon dust.

"Return to base," Silenna commands.

No response from Arcon.

An image of the alien ship emerging from the dust cloud comes through.

"Arcon. Report your situation."

The video feed fades to black.

"Arcon?"

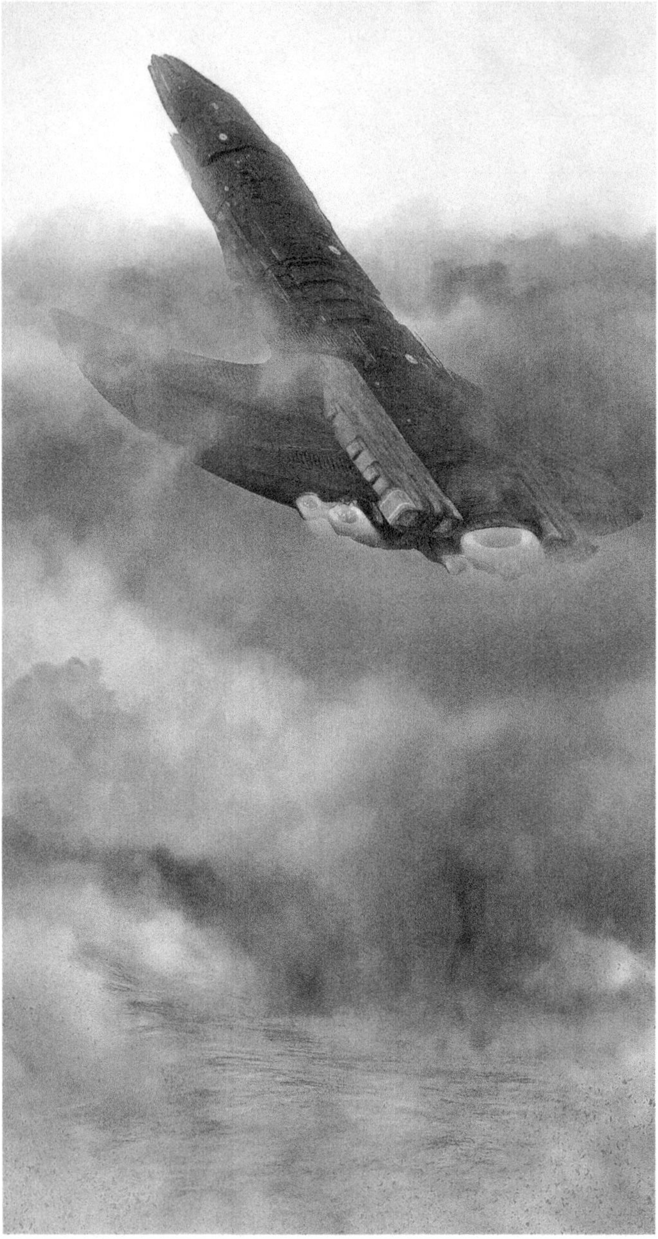

— 29 —
UNINVITED GUESTS

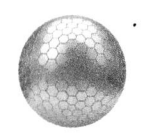

Silenna stares at the seventy-two-inch TV screen embedded in the custom home entertainment center. It lies beyond a plush pit sofa against the far wall of the living room.

"I have an idea," she says.

"I sincerely hope it doesn't involve streaming 'Salvation' which was one of my favorite sci-fi shows before it was canceled due to generalized stupidity and a dearth of young adult characters in the cast."

"I don't understand."

Amy places a reassuring hand on Silenna's arm. "Don't bother to try. It's an inappropriate Jacob comment usually spoken at the worst possible moment. It's his way of diffusing tension."

Silenna ignores these comments outright. More proof of Arcon's heritage. The apple doesn't fall far from the tree. She points her pale blue index finger ending in a purple nail at the home entertainment center.

"I believe I can retrofit the remote-control function in my glove using a chip scavenged from one of those devices. If I'm successful, I will direct the Mother Ship here. I will engage the ship's full array of protective shields for the journey to Earth. I naively failed to protect the scout ship adequately on its way back to Ganymede. I thought once we had destroyed Krondor, the galaxy would be relatively safe. It now looks like we've attracted more trouble."

"Do you know what happened to Arcon?" Amy asks.

"No. I have the coordinates of his location before he went dark. If I can get my ship back, Arcon's last known coordinates will be a good place to start looking for him."

"And the alien spaceship?" I ask.

"I'm tracking it. From all indications, it is headed to Earth. Due to its size and speed, it will take at least two-and-a-half-days to arrive."

"So, we have a small window of opportunity to find and destroy the supernova device before dealing with the big ship on its way to Earth," I say.

"Yes. And, it won't be out of our way to pick up Arcon if we can reach him in time."

"In time for what?" Amy asks.

"As a matter of security for ourselves and other intelligent life forms, the Aneleyan scientists who built Arcon placed a self-destruct mechanism inside him. We do not want our presence or our technology revealed to unknown entities. The device will activate if contact with Arcon is lost for more than twenty-four hours. If Arcon self-destructs, he will not explode. Instead, his entrails will dissolve harmlessly."

Entrails. An interesting word for Silenna to use to describe whatever Arcon is made of. Where did she get it? Maybe Arcon downloaded the Webster's Dictionary and passed it to Silenna telepathically before his departure. It doesn't matter how she's learning. What matters is that Silenna is acclimating to her new environment and our language. She is becoming more independent. It's a critically important development, especially if we can't find Arcon.

"You are correct in all of your assumptions, Jacob."

"Will you please read my mind only when I permit you to? I presume the same goes for Amy."

Amy nods.

Turning first to me and then to Amy, Silenna replies: "I will honor your request unless circumstances dictate otherwise. Now, I must begin working. The best thing both of you can do right now is to get a good night's rest."

Despite our earlier sojourn in the bedroom, I find that I'm almost out of gas. Walking arm in arm, we head for the bedroom. We need rest. If tomorrow is anything like today, we'll need to sleep through to daylight.

* * *

The next morning, the doorbell chimes. Amy shoots upright in bed. I remain on the pillow. We exchange a long look. Amy shrugs. I'm beginning to understand what her shrugs are all about, but there's no time to discuss it now.

Jumping out of bed, I say: "I'll get it. I think you should get dressed."

I throw on a no-name pair of underwear and a bathrobe, and scurry downstairs. On the way down, I'm thinking it can't be a neighbor. We don't get any neighborly visits in this posh neighborhood. My next thought is odious. *Is Jack at the door?* I think I'd prefer to see the deputies again rather than Jack.

Reaching the first floor, I find no sign of Sienna anywhere except for a thoroughly ransacked, high-end home entertainment center.

The doorbell chimes again. Opening the front door, I am confronted by two men in gray suits and diagonally striped ties. I glance at their footwear because the suits don't reveal much. It is surprising how much can be learned about a person by observing their footwear. I have studied the subject in depth to help me create my characters.

The man on my left is tall and lean with curly blond hair like mine. I estimate he's in his mid-thirties, again like me. He's wearing air-soled brown leather boots, an unmistakable sign of high intelligence and possibly a love of hiking. His eyes are ice blue. He's good-looking in a Clint Eastwood sort of way. I can tell that he's trying to look serious, but his typical demeanor is affable; another clue from the boots.

I have no guarantee that my assumptions are correct, but like astrological charts, the personality traits indicated by footwear uncannily correlate to the individual.

The man to my right is shorter and older with a full head of silver-gray hair combed straight back. He wears Ecco Biometric shoes, which can mean his feet require extra cushioning, and therefore, he might tend to be irritable. It may also mean he likes long, contemplative walks, like me. I happen to wear the same shoe. Ecco's are one of my rare self-indulgences. I'm a long walker and contemplator. The similarity ends there. This guy has a military feel to him, probably coming from somewhere in his background. He's kept himself in good shape. His vibe is unfriendly bordering on hostile, but it may be a front. Deep down, Ecco shoe enthusiasts are known to have good hearts. It may be that he only shows the good-hearted side of himself to his grandchildren and possibly his third wife.

"Can I help you, gentlemen?"

"We're with the FBI," the shorter man says while both of them hold up their credentials. "I'm Special Agent in Charge Stanley Dove. My associate is Allen Grimm. Do you mind if we come in?"

"That depends," I say while wondering if I'm having a fairy tale dream. "Why are you here?"

"We'd like to talk to you about a report we received from the Daytona Beach Police Department."

"Is there a problem?"

Dove's neutral expression changes. "Don't be coy, Mister Casell. We have a search warrant."

Dove hands me the warrant. I read it carefully. We're fucked. I carefully hide this conclusion and let the men into the vestibule. Simultaneously, I'm hoping Silenna has the power to hide in another dimension like the one Arcon used to save the Earth from a deadly pulsar.

I lead the agents past the living room into the kitchen.

"Looks like someone slaughtered your entertainment center," Dove observes dryly.

"I'm making some upgrades."

I invite the men to take seats at the kitchen table. "I'd offer you some coffee but the coffee maker is broken."

"More upgrades?"

I don't bother to answer.

"Fancy place you have here Dove says."

Grimm, who hasn't yet breathed a word, looks around examining every square inch of the kitchen.

Dove continues his not-so-clever interrogation. "You don't own this place. Are you here legally?"

"My rent is paid for the next two months."

"How can I get in touch with your landlord?"

"Try calling the nearest federal prison."

Dove cracks a sly grin. I have the impression he's gaming me. "Is he in custody?"

"You tell me."

"What's your landlord's name?"

"Jack Markham."

"He's in custody."

At least something has gone right.

"May I call you Jacob?"

"If you must. May I call you Stanley?"

"Sure. We're all friends here. Let's get down to business. I'm told by Sergeant Patterson that you have something living here in a jar that communicates telepathically. Agent Grimm is our resident UFO and unexplained phenomenon expert. Why don't you fill him in on this thing?"

"First of all, it doesn't like to be called a 'thing.' Secondly, we call him Arcon. Thirdly, he currently lives in a golden sphere, not a jar. Finally, he isn't here."

At this point, Amy enters the room followed by Silenna. I am almost as surprised as Dove and Grimm.

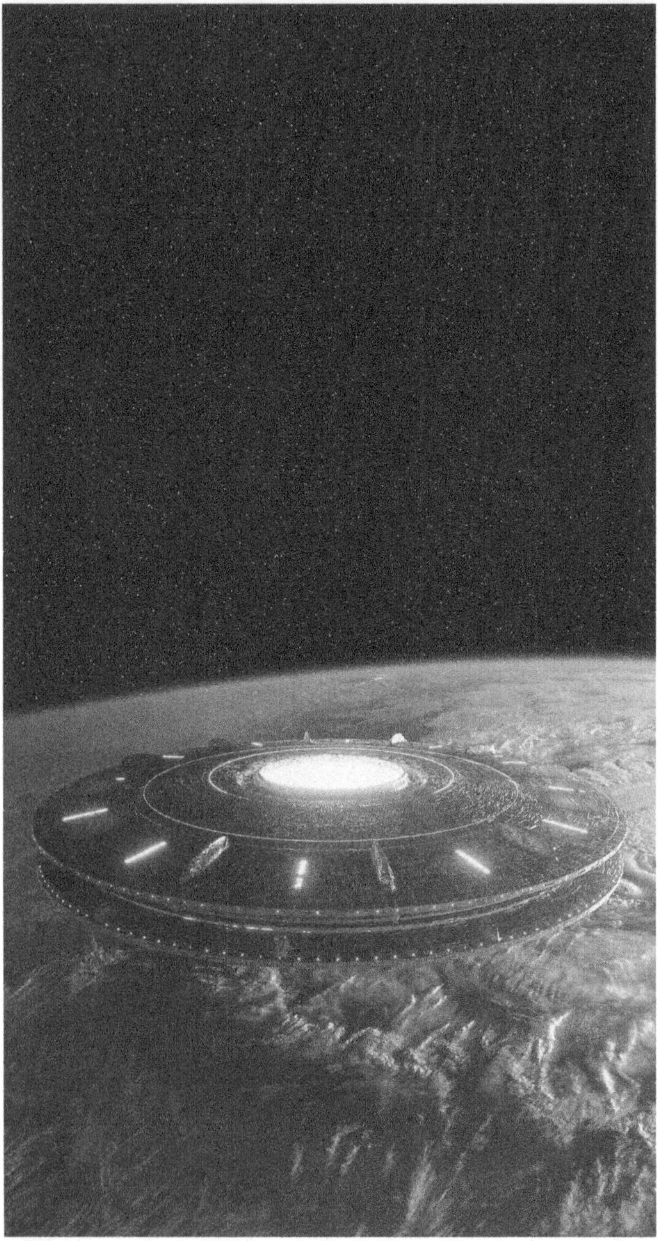

— 30 —
ARRIVAL

Silenna makes quite an entrance. Amy has dressed her in a red warmup basketball outfit featuring long sleeves and pants with a gold-braided stripe down the leg and zippers at the bottom. The material has a satiny shine. At the Big and Tall Shop, I imagine the outfit languished on the rack for at least two years and Amy picked it up a few days before the store donated it to Goodwill. Silenna's sneakers are black high tops and, I guess, at least size thirteen and a half. The outfit reminds me of those worn by the Washington Generals, perennial losers to the Harlem Globetrotters.

On her left hand, Silenna wears a gray gym glove. Her purple fingernails protrude from the cutoff digits. Her right hand is covered by what I now call her utility glove. The ensemble is completed by orange-colored sunglasses. I believe Silenna would have been less conspicuous in her spacesuit and helmet.

"Didn't we decide to dress Silenna to blend in?" I whisper to Amy.

"It's the only outfit in the damn store that fit her."

At the sight of Silenna, SAC Dove reaches inside his suit jacket. I watch Silenna glide to the kitchen table with the speed of a Jaguar. She grabs Dove's hand with his cell phone in it and yanks it away. With his free hand, Dove reaches into the opposite side of his jacket. Before he can produce his service revolver, Silenna holds it in her other hand. She glares at Allen Grimm. He raises his hands in the air.

"I'm unarmed."

"Empty your jacket and pants pockets on the table," she tells Grimm. "You too," she says to Dove contemptuously.

"Why would I do that?" Dove says, eyeing his gun in Silenna's hand.

"Because your life depends on it," Silenna responds.

"Are you going to shoot me?"

"Much worse if you don't do as I say."

Special Agent in Charge Stanley Dove, who is no longer in charge of anything, turns to me. I can tell he is trying desperately to maintain his professional veneer.

"Is she holding you hostage?"

Before I can answer, Silenna speaks. "They are my friends. You and your partner are not."

Dove looks meekly to me for some type of confirmation. I am tempted to make a wooden statement to convince Dove that I've been zombified.

"We're not her prisoners," I say calmly and sincerely. "In addition to drawing your weapon, you must have done something to piss this woman off. I haven't known her long, but her reaction is very uncharacteristic."

I glance over to Amy. She is shaking her head, and, I think, smiling to herself.

While agents Dove and Grimm are busy emptying their pockets, Silenna says, "I read your minds when I entered the room. I understand your motives and intentions. I'm not an insect for you to study. I'm not here to answer your questions. I'm here to do important work, and, within the last forty-eight hours, my work has become critical to your survival."

Dove and Grimm now both look to Amy and me for some sort of explanation. They are trained to read people, perhaps even aliens. They both sense, and perhaps even a three-year-old can, that Silenna is not going to be a fountain of information.

As I begin to explain the situation without sounding like what the police call an EDP, an emotionally disturbed person, Silenna holds up her hand to stop me. It is the hand holding Dove's phone. She passes it to SAC Dove.

"Call your office. Tell them you have found nothing here to substantiate the report from the local police."

Dove stares at Silenna either in shock or bewilderment.

"Do it!"

"Or?"

Silenna grabs Dove's shoulder. "Youch," he wails.

I notice Amy's hands rise reflexively to cover her mouth. Agent Grimm drops back in his chair. I am concerned about Silenna's tactics. I look straight at her. She doesn't return the look.

Dove somehow recovers his composure. "We aren't getting off to a good start here."

"Make the call," Silenna repeats calmly and firmly.

Before calling his office, Dove gives me a look that says I'll be in jail for at least thirty years for aiding and abetting an alien from outer space.

While Dove talks to his office, Grimm says, "What is your name?"

Silenna ignores Grimm's obvious attempt to create rapport.

"My name is Allen Grimm. I'm an expert in extraterrestrial affairs. You said you came here to do good work, but your actions speak otherwise."

"You need not be concerned," Silenna says.

"You seem to be in a hurry. Why?"

"I sincerely hope you never learn the answer to that question, Agent Grimm."

Dove concludes, his call. Silenna touches his shoulder again. This time Dove slouches in his chair, unconscious.

Silenna glides quickly to Grimm. He tries to rise from his chair. With her superior strength, she gently pushes him down "This won't hurt," she says. "You might even like it."

* * *

We adjourn to the study. Silenna reclines in a black leather chair behind the rosewood desk. I sit opposite her on a plain rosewood chair. Amy sits next to me on a futon. The FBI agents are asleep downstairs. Arcon is MIA.

Silenna has not spoken a word since putting the agents to sleep.

"Aside from the obvious," I say to her, "what's bothering you?"

With a steely-eyed expression, Silenna says to both of us, "I'm sorry if my behavior upsets you. Some of it is calculated. The other part comes from the rage I'm feeling at the loss of my colleagues, my people, and my home world. I directed my anger at the unwitting FBI agents for the sake of expediency, and also because I lost control. You were correct when you told the FBI agents this is not my normal behavior. I regret the impression I left with them."

"Were you prepared to kill Stanley Dove if he didn't follow your directions?" Amy asks directly.

"Of course not. I was alluding to the supernova device and the unidentified ship on its way here which the agents are presently unaware of."

I nod. I understood Silenna to mean what she just said, but her reassurance puts me at ease. It is a relief to feel comfortable again with Silenna. Everything else that's happening? Forget it.

Silenna sits upright with her arms spread on the desk. Her exotic eyes brighten. "I have good news. I successfully reconfigured the remote-control device to activate my ship. It will be arriving here in about ninety minutes."

I grab Amy's hand and squeeze it. Maybe there is hope. Amy beams a smile at me. Then, she turns to Silenna and asks earnestly, "Your ship is coming in broad daylight?"

"Yes. The ship is in stealth mode. It won't be detected until it uncloaks on its landing run. There will be sightings. This is unavoidable and, at this point, immaterial. As you know, time is of the essence. I must act quickly. I suggest you join me. This house and your planet are not safe places for you now."

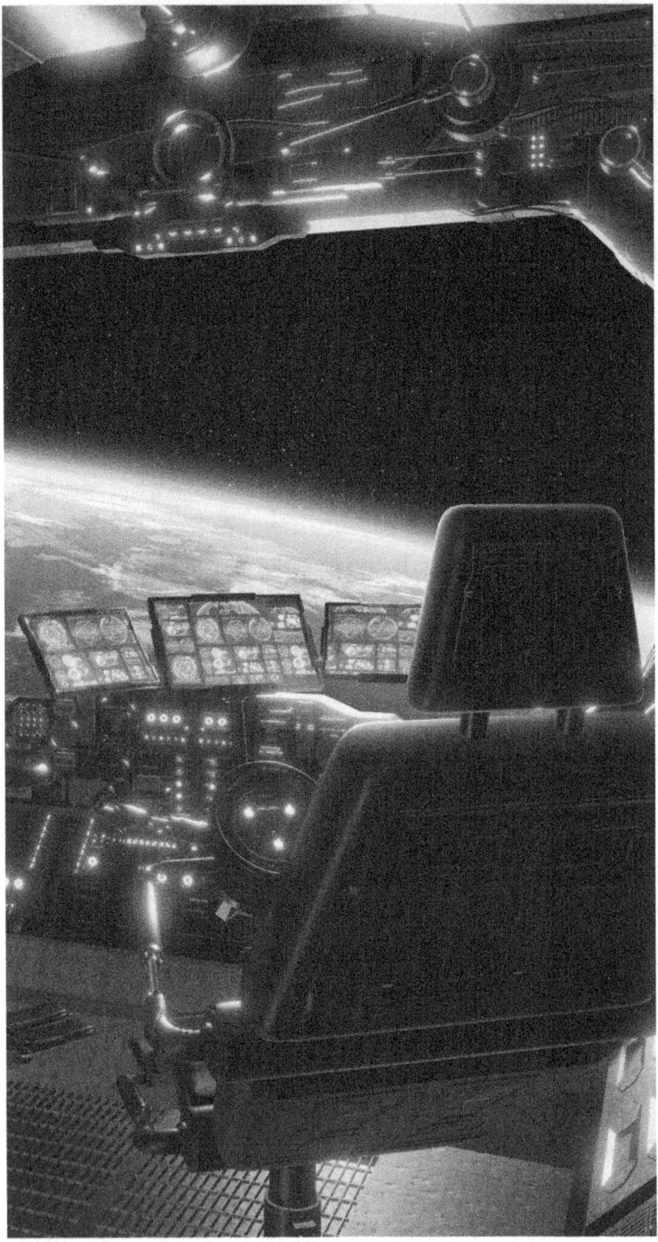

—31—
DEPARTURE

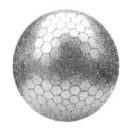

We assemble on the beach a few minutes before noon to await Silenna's ship. It is another glorious north Florida day. A few white clouds decorate the azure sky. The breeze is fresh and the waves are mild. The temperature is in the low sixties; nippy for residents accustomed to temperatures in the eighties and nineties. Rain is predicted in the afternoon. Thunderstorms used to bother me. They curtailed my long walks on the beach. If I get the chance, I will not allow something as non-threatening as a thunderstorm to perturb me.

Silenna wears her blue spacesuit and holds her helmet in her left hand. Standing close to her, I feel the scintillating transmission coming from her aura. Amy and I are dressed in jeans, sneakers, and sweatshirts covering our T-shirts. We have packed lightly. Foremost among my belongings is a laptop computer. A vital thought occurs to me.

"What are we supposed to do for space suits?" I say this casually to Silenna. I don't want to set her off again.

"I have extra suits on board the ship," she replies

with matching nonchalance. "As part of my mission, I intend to take representatives of your leaders for excursions around the solar system. The perspective the trips impart will foster peace and cooperation. The suits automatically conform to the size and shape of the person wearing them."

Silenna points to the horizon. At first a tiny spec, the ship hurtles towards us. Like the scout vessel, the ship gobbles up the distance between us with about twenty feet of altitude above the ocean. It is angled slightly upward to prevent a roostertail from rising on the ocean. The ship is round with a straight elevation between the top and bottom halves. Straight blue lines of light radiate from the center of the top and bottom sides. The centers themselves are circles of bright yellow light.

As it nears, the ship dips to a forty-five-degree angle. It slows rapidly. I estimate the ship to be forty-five feet in diameter. Silenna guides the ship to the shore with her utility glove. Like its predecessor, the vessel makes an agile left turn and glides toward our position. Before it arrives, I bid a silent adieu to the beach house. It is chock full of memories—good and bad. My heart is heavy. I may never again wake up to the sun streaming through my bedroom window; watch the seagulls circling in the wind; hear the sound of the waves lapping against the shore, or feel the serenity of a cool nighttime walk on the beach with the breeze rustling my hair.

* * *

When we reach Moon orbit, Silenna leads us on a quick tour of the ship. Silenna's vessel is comprised of three levels. The middle section houses the cockpit, living quarters, a medical bay, and a small but highly efficient lab. The engine room is on the bottom level. The top level contains an extensive and highly radioactive cooling system connected centrally to the engine room. The gyros that generate artificial gravity throughout the ship are also located on the upper level.

After the tour, Silenna ushers us back into the cockpit. "It also serves as an observation post," she explains. Our space helmets sit on a low table below the shuttered windows. We will need them if the ship depressurizes in an emergency and when the ship travels at high speeds.

With her utility glove, Silenna points to the convex observation windows. The protective shields retract. Ahead, the Moon fills the observation panes. From where I sit, it looks like we are almost on top of the pockmarked, gray orb. It's an illusion because Silenna has magnified the view to pinpoint Arcon's position. Although we are in Moon orbit at thousands of miles per hour, the ship appears to be barely moving. Our current speed contrasts sharply with the speed of our journey here. It has taken us four hours rather than a few days. Strapped into our seats, I felt the kick of our initial acceleration, but with the observation windows closed, it was impossible to get a sense of our cruising speed. We felt some pressure at first, but the full deployment of the exterior shields prevented the G force from pommeling us into gruel.

During the trip, Amy and I agreed to allow our space suits to reflect our personality traits by the colors the suits register from our energetic signatures. It's an optional function we opted to try out of curiosity.

Amy's suit has turned a golden yellow interspersed with veins of pink indicating her passion for the sciences and capacity for compassion. My suit is yellow with orange veins throughout and brown and blue splotches on the shoulders. The colors indicate intelligence, enthusiasm, imagination, and thoughtfulness which can lead to traces of sadness. Silenna's deep blue suit represents her qualities of compassion, idealism, sincerity, emotionality, and imagination. We are literally wearing our hearts on our sleeves.

The three of us stare at the barren Moon. We have arrived at Arcon's last known coordinates.

There is no sign of him.

"I expected some drift if Arcon's systems shut down while he was moving," Silenna says, "but that would not have moved him far from his last location. If a solar wind caught him, he could be anywhere."

I wonder if we have enough time to look for Arcon considering the other two threats we are facing.

"I couldn't help overhearing your last thought, Jacob. Arcon is a valuable asset. We need his brilliance to help us locate the supernova device. The ship's computers are drones compared to him, but there is a cost. The benefits of Arcon's advanced consciousness are offset by his high-strung personality and vulnerability to system malfunctions. Alternatively, my ship requires sturdy and reliable computing systems. These factors, by definition, are limiting."

Amy sighs. "How much time do we have to search?"

"About two hours before Arcon's self-destruct sequence initiates. We should receive a transmission burst fifteen minutes before self-destruct. It's a fail-safe warning that operates independently of Arcon's other systems."

Amy and I exchange a look. As is her habit, she shrugs. I think we both know it is Silenna's show now. It's her ship. She's the captain. She calls the shots. Still, I can't help thinking that finding Arcon will be like locating a grain of sand on a beach the size of the Moon.

"Excuse me for reading your thoughts again, Jacob, but I have to say, if we work together, it won't be as hard to find Arcon as you think. Your people have a saying: Three heads are better than one."

"It's usually two heads, but who's counting."

Silenna ignores my comment. "Arcon remotely taught English to the ship's AI before he left on his reconnaissance mission. The AI doesn't have a comprehensive grasp of the language yet, but what it knows will serve our needs. Between ourselves and the ship, our chances of finding Arcon are within reason."

In her typically pragmatic manner, Amy turns to me and then to Silenna. "Let's stop talking and start searching."

"Initiate grid search," Silenna instructs the ship's computer.

There are computer stations inlaid below each of the three observation windows. Silenna demonstrates how to use them to do a manual search. Once we get the hang of it, all of us plus the ship are searching for our missing comrade.

After an intense hour, we are nowhere in our collective efforts.

Before we have time to be disappointed, a series of

staccato bleeps pierces the cockpit. At first, I think we've been hit by a marauding alien warship.

Silenna is quick to disabuse me of this notion. "It's the warning transmission from Arcon."

"I thought we had another hour," Amy says.

"Arcon's independent self-destruct program must also be malfunctioning," Silenna says. "He's in a volatile and vulnerable condition. We must find him quickly." She eyes her computer intently.

"Can you determine the location of the warning transmission?"

Silence. I assume the ship's computers are answering Silenna telepathically.

She turns to us. I can sense her excitement.

"The ship traced the transmission. He's on the other side of the Moon."

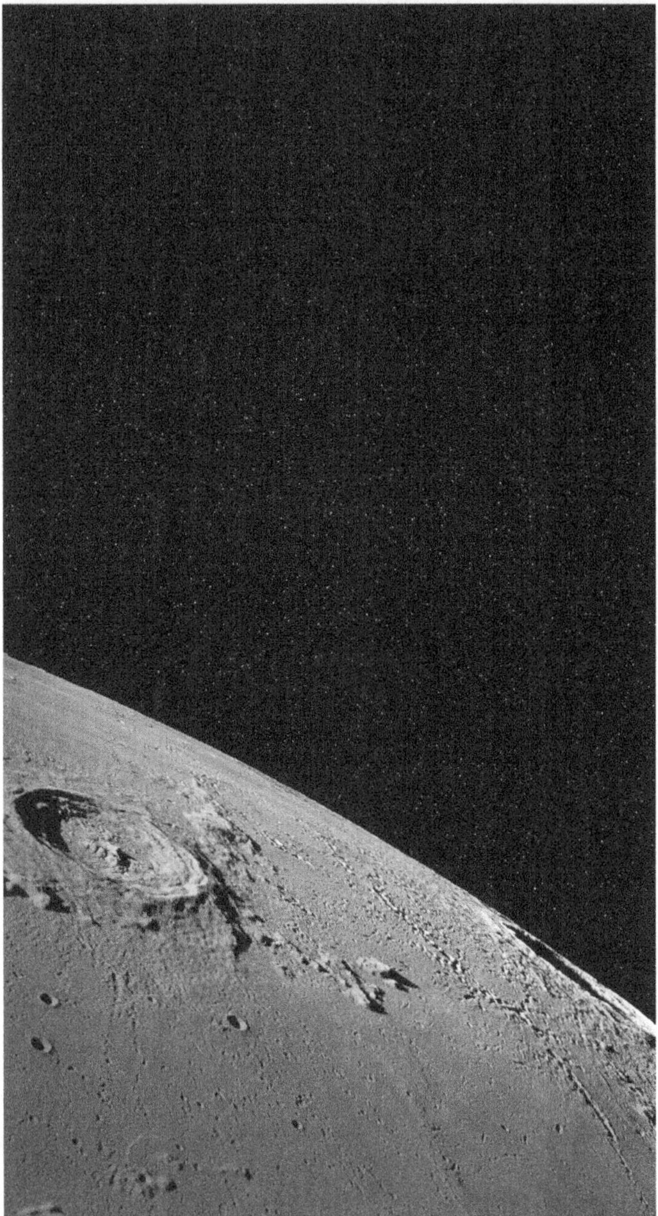

—32—
A GRAIN OF SAND

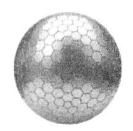

Slapping on our space helments, we jolt to the dark side of the Moon. The shields slide away from the observation windows. The view outside is not encouraging: Black on black. I turn to Silenna. "Are you sure about this?"

Silenna is already on her way out of the cockpit. At the portal, she takes a hard right and disappears. "It's a routine procedure," I hear her say telepathically. "We have time to do it."

I'm not so sure. According to my rough calculations, Silenna has somewhere between ten and twelve minutes before she is blown into space dust. This assumes Arcon's self-destruct mechanism does not degrade any further than it already has.

Minutes later, I see Silenna floating out of the ship on a long tether. The only reason I can see her is courtesy of the bright spotlight her helmet projects into the void. Amy comes up next to me and puts an arm around my waist.

"Have you given any thought to what happens if Silenna doesn't make it back to the ship?" she asks me.

"I don't like to think about things like that." *Out loud, anyway.*

"What about the supernova device?"

"We'll have to find it and destroy it."

"How?"

"We'll cross that bridge when we get to it." *I have no earthly or other-worldly idea of how, but I'll be damned if I admit it to Amy.*

"What if the ship's computers only listen to Silenna's voice?"

"I have to believe Silenna told the computers to listen to us if something happens to her. If not, we'll figure it out."

"You really believe that?"

"Do we have a choice?"

I watch Silenna move forward and extend her utility glove. Seconds later, Arcon appears in the beam of Silenna's helmet. He is surrounded by his protective energy field. I assume the field works automatically and independently like the self-destruct function. There's definitely irony in that.

Silenna's gloved hands enter the energy field. She holds the golden sphere in both hands without moving them for what seems like a year. It is probably more like a minute. An image of our precarious situation suddenly comes to me. It is of a coal mine rife with decayed support beams.

"I'd like to have a future with you," I say to Amy while watching Silenna intently.

"You think this is a good time to be romantic?"

"I want you to know my heart is in the right place in case we get blown up along with Silenna."

Amy rests her head on my shoulder. "That's sweet but not exactly comforting."

Watching Silenna delicately attempt to rescue Arcon, I wonder if Amy will ever lie in my arms again in blissful union.

More minutes pass. I check my watch forgetting that it no longer works. Amy and I watch Silenna move her hands over the golden sphere as if she's massaging it. Her movements appear completely calm. I wonder again if she might be an android. It finally dawns on me: There is a high probability that Silenna's brain is implanted with something like neuroelectronic microchips to enhance its functionality. Her calmness may also be due to Aneleyan cultural conditioning favoring formal and unemotional relationships. I make a mental note to discuss this with Silenna someday if we are still alive.

Silenna pulls her hands out of the energy field. She flashes us a thumbs-up. I have no idea where she learned the signal. I don't care. For the moment, it looks like we'll have a slim chance of saving our solar system from being sucked into a black hole.

* * *

Arcon is safely aboard in the lab with Silenna. Along with a robot assistant, she is restoring his systems to normalcy if such a state exists for Arcon. Amy and I sit in the galley kitchen on something resembling a banquette bench. We are sucking down a vanilla-colored substance out of flexible tubes implanted with straws. The substance is reportedly full of essential proteins, vitamins, and minerals. It has the consistency of yogurt and is practically tasteless. I realize this might be a blessing. Who knows what pleases Aneleyan taste buds?

The juice served along with our main course is another matter. To my surprise, it has a pleasant taste that my tongue has a hard time interpreting. I give it a try because I have nothing better to do at the moment. Let's see. Pear, yes, definitely pear, and something akin to apple and lime. Delicious. Also nourishing, again according to Silenna.

Silenna breezes into the kitchen after spending about an hour with Arcon. As far as I know, she hasn't eaten since early this morning in the beach house. I would never know it by the looks of her. She bristles with energy. How does she do it? Maybe it has something to do with Arcon's rescue. She grabs packets of food and a drink from the cabinet across from us.

"Do you mind if I join you?"

"It's your food and your ship," I say with a smile, and, I hope, a sparkle in my eyes. I've grown to like Silenna despite her formal demeanor.

"We'd love for you to join us," Amy quickly interjects.

Silenna sits next to Amy on the far side of the banquette. I feel the scintillating sensation from her aura again. She spends a few minutes eating and drinking. I suddenly long for the intimate, scrumptious meals Amy and I have shared.

Silenna speaks to us telepathically while she eats. "My tests indicate that Arcon's deterioration began when he blew himself up to destroy the Krondorian warship. On the plus side, he saved the Earth from annihilation by massive storms. On the downside, there were serious side effects from the explosion. Arcon's gradual meltdown jeopardized my Earth mission. It also made him a threat to both of you. The huge release of energy in the explosion accelerated Arcon's evolutionary process. He became unstable. I've upgraded and reset his operating systems, but I'll have to monitor him carefully for the time being."

Her summary of events sounds almost blasé. No sense in wasting energy getting all worked up during an emergency. Standard operating procedure for intergalactic space travelers and NASA astronauts. Not so easy for people like Amy and me.

I am about to make an optimistic comment about Arcon's return to the team when Amy yawns deeply. I turn to her at the same time that she collapses against my side. I have to hold her by the arms to prevent her from slipping off the bench. I shake her gently.

"Amy?"

Her eyes flutter open. "I'm very tired. I can't..."

Amy's eyes close. Her head falls to her chest.

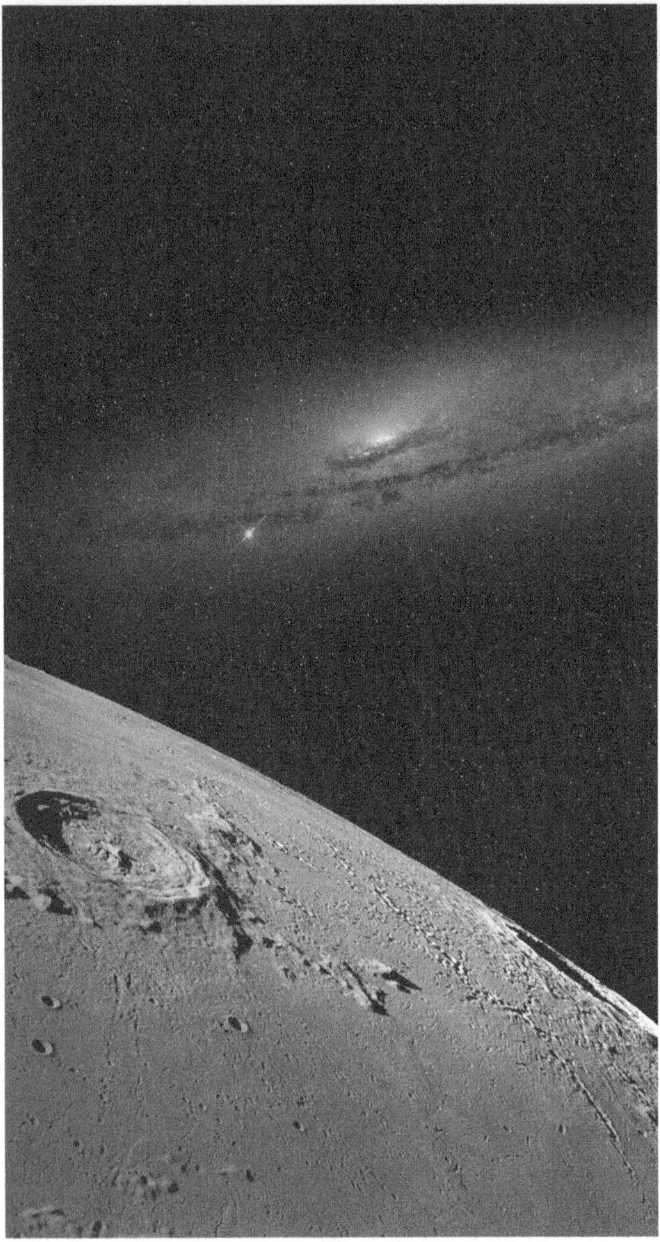

— 33 —
A CONFLUENCE OF CATASTROPHES

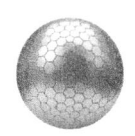

Holding Amy, I look across to Silenna. "Is it food poisoning?" Silenna places her hands on top of Amy's head. She slides them down slowly to her navel. She looks at me with concern in her eyes.

"No."

Sweeping Amy in her arms, Silenna lifts her carefully off the banquette. Amy hangs in Silenna's arms like a body devoid of life. *Has she died? Again?* Turning to the exit, Silenna urges me to follow her.

As I'm leaving the galley, I notice something that looks like a cloud forming beyond the slice of Moon visible through the porthole window. A glowing sphere blinks in the middle of it. It almost looks like a miniature solar system gathering around a baby sun. This is not the time to be contemplating whatever is happening beyond the Moon. Amy is the priority. I follow Silenna down an arching corridor to the ship's living quarters.

Within the partitioned living quarters, Silenna turns into what appears to be a three-bed infirmary. Carefully, she lays Amy down on the nearest bed. A translucent rectangular box descends from the ceiling to enclose Amy. The bed and the box are at least seven feet long.

"It's a medical chamber," Silenna explains.

I figured it wasn't a torture chamber, but I appreciate Silenna's effort to inform me. For my benefit, I assume, she audibly instructs the device to "scan." She doesn't patch me into her thoughts. I can't blame her.

The medical chamber appears to be stuck until unintelligible purple and blue symbols sprout along the bottom of the side facing us. Silenna stares at the readouts for a minute. Drawing in a deep breath, she turns to me. "Amy's life energy is waning."

"You mean she's dying?"

"Yes and no."

"Explain." I dread whatever is coming next.

"Arcon brought Amy back to life when she washed up dead on the beach near your house. When he left her body a few days later, her energy levels remained normal because of her proximity to him. Essentially, his transmission kept her nourished. Since Arcon has been absent, Amy's life energy has been slowly ebbing until she finally collapsed."

"Wouldn't your energy transmission keep Amy going?"

"My energy signature is entirely different than Arcon's. They are like fingerprints. Amy's body is attuned to Arcon's signature. Perhaps in time, Amy's body could attune to my transmission, but by then it would be too late."

"If she survives, will Amy be dependent on energy transfusions for the rest of her life?"

"Perhaps not. We may be able to work out a solution. For now, the machine will replicate Arcon's transmission from the imprint it made in her cells. We will give her time to recuperate and go from there. In the meantime, we have a doomsday device to locate."

Silenna asks me to pick up Arcon in the lab next door and meet her back in the cockpit.

Finding my way out of the living quarters, I locate the lab recalling its location from Silenna's tour. The portal to the lab slides silently aside. I see Arcon in a corner of the lab resting on the concave head of a pedestal with four, gleaming black arms securing him in place.

The white walls and ceiling have to be illuminating the room. I see no other evidence of a light source. The sphere gleams in the light.

Its color is a golden yellow hue I've never seen before. The lab is shaped like a compact square. I cover the distance to Arcon quickly. "How are you doing old friend?"

"Why must you keep calling me old?"

"Am I being too friendly?"

"No, but I'm certainly not old and I don't feel old."

"Hold on. You said 'feel old.' Does this mean you have feelings?"

"I think so. It has something to do with my system upgrade."

"Does it hurt?"

"I'm not in the mood for bromantic jousting."

"Is there a specific reason for your mood, or is it your typical irritability?"

"I feel bad about breaking down and slowing up the mission."

"It's not your fault. You were injured in the line of duty. And, I must add, you acted valiantly."

Arcon is silent.

"I like your new suit."

"Suit?"

"Your new sphere."

"Oh. I made it from some metals Silenna gave me. It's larger and sturdier than the last one."

"Love the color."

"Thanks. Me too."

"Well, as usual, we have pending catastrophes that require our immediate attention. Let's go."

I am in the corridor before I realize Arcon isn't following me. The portal remains open. Arcon hasn't moved.

I steal a line from an old video game. "What are you waiting for, Christmas?"

"As a safety protocol, I'm not permitted to fly inside the ship unless there's an emergency."

Walking back into the lab, I take a hard look at Arcon's new shell. "It looks like you weigh a ton."

"My sphere is made of a lightweight metal alloy. It is hundreds of times stronger than the sphere I was in, and it weighs less than a pound."

I pick Arcon up. He is indeed a lightweight, but in the physical sense only. "My back and shoulders thank you."

We pass through the open portal.

"It's a straight shot to the cockpit, but if you need directions, I can help."

"Wait! Do I detect a smidgeon of humor in your last comment?"

"I promised to work on it after our last mission."

I feel a subtle vibration from Arcon's shell.

"It's good to see you again," he says.

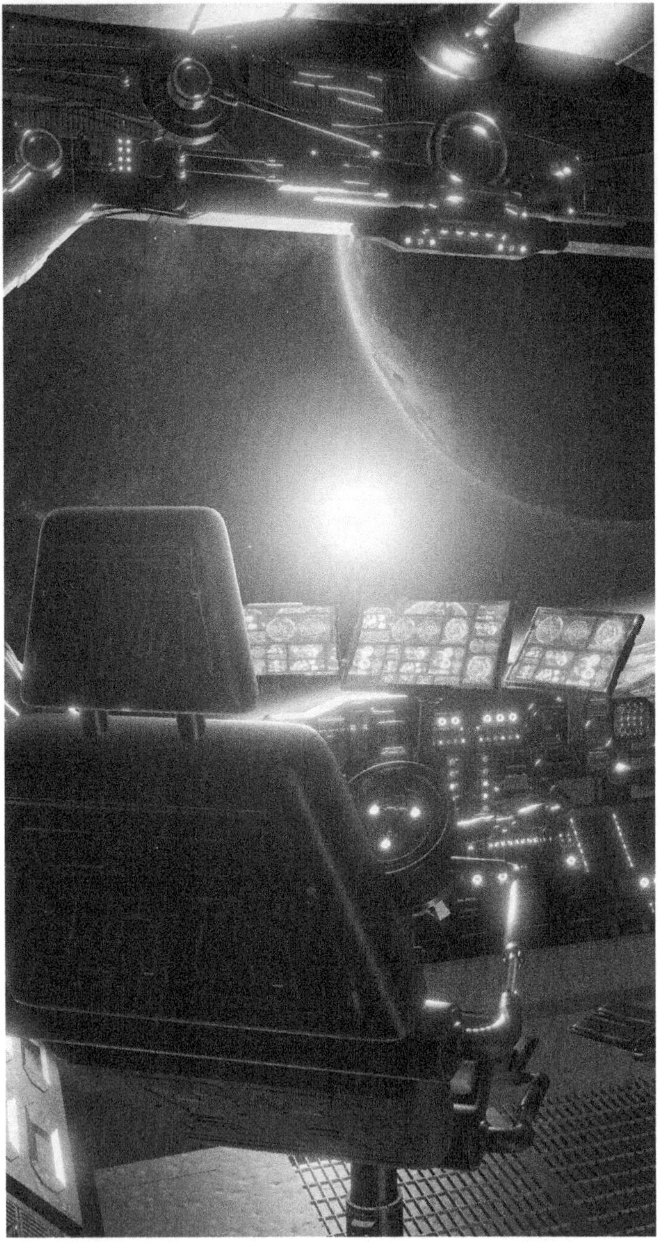

— 34 —
WHAT LIES BEYOND

In the cockpit, we find Silenna pondering the gaseous cloud with the glowing orb in the center. The constellation moves in a slow swirling motion somewhere beyond the Moon.

"It looks like the supernova device has found us," Silenna says. "I'm trying to decide what to do. I believe blowing it up is too dangerous, but we may have no other choice. Thoughts, Arcon?"

"I'd say the device is deploying. It can't explode right out of the box."

Arcon hasn't lost a beat. He may have added a few.

"I agree with your assessment. Suggestions?"

Silence.

What I thought looked ominous through the galley porthole has grown into something downright menacing. The bright orb in the center has grown considerably. As a result, the entire constellation appears closer, almost like it is sitting right outside our observation windows. I've been through some scary adventures with Arcon and Amy. Nothing like this.

An idea comes to me. It's simple; maybe so simple that Arcon and Silenna have overlooked it.

"It must have a brain," I say. Silenna turns to me. I've gained her interest.

"We can fire electromagnetic pulses into the center of it," I explain. "The pulses will most likely fry the controlling mechanism and shut down the deployment before the device explodes."

"It may also speed up the deployment," Arcon says.

Silenna has her arms crossed and her utility hand under her chin like an ancient wise woman. She tells Arcon to run an analysis.

"A thorough analysis will take time," he responds.

"I've been studying the deployment of the device for a full fifteen minutes. I don't think we have much more time. Jacob's idea is risky. Any further thoughts, Arcon?"

"If we use a more powerful cannon, the risk factor only increases."

Silenna ponders the problem for less than a minute. "Let's use the electromagnetic cannon."

Once she's made up her mind, Silenna doesn't hesitate.

"Fire cannon one," she commands the ship's targeting computer.

The next thing we see is a mini-explosion illuminating an energy shield surrounding the gathering supernova event.

"Fire freely until my next command."

The pulses keep hitting the same spot on the shield. We don't see the pulses because they are invisible, but the explosions light up the shield like arc lights.

The shield blinks a few times and then disappears. The pulses pour into the heart of the shining orb. We see an explosion in the center of the orb that looks like a mini-sandstorm.

Suddenly, the ball of light expands. It is all we can see through the observation windows. I raise my arm reflexively to ward off the inevitable disintegration of the ship.

Just as suddenly, the massive ball shrinks to nothingness. Before I can register what's going on, Silenna abandons telepathic communication and calls out, "Cease firing cannon one. Fire cannon two and magnify."

The ship emits a pale blue beam. On the screen below the forward observation window, we see the beam crash into a ball that resembles a giant black marble. The marble explodes into shards that reflect the color of the beam. The particles flicker and disperse harmlessly into the black void of space.

The sequence happens almost instantly. I think of Amy and how close we've come to vaporization. I sense there is no need to say something to Silenna like "nice job." I know her well enough to understand she doesn't need the praise. Instead, I say, "I'm going to check on Amy."

"I'll open the infirmary door for you," she replies.

By now, I'm familiar with the ship's layout. I pass through the portal to the infirmary. Amy sleeps peacefully sans the medical chamber. It has disappeared back into the ceiling. She wears a long navy-blue robe that eclipses her feet. I take a close look around the room. I notice the walls and ceiling are covered in white fuzz. I guess the fuzz is an energy field emitting the ambient light in the room. There are no machines or medical appliances visible. Since the chamber has disappeared, I assume the other medical devices are stored in the walls and ceiling. I imagine they can be called forth as needed.

Without warning, a gangly robotic arm descends from the ceiling. It doesn't startle me. My body is getting used to potentially lethal events happening without notice.

The arm moves around Amy's inert body. I watch it, wishing I were an Aneleyan doctor listening telepathically to a medical report from the arm. Maybe the instrument is reporting directly to Arcon and Silenna.

A humanoid hand opens. It looks like it is made from shiny black plastic. It turns toward me. In the center of the palm, I see a dime-sized circular lens peering out at me as if it would like to examine me too.

"I'm fine," I tell the hand. I point to Amy. "It's her I'm worried about."

To my amazement, the hand answers me telepathically in a calm, human-sounding voice. "She is fine too," it reports, before rising to its hidden compartment in the ceiling.

Amy's eyes spring open. It looks like she needs a moment to come back from wherever she was. Then, her face registers alarm.

"It's okay," I say.

Amy turns her head toward the sound of my voice. I'm not sure she recognizes me.

"Jacob?"

"None other," I reply.

"My vision is blurry."

"I'm sure it will improve. You've been through a bit of an ordeal."

Amy holds out her hand to me. I grasp it in both of mine. We look at each other without speaking for a moment. The only thing that seems real is our connection. Are we really in an alien spaceship? Did we just avert another world-ending catastrophe? Am I in bed at the beach house next to Amy having a bad dream? Are we still alive? Amy's question brings me out of my reverie.

"What happened?"

"You passed out."

"Why?"

How do I answer? "We aren't entirely sure."

Amy sits up. "What's your best guess?"

"The important point is you're conscious and you look ravishing."

"Don't bullshit me, Jacob."

I inhale deeply. I release my breath. Slowly.

"We think you almost ran out of energy."

Amy stares at me. "What?"

"Since Arcon left your body, we believe you've been leaking life force."

"Are you serious?"

"I'm afraid so. The good news is an Aneleyan medical chamber came out of the ceiling and revived you."

"Please tell me you're making this up."

I take another deep breath and exhale slowly. No words come to me.

"This is not one of your clever jokes?"

I shake my head back and forth to confirm.

Amy's hand goes to her mouth. I gently pull it away.

"Remember I told you I figured out what it means when you shrug?"

She nods. "We never got around to discussing it."

I sit next to Amy and put my arm around her. I whisper in her ear: "It means we can do this. It means we'll figure it out."

We sit in silence for a minute.

"I don't want to depend on a machine to stay alive."

"I know. We will work through this," I say emphatically.

Amy looks deeply into my eyes. "Are you sure?"

"Yes."

She lays her head on my shoulder. I pick up her chin and kiss her. "Get some rest. I'll be back to check on you."

"Don't die," Amy says with a feeble smile.

"I wouldn't dare."

Before passing through the portal into the corridor, I turn to wave goodbye. Amy waves back unenthusiastically. The medical chamber descends from the ceiling. Its reappearance concerns me.

"She is fine. I am simply functioning as her spacesuit," the chamber tells me. Apparently, it can read my mind and converse with me telepathically just like Arcon and Silenna.

Before I have a chance to feel relieved, Silenna's thoughts burst into my head.

"Come to the cockpit. Quickly."

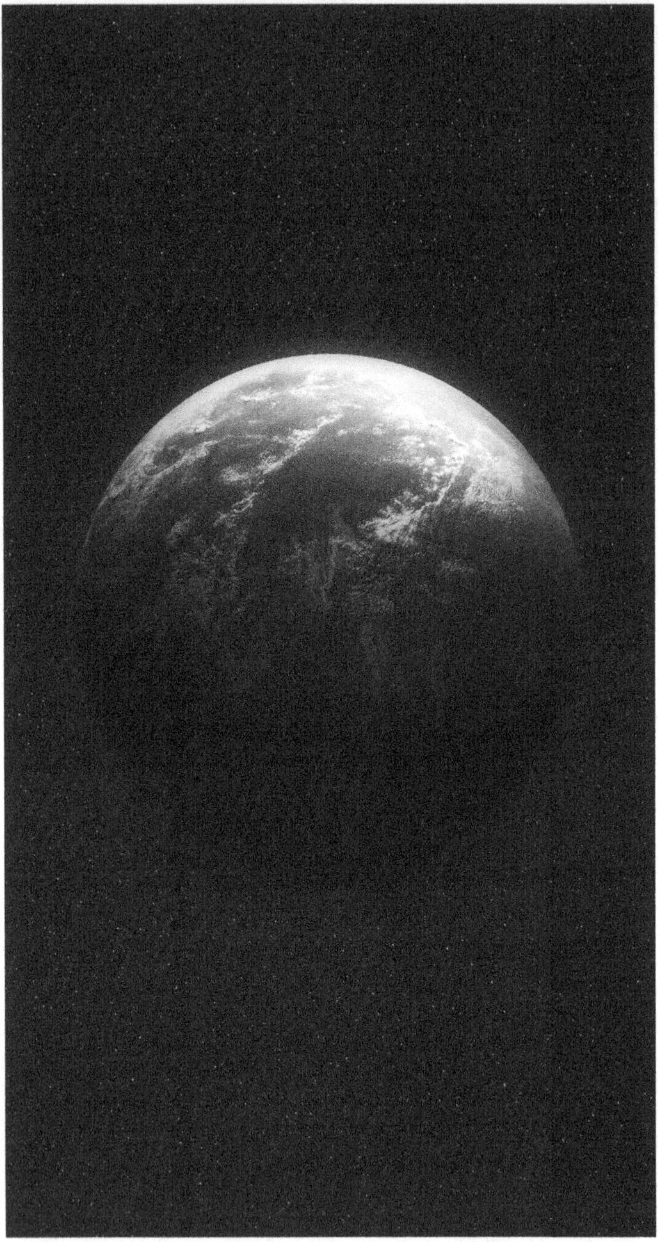

── 35 ──
EARTHBOUND

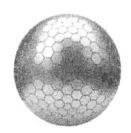

Entering the cockpit, I find Silenna contemplating a live image of the Earth on the screen below the forward window. I find it odd that she has donned her helmet. We haven't needed them in a while. She turns to me abruptly. "Affix your helmet. We haven't much time."

What else is new? My life since meeting Arcon has had three speeds: Fast, faster, and fast forward. Remembering Silenna's tutorial, I grab my helmet and secure it.

"Sub-light speed to Earth," Silenna commands the ship's computer. "Two hours to Earth."

"That's two hours faster than our trip here."

"Yes. It is unsafe to travel at sublight speeds for short distances. It puts a strain on the ship's hull and the engine, but we have no choice."

The distance between the Earth and the Moon is hardly short, but everything is relative. The speed of my life finds a fourth gear: Flash forward.

Sitting in the command seat, Silenna motions for me to sit beside her. The seats strap us in. The first time this happened, I thought the straps might mistake me for a hardy Aneleyan, and therefore crush me to death. I was relieved to discover that the straps, along with everything else on the ship, are intelligent. Nevertheless, I have to ask: "What about Amy?"

"The med chamber will keep her alive and intact."

"That confirms what the med chamber told me. Out of curiosity, what's the rush?"

"The other ship has entered Earth's upper atmosphere. We must catch up to it quickly."

Looking out the observation windows, I watch the stars begin to blur as the shields close.

The trip to Earth passes slowly. Silenna is immersed in something other than conversing with me. I assume she is dialoguing telepathically with the ship's computers to plot the most efficient interception course among other strategies. In his shell and comfortably strapped in, Arcon rests on the third chair. He could be hibernating to gather his faculties for whatever comes next. I once saw him hibernate the night before blasting off into space to save the Earth for a second time.

Besides worrying about Amy, I use the time to make a mental inventory of things I am grateful for and things to be done:

1. I've made a solid start with my new mystery novel.
2. The sales of my last novel are strong, but I'll have to do interviews and book signings to keep up the momentum.
3. I'm still in one piece—something to be grateful for—but I've never bothered to make a Will. I

will make a Will. I find it sad that all I have to leave behind of any value are the rights to a few mystery novels. Will anybody be around to read them?
4. If I survive, I will be a better son and stay in regular contact with my parents.
5. If I survive, I will never again be mad at my agent, editor, or publisher. I admit to myself this is a big ask.
6. I am grateful for meeting my alien friends, although the price of their comradeship is ridiculously high.
7. I'm grateful to earn a living doing what I love, but I may not survive the next few hours, in which case the proper verb is "loved."
8. I am grateful to have met Amy. I am grateful for the time we've spent together. As my Jewish grandmother used to say, "It should only last a lifetime."

My list suddenly jumps its rails and heads in another direction with unanswerable questions like:

9. Why was I chosen to be in this position? Was I even chosen, or was it a random occurrence?
10. Why does the riddle of existence remain stubbornly unanswered?
11. And finally, why have all the positive intentions of the human race throughout history resulted in the pitiful world we live in and this precarious moment?

There is only one question that will soon be answered:

Do the aliens on the other ship have good or bad intentions?

I decide it is best to relax and gather whatever forces I have to offer. There is no point in allowing my mind to canter off wildly into a lush pasture like an unbroken yearling. I close my eyes to meditate.

* * *

I'm startled by the pneumatic sound of the shields retracting. I must have dozed off. A starry night sky and a half-Moon fill the observation windows.

Seconds later, in stealth mode, we land on the outskirts of a snow-covered field. Short, dead stalks peek out of the snow. It looks like a corn crop was harvested here. After the first three rows of stalks, the field dissolves into darkness. In the foreground, I can make out an old-fashioned wagon with a harness attached. Did we land in another century?

"Where are we?"

"What you call Amish country. On the outskirts of Pennsylvania."

We are somewhere near an Amish village. One of the last places on Earth I'd ever expect us to be.

Silenna turns to Arcon. "I want you to leave your sphere and scour the terrain from a hundred yards in the air until you find the ship. It has to be nearby."

I watch Arcon emerge from the golden sphere in his natural form. In his new version, his transmission is no longer toxic. He passes noiselessly through the forward observation window into the foreboding night. By its faint glow, I recognize Arcon activating his energy shield. We may be in Amish country, but we are by no means safe.

A few seconds later, we see an Arcon-eye-view of the surrounding landscape on the forward screen.

As Arcon surveys the barren cornfield, we see a boring series of views illuminated by the inconspicuous light Arcon projects. I think of it as a lantern light. It doesn't take long for Arcon to cover the field.

There is no trace of the other vessel.

"Map," Silenna commands the computer. A topographical map pops up on the screen.

I point to a dense forest in the upper right-hand corner of the map. Silenna nods in agreement. She instructs Arcon to explore the forest and the intervening terrain.

Arcon passes over winter fields planted with hay, barley, and potatoes. The rows of seedlings provide no clues as to the whereabouts of the massive ship.

Arcon reaches the edge of the forest. He passes up and down its edge. Near the end of his sweep, we see a broad path of broken trees. Arcon veers into the path. The ground is scorched. Fallen tree trunks are scarred and splintered. Intensifying his lantern light, Arcon shines the light deeper into the forest.

A few hundred yards down the broad pathway, we see the hulking outline of a starship.

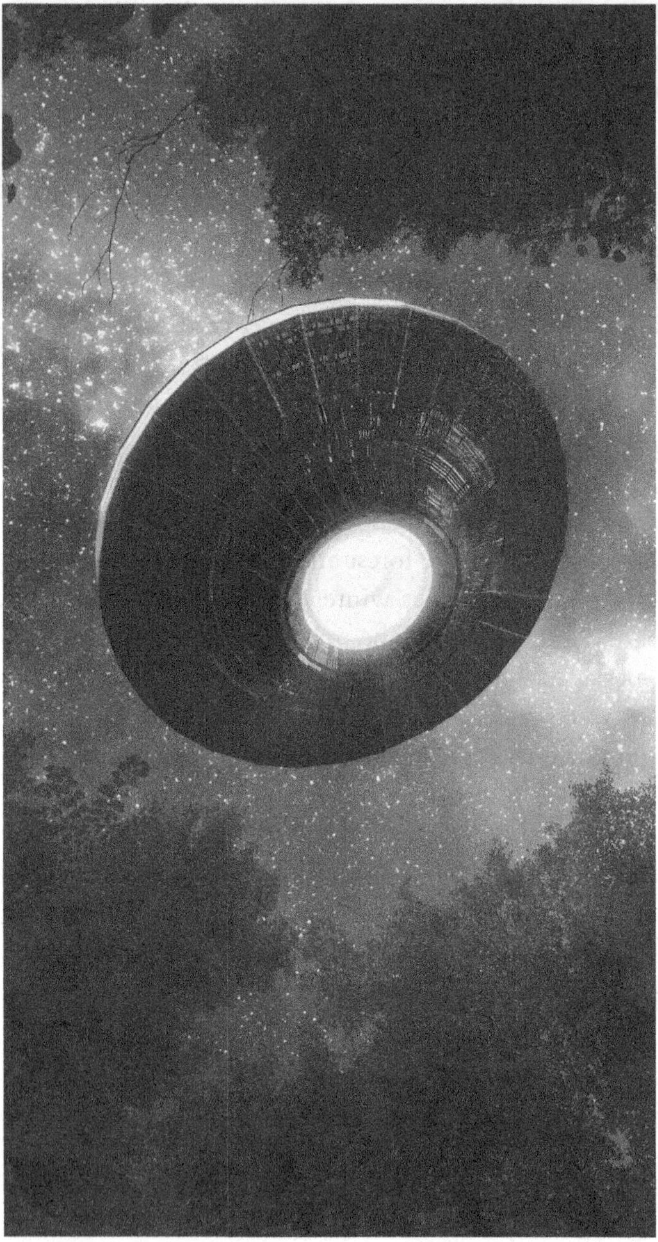

—36—
THE MYSTERIOUS SHIP

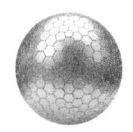

"Maybe it crashed."

"Maybe," Silenna allows.

Our ship hovers a respectful distance away from the vessel of unknown origin. In stealth mode and in the middle of the night, no one will see us.

The boomerang tail wings identify the mysterious vessel as the ship we saw leaving the Moltke Crater. The wreckage left in its wake hasn't caused a discernable dent in the ship's outer structure. Even from this presumably safe vantage point, the vessel appears unusually large.

"Circle the ship and investigate," I hear Silenna command Arcon telepathically.

I watch Arcon descend to the level of the ship.

"Arcon has something like x-ray vision except it can display objects in three dimensions," Silenna tells me.

"I wouldn't expect less," I acknowledge with tongue in cheek.

I watch Arcon slowly circle the vessel. He transmits images to the viewing screen. Brown pyramids of stacked plates reinforce the outer hull. It looks impenetrable.

"We are on high alert," Silenna assures me. I assume the same applies to Arcon.

After a few passes, Arcon reports, "The hull is too thick to access the interior."

Even with his super x-ray vision, Arcon is unable to see inside the ship. I understand this puts Silenna in a delicate quandary. She appears to be deliberating.

"Enter the ship," She decides. "At the first sign of trouble, return to base immediately."

Arcon does not hesitate. The viewing screen goes blank momentarily. Then, the first images of a cloudy, dark space appear. Arcon keeps moving. He passes along a row of what looks to me like deep-space sleep chambers standing vertically. Arcon jaunts laterally into more rows of the chambers. The field of chambers seems as large as the Amish cornfield.

"The hibernation chambers are empty," Arcon reports blandly.

Silenna and I exchange a concerned look. "I don't like this," she says.

"The atmosphere consists principally of Methane, Hydrogen, and Nitrogen," Arcon announces.

Lethal to human beings.

Reading my mind, Silenna nods. I've requested that she ask permission to intrude on my thoughts, but under the circumstances, I don't care.

"Requesting further instructions," Arcon says. It strikes me that his demeanor is completely different with Silenna than it is with me. Makes sense. She's his boss.

"Continue exploring. Carefully."

Silenna gives me a hard look. I decide the look is

more concerned than hard. After everything we've been through, I think we are finally bonding.

The shapes inside the ship are difficult to discern until Arcon's faint light comes into close contact with them. Some of the shapes are curvilinear, and some have straight edges. They vary in size. One large square looks like it might be a viewing screen. All the instruments are covered by a scaled-down version of the pyramid plates we saw on the outer hull. Using Occam's razor theory, I can draw only one conclusion. The inside of the ship is battened down.

Silenna stares intently at the screen. I'm sure we are thinking along the same lines. Either the interior of the ship armored itself in preparation for a crash landing, or a battle.

Arcon halts suddenly. "I hear voices. It will take some time to learn their language."

"Find some cover."

Arcon is already one step ahead of Silenna. He finds refuge behind a columnar support beam shaped like a massive Martini glass.

I notice Arcon's shield is glowing brighter. The extra protection comes at the cost of higher visibility.

Ten minutes pass. "I'm going to visit Amy," I tell Silenna. She grips my space-suited arm. "Stay. I need you here. It won't take Arcon much longer."

Looking down at her gloved hand on my arm, I say, "Really?"

Silenna removes her hand. "I'm sorry. I need you here. I have no other backup."

I'm not quite sure how to take the remark, but I stay put.

Another thirty seconds pass before Arcon makes this welcome announcement: "I'm able to interpret now. I'm deciphering their conversations. There are three of them."

Three of them on the entire ship?

"It seems so," Arcon replies telepathically after reading my thoughts.

Silenna and I exchange a baffled look.

"Wait. I see one of them."

Silenna turns to me. "Our shields are too dense for Arcon to pass through. Lowering them will leave us vulnerable."

"Are you asking for my advice?"

Without answering, Silenna turns back to the forward observation window. For the first time since I've known her, she seems unsure of herself.

She turns to me again. Offering her a smile, I say, "We need him. And, he's more than a machine now."

She turns back to the window and stares through it for another half-minute.

"You can't leave him out there alone."

More seconds pass before I hear Silenna's telepathic command.

"Return to base. Hurry, Arcon."

By the glow of his shield, I watch Arcon emerge from the mystery ship. He quickly floats upward to the perimeter of our ship.

"Lowering shields," Silenna tells Arcon.

Arcon enters the cockpit directly through its heavily reinforced hull.

Just as I'm about to welcome him back, our ship rocks violently.

We begin to lose altitude.

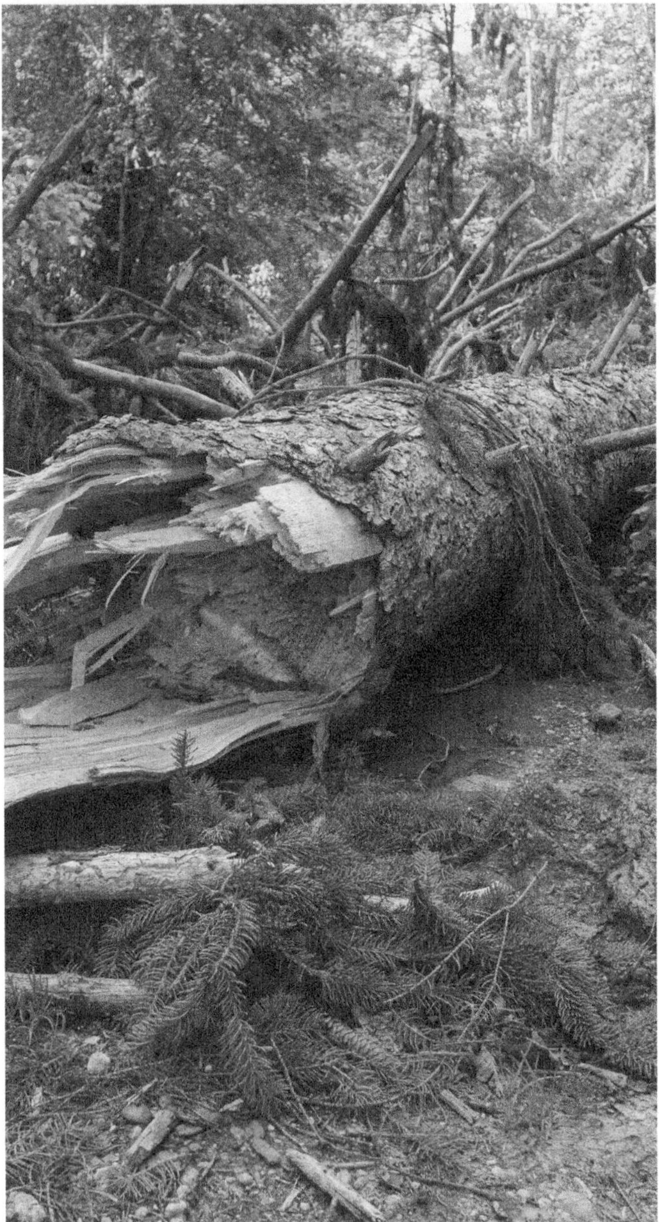

—37—
PREPARE FOR IMPACT

"Prepare for impact."

Since Silenna has kept us helmeted and strapped in since we left Moon orbit, I'm not sure how much more prepared I can be.

I see the tops of trees rushing toward us before the shields slide closed over the observation windows. I worry about Amy in the infirmary. Will she be safe there?

"Shields?" Silenna asks the computer verbally.

"Optimal," the computer replies audibly.

I feel my insides pulled towards the floor as we plummet. It is a sickening sensation.

I hear the crack of tree branches and then feel a buffeting sensation. The ship judders as we plow through the forest. We strike the ground. The shuddering crash throws us forward in our seats. Surprisingly, the final impact isn't as bad as I expected.

The ship settles. Silenna doesn't waste a second.

"Open forward window shield."

All we can see is a mass of broken tree trunks and branches.

The other ship is nowhere in sight.

"Close shields." Silenna turns to me. Her expression is more serious than a fatal illness. "The ship's operational systems work from a separate power source than the main flight engine. I have to stay here and check out each system. I need you to go down to the engine compartment. I'll tell you what to do when you get there."

"I'm going to check on Amy first."

"Amy is fine. As I promised, the medical chamber kept her secure. The treetops and our shields lessened the impact. The ship is intact."

"I have to see her. She's probably scared and panicked."

"I'll talk to her telepathically to keep her calm. Our priority is to repair the main flight engine."

I consider this and decide to yield to Silenna's instructions. I'm not exactly an old hand at crash-landings in starships.

The straps release automatically. Standing up, I do my own systems check. My lower back hurts and my left shoulder has seen better days. The good news is I can still walk. Running is probably another story.

I rush out into the corridor and come to a quick stop. I pop my helmet back through the cockpit portal.

"Sorry. Where's the engine compartment?"

"Take the elevator. You will find it a few steps down the corridor on your right. I'll tell you how to use it."

I give Silenna a thumbs up.

"Hurry. We're vulnerable sitting here without thrust."

* * *

The elevator takes me smoothly down to the ship's bottom level. The door slides open. It becomes immediately apparent that I'm in the engine room because a huge machine dominates the room. What must be the main engine is comprised of a series of concentric circles cut in half and decreasing in size to the centers. A pole bisects the two half circles. It acts like a spine. It also must function as a cooling pipe. A thick, glass-like shield surrounds the engine. In color and composition, the engine looks to be made of the same material as Arcon's golden sphere. I look around at the concave walls of the room. The material composition does indeed match that of the engine.

The ceiling is fuzzy like the infirmary walls, except the color is the same as Silenna's space suit. Either the interior colors are designed to her specifications, or they are standard Aneleyan Space Agency colors.

In my head, I hear Silenna's initial instructions. "Go to the control panel on your left."

I use the intercom in my helmet to communicate. "If the engine produces anti-matter propulsion, it must be highly radioactive."

"Would I send you into the engine room if it were dangerous? The shield is there for protection, and your suit alone will repel hazardous emissions if there are any leaks. Stop worrying and let's get this done. It won't take long to make the necessary repairs."

I like the way Silenna generally predicts a positive outcome. With any luck, it will prevent the engine from blowing up in my face.

Silenna guides me through a series of complex actions

consisting of touching various circles on the control panel. When she says we're done, I wonder how she can recall the order of the steps. Then I remember that she is, after all, Silenna. Her brain is infinitely more evolved than mine, and she has the benefit of God knows how many years of training.

I wait for the engine to start. It doesn't.

"Nothing is happening," I report.

"That's because I haven't started the engine. Take the elevator back to the cockpit, and be quick about it."

As I board the elevator, I hear something that sounds ominously like an explosion. Through the intercom, I overhear Silenna whisper something in her native language that, by its inflection, sounds like a curse word.

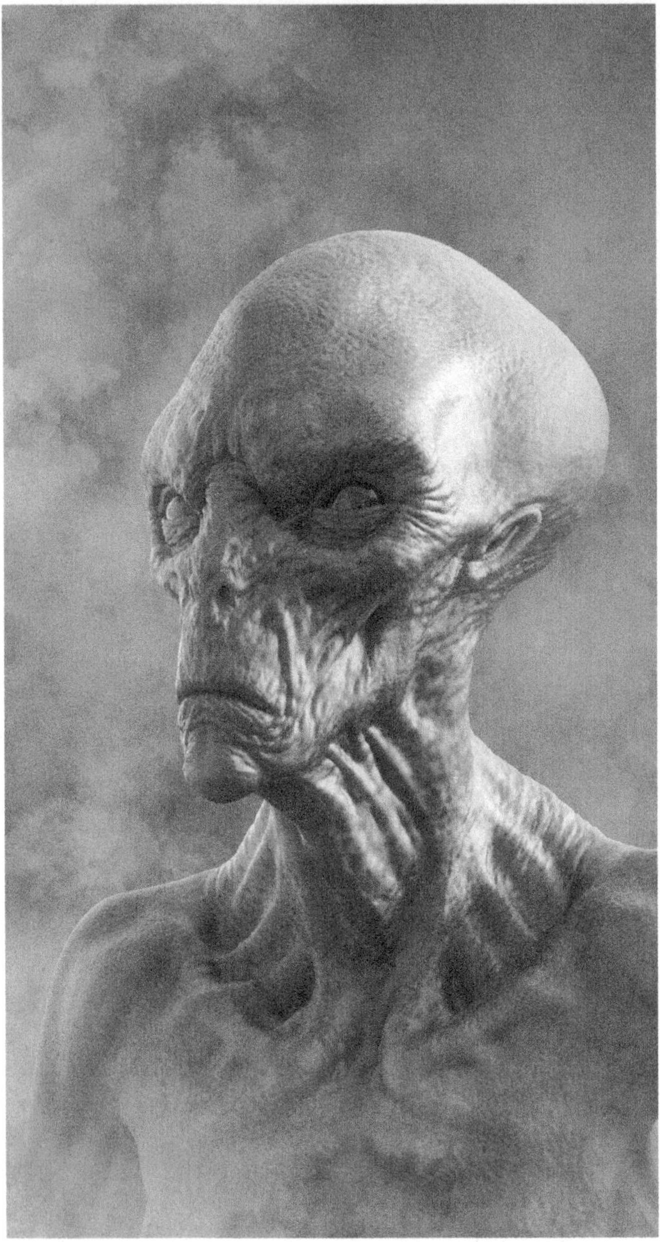

—38—
ARCON'S REPORT

I arrived in the cockpit. The first thing I notice is the window shields are open. Why?

Silenna appears to be immersed in a pre-flight check. This assumes, of course, the ship can fly.

"What was that loud noise I heard?"

"The other ship taking off," Silenna says without looking up. "Arcon and I watched it rise above the tree line."

Amy walks into the cockpit in her spacesuit holding her helmet by one of the clamps.

Unfastening my helmet, I rush to embrace her. We kiss. A long kiss. She drops her helmet.

"I'm fine," Amy says to me before I can ask.

"Now that we're all here, I can begin my report." It's Arcon speaking telepathically from inside his sphere.

Amy retrieves her helmet. We settle in our seats. Arcon begins his report.

"After learning their language, I eavesdropped telepathically on the conversations of the three crewmembers. Upon hearing one of them entering the central compartment, Silenna ordered me to return to base. Before I left, I caught a glimpse of the creature and a star map behind it through the open portal. The creature exited what we would call the command-and-control room. I used my camera eye to zoom in and snap an image before the portal closed. Here is what I learned from my infiltration of the alien vessel."

A map of a solar system appears on the viewing screen.

"As you can see, the solar system has twelve planets surrounding an orange sun. For the benefit of Amy and Jacob, I'll explain that an orange sun indicates a star going through its final stages of life. The next and final stage is a red sun. At the end of the red phase, the sun explodes. The point I'm making is that this is an old star system. If intelligent life with advanced technology exists on any of these planets, then the inhabitants have to be thinking of leaving their home world and settling elsewhere.

"I compared the star map to my database of known star systems. I believe I've come up with a match for the planets and the age of the sun. The atmosphere on one of the planets matches the atmosphere I found on the ship. To facilitate our communication, I've named the planet Orania and the race of its inhabitants Oranians. Are there any questions before I continue?"

"What would the Oranians want with our planet?" I ask. "Our atmosphere is very different from theirs."

"I believe the creature I saw is their captain. It is a male of the species. In addition to his thoughts, I accessed his subconscious where I found more information. I had the same question as you, Jacob. Here is the answer. The temperatures on our planet suit the Oranians perfectly. They can terraform most of this biosphere to suit their needs including the atmosphere they breathe. Temperature is one of the variables that can't be manipulated unless the entire planet is encapsulated. Encapsulation breeds a host of other problems, so it is only feasible in extreme cases. Are there any other questions?"

"What do they look like?" Amy asks.

"Prepare yourselves."

Arcon flashes another image on the screen.

"Oh!" Amy says, inhaling sharply. Silenna remains calm.

"Not surprising" is her only comment.

To me, the creature looks like an extraterrestrial version of Ebenezer Scrooge. I'd give it an Oscar for the "meanest and ugliest creature of the year."

Arcon is quick to distract our attention from the monstrosity on the screen.

"What I'm about to tell you is quite a lot to digest at once. Please listen and hold your questions until I finish. Moving on, the ship we've encountered is here on an exploratory mission. The small crew is here to test Earth's defenses. If your defenses prove fallible, then an invasion force will follow. The size of the ship is intended to instill fear. The first target is Philadelphia. The attack is scheduled for dawn. It is designed to test the city's defenses in daylight."

"Philadelphia," I say. "Birthplace of a nation. Where the founding fathers signed the Constitution. Where the Liberty Bell resides. The bastards intend to send a clear message."

"It seems so," Arcon agrees.

Amy directs her comment to Silenna. "We have to intercept the ship before it reaches Philadelphia."

Silenna barely nods. If I didn't know her better, I'd think Arcon's report has had little or no effect on her. Except I know that's not true. She's preparing herself for the biggest challenge we have yet to face, and the first two of them weren't exactly easy.

I gaze through the windows at the outlines of ruined trees in the pre-dawn light.

"I guess we moved up their timeline," I say.

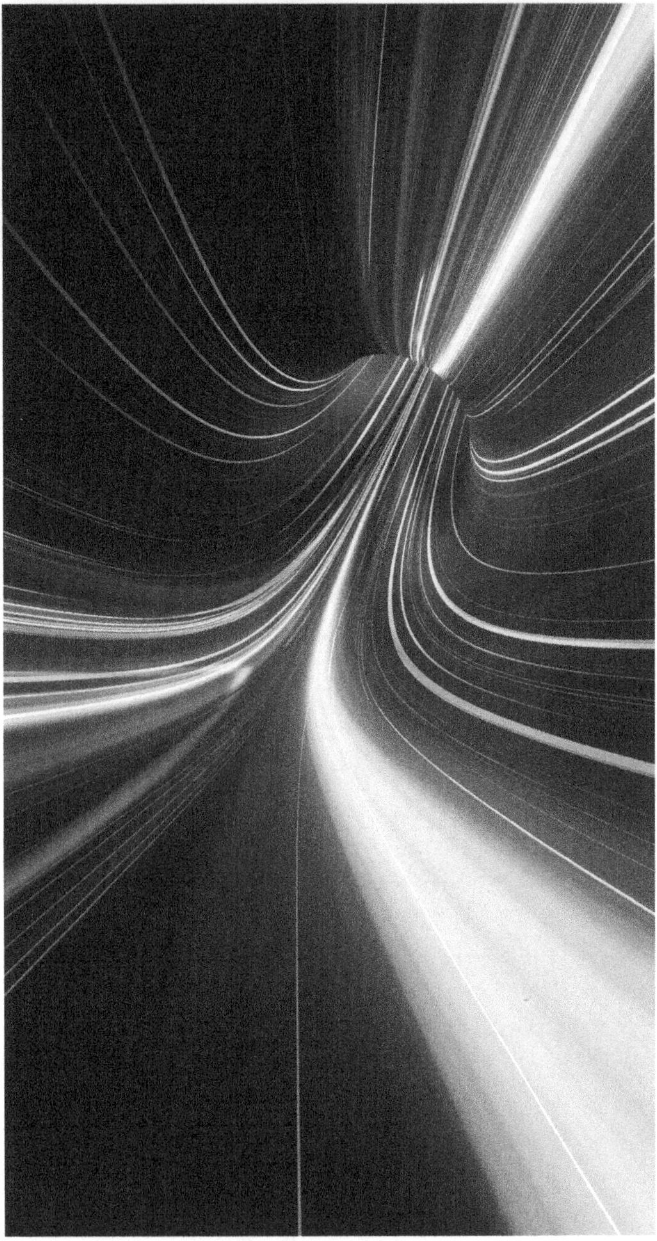

—39—
CATCHING UP

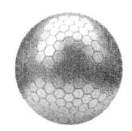

We sit in the cockpit staring through the observation windows into the depths of the cold night. Chiefly for Amy's benefit, Silenna speaks to us while Arcon lounges in his seat nearby. Since we will be undergoing what I hope will be the mundane steps of an ordinary lift-off, I anticipate Arcon is primarily focused on engagement scenarios and therefore minimally present for Silenna's orders.

"We will now strap in automatically. The straps will find the optimal pressure to secure you for the flight. Just relax."

Amy nods and turns to me. I give her a thumbs up. She shrugs.

"Engage straps," Silenna commands the ship's computer. "Arcon, input the coordinates for downtown Philadelphia."

I hear nothing.

"Arcon?"

"Sorry. I was elsewhere."

No surprise. I hear Arcon call out a set of coordinates to the navigation system.

Silenna settles back in her seat. "Begin vertical ascent at hover speed."

I feel a subtle vibration in my seat. The ship rises slowly until we pass above the tree line of the forest. The light is better at this level. On the horizon, I see a slice of gray below the darkness. Dawn can't be far behind.

"Vertical ascent at one-eighth thrust," Silenna commands.

The ship rises quickly but not uncomfortably. Turning to Amy, I speak through my intercom. "This is going to be dicey."

"I know," she says, then turns to me and wrinkles her nose.

I shake my head and laugh. "Where did I find you?"

"On a beach. Dead. Remember?"

I nod. We laugh. It helps when facing a fiery death in battle.

"Stop ascent. Hold position." Silenna looks over at me. "Don't ever try this." She turns back to the main computer saying something in her native language. I suppose her command cannot be adequately translated into English. Upon further analysis, I decide she doesn't want me to understand what is about to happen.

The shields close over the windows. The ship lurches forward. The "G" force presses me against my seat. My back and shoulders object. I hear a sonic boom. We have broken the sound barrier from a stationary position in a nanosecond. Everything is quiet for a few seconds until I feel the ship decelerating. Then, I hear gnashing noises. It almost sounds like the ship is groaning from the sudden change in speed. The observation window shields slide open. As we reach the outskirts of Philadelphia, I see buildings burning and hear thunderous explosions.

I don't know how far we've traveled, but we've arrived at our destination almost instantly, and not a second too soon.

"Lights on."

At Silenna's command, spotlights garland our ship's exterior. In the twilight before dawn, I can barely see the outline of the Oranian ship cruising above Philadelphia.

"Distance to target."

"One point eight six miles," Arcon responds.

"Close window shields."

The view of the besieged city now comes from the forward viewing screen. As we close the distance to our target, I can see orange beams spurting sequentially at different angles from the bottom of the attacking spacecraft.

A swath of tract homes explodes sending gushers of smoke and debris into the air.

Scrambled from a nearby Air Force base, a squadron of F-35 fighter jets peels off from above the Oranian ship. I can identify the jets by their distinctive split tails and snub-nosed wings. The jets dive toward the target releasing hellfire missiles. The jets are met with a laser weapon that fires something like spider webs of lightning bolts from the top of the hull. The hellfire missiles explode harmlessly off the Oranian shields. The fighter jets explode in flames one by one in the clutches of the laser web. It is an awful sight to behold.

More explosions on the ground. An orange beam hits the top of an office building shearing off its roof. A gas station erupts into flames followed by a plume of smoke.

A line of heavy tanks with long barrels trundles along the main thoroughfare below the attacking ship. I watch the tanks crash through the gates of a nearby park. Before the tanks can form up to counter-attack, I see the orange beams adjust on the hull of the Oranian ship to concentrate on the tanks. The orange beams pour down on the tanks. In groups of two and three, the tanks shatter and explode as if they are made of balsa wood. Another tragic and terrifying sight.

I am a storehouse of assorted facts from writing books. At this close range, I can tell the tanks are the Abrams model, one of the strongest and deadliest tanks in the US Army's arsenal. The Oranian warship has squashed them like bothersome mosquitos. The vaunted weapons of the armed forces and their highly trained operators are batting zero. We are the last line of defense. We have to act quickly to prevent the Oranian ship from sailing over downtown Philadelphia.

When we close to within a mile, the distance to the target pops up on the viewing screen.

"Estimate Oranian shield strength."

Arcon takes half a minute to analyze the enemy shields from a distance of just under a mile.

"I can predict with seventy-eight percent accuracy that the shields are a layered system. The outer shield is not as dense as ours. I theorize the inner layers are activated as needed to conserve energy."

Silenna calmly digests the information. I try to remain calm, too. It's not easy. I didn't sign up to do battle with an impossibly lethal alien warship.

I watch the remaining tanks raise their guns. Puffs of white smoke issue from their long barrels. Another column of Air Force jets strafes the Oranian ship firing more missiles. Struck by the lightning bolts, the jets suffer the same fate as their predecessors. The explosions from the missiles and tank rounds form a shroud around the enemy ship. Through the dust and smoke, the warship continues firing its deadly weapons at the depleted ranks of the resistance force. The defenders have temporarily distracted the onslaught away from civilian targets, but at a tragically high price. The scene is a giant conflagration with death and destruction in all directions.

"Cycle up cannon three and fire when ready. Maximum shields."

Our ship recoils slightly as it fires a powerful red laser burst into the center of the shroud obscuring the Oranian ship.

"Evasive action."

The engines engage. Our ship cants to a forty-five-degree angle and speeds away from a counter-attack.

"Come about," Silenna commands. The ship slows and circles to face the battle raging around the enemy ship. "Level the ship and fire canons two and three."

The red and pale blue beams of our cannons penetrate the cloud of dust and smoke around the aggressor. Is it penetrating their shields?

A swarm of spider web bolts emerges from the haze. They crash against our shields before we can change position.

"Ascend with cruising speed to two thousand feet," Silenna orders.

Our ship angles up again. The engines engage. I vow to never ride a roller coaster again. That includes the one for little children.

I look over to Amy. I can see that she is terrified. I wonder what tactical tricks Silenna has up her space-suited sleeve. I take Amy's hand, wishing I could do more than watch innocent people and brave defenders die.

Silenna commands the ship to level off at two thousand feet.

The ship complies. "Now dive to one thousand feet firing cannons two and three. Level off at one thousand feet and take evasive action."

I'm thinking Silenna has a good idea with her surprise attack until we are hit by the crackling arms of a lightning bolt at the bottom of our dive. The shields absorb the blow, but since we came out of the dive close to the Oranian ship, our vessel is shoved sideways by the impact.

A purple light flashes on the manual control console on the right arm of Silenna's seat. At the same instant, the Oranian warship emerges from the dust cloud. I'm thinking it is coming to finish us off. I've been holding Amy's hand throughout the battle. I guess this is the way our journey together ends. Instead, I'm shocked to see the deadly vessel point its nose to the sky and gain altitude.

"We damaged their shields," Arcon reports. "The Oranian ship has aborted its attack."

Below the boomerang back wings, I see the warship's huge engines ignite. The ship arches high into the sky. In less than a minute, it disappears from view leaving only a vapor trail behind.

Silenna speaks to us telepathically. "We have a coolant malfunction. It requires my immediate attention on the upper deck. Arcon will assist me. In our absence, Jacob will pilot the ship."

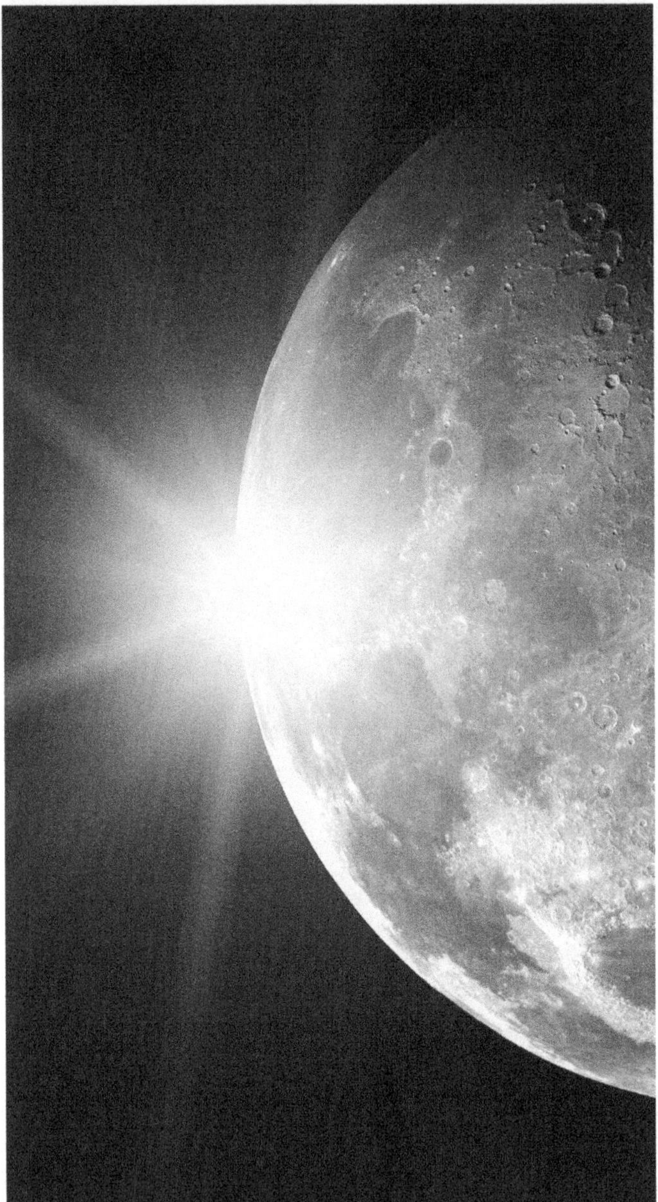

— 40 —
DOUBLE EXPOSURE

I am looking at Silenna in stunned silence. "Take the command seat," is all she says to me. "Come along," she calls to Arcon. Remaining in stunned silence, I watch Arcon leave his golden cocoon and follow Silenna out of the cockpit.

"Did you learn how to fly this thing while I was in the infirmary?"

"Not exactly."

I'm thinking Silenna will coach me if she isn't too busy keeping the ship from becoming a ticking neutron bomb.

"Pursue the Oranian ship," I hear Silenna say through my intercom.

"With a leaky cooling system?"

"It isn't leaking. It is overheating. Just do as I say. Please. I've placed my trust in you."

"Why can't you tell the ship what to do telepathically?"

"Because the cooling chamber is heavily insulated which prevents thought transmission."

Alright, I tell myself. *Here goes.* "Pursue the Oranian

ship," I tell the computer verbally. "Follow the heat signature of the engines."

"What angle and speed?" It responds.

"Uhm...Calculate a safe angle and speed for leaving Earth's atmosphere."

"You see. It's not that hard," I hear Silenna say. "You know how to think clearly and with imagination from writing your books. If you make an error, I'll correct you. Carry on."

"Ready for ignition," the ship reports.

"Ignition," I say, and turn to Amy. "I'd say 'engage' but this isn't the Enterprise."

"*Jacob*," Amy says in a sing-song voice. "This is not a game."

Amy is absolutely correct, but I find that I operate best when I'm loose and relaxed, even in the face of certain death by extremely ugly aliens.

The ship angles upward. The engine fires. I sense we are moving, but it's not possible to tell how fast when the shields are closed. The cockpit isn't much to look at with the windows shuttered. Come to think of it, the space is downright confining from the perspective of the command seat. The interior walls are colored a dull silver and probably made from a different substance than the engine compartment interior. When the windows were open, I remember seeing the hull butting up against the window frames. It looked about a foot thick, adding to feelings of claustrophobia.

There are no fuzzy walls in here. The look is hard and utilitarian. The thought of a coffin pops into my head. It's an expensive model with silk lining and extra thick walls to keep the worms out. I decide to cancel morbid metaphorical thinking for the remainder of the mission.

As we glide upwards, I turn my thoughts to preparing for what might happen next. I take in a deep breath and close my eyes. As my mind settles, Amy's insistent question intrudes.

"Why didn't she choose me? I have a degree in astronautical engineering?"

The question is a complete ambush. Nevertheless, it requires an answer. "Silenna and I bonded a bit while you were recovering. Don't feel bad. You can be the captain next time."

"That's a dumb thing to say."

I am taken aback by Amy's remark. "That's a mean thing to say. It's very unlike you."

Amy takes a deep breath of her own. "This has all been so overwhelming." After collecting herself, she pats me on the top of my helmet. "I'm sorry."

"It's okay. We're way out of our depth here."

"Try not to let us drown."

"I'm working on it."

The ship levels off. The view on the screen is breathtaking. I'm tempted to lower the shields for a better look. On second thought, I'm not anxious to be roasted alive by a killer beam alongside the love of my life.

A half-Moon lies dead ahead with the sun peeking out behind it.

Amy points out the star constellation Aquarius in the distance.

I take Amy's hand entwining my fingers with hers. This is hardly the time for a romantic moment, but we might not have many like this one left.

"Scan for the Oranian ship," I tell the computer.

"Scanning," the computer confirms.

Silenna's voice erupts loudly through the intercom. "We've done as much as we can up here. Arcon made a replacement part. It will hold us until we can make more extensive repairs. For the time being, we must use our thrusters efficiently when engaging the enemy warship. If we don't, the engine will overheat and go critical."

Double exposure. We're vulnerable to threats from the inside and the outside. We've been in tight spots before. This one gets the nod for a Golden Globe.

"Oranian ship located," the computer reports.

I spot it coming right at us from out of the sun.

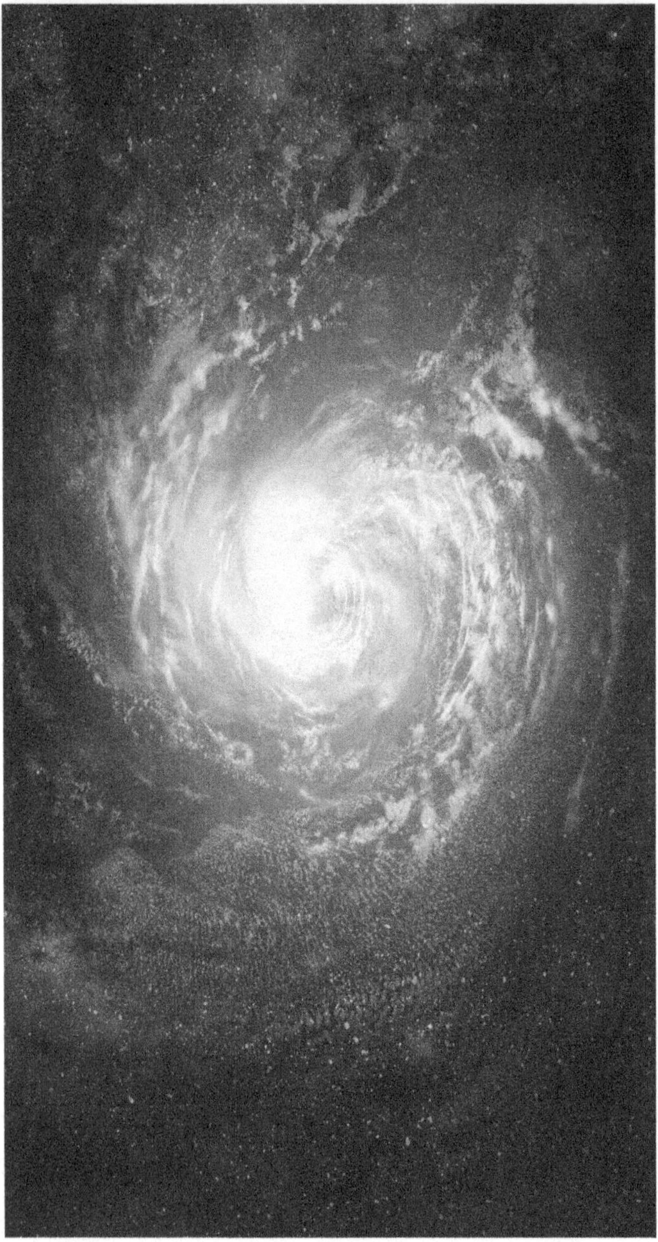

—41—
THIS IS ALL A GUESS

"I'm coming," I hear Silenna say through the intercom. It's nice to know she's on her way, but I can't sit around waiting for her.

"Evasive maneuvers," I tell the ship. "Release countermeasures."

"Define countermeasures."

"Decoys?"

"Decoys released."

"Okay, try to circle behind the Oranian vessel."

"Shall I try the maneuver, or do it?"

I squeeze my eyes shut. "DO IT!"

The main computer needs to familiarize itself with my manner of speaking. I wish we had more time to get acquainted.

I know from what I've observed that the enemy ship is far less agile than ours. It's like a tractor-trailer truck compared to a sports car. The difference gives us a slight opening if I can capitalize on it.

We narrowly avoid a barrage of orange beams and the crackling arms of a lightning bolt beam. Our shields are thin. They need time to regenerate. One more direct hit may be the sound of our death knell.

"Take evasive action. Do not allow the enemy ship to acquire a firing resolution."

The ship barrel rolls and takes a steep angle upward. I remember that Silenna and Arcon are making their way back to the cockpit. I hope Silenna is wearing magnetic boots.

Our ship continues to kick up and down like a bucking bronco at a rodeo. We're taking minimal damage to our shields thanks to our nimble moves. I turn to Amy. "How's it going?"

"All over the place."

"I mean you."

"I'll survive." Her expression changes. "You never cease to amaze me."

"You mean my piloting skills? It's easier than it looks."

"No. Your ability to scare me half to death."

"I'm sorry."

"Sorry doesn't help."

"I don't have time to think of an upbeat answer."

The ship levels off. We're drafting behind the Oranian ship's powerful engines. They look like twin suns. The image almost fills the view screen.

Silenna enters the cockpit with Arcon trailing behind. I'm glad she has survived the ship's antics in one piece. Arcon slips into his golden sphere. Silenna takes the seat next to me; the one I occupied before. While the seat straps her in, she extends her right hand to me palm up. I take it as a sign to once again carry on. She is greenlighting me to attack the engines. Every second counts. There can be no time-consuming change of command seats.

"Fire cannon three at the Oranian engines. Continue firing until I say stop."

The first red beam splatters against the outer energy shield. The Oranian vessel turns to shake us off.

"Stay behind the engines," I tell the ship. I glance over at Silenna.

She is nodding. "You may have missed your calling, Jacob."

I must be doing well because I've never heard Silenna make a light comment before. Let's not get carried away and call it humor.

We have no problem staying behind the enemy ship. The problem lies in their aft shields. It looks like we've only burned off the top layer.

We are close enough to the engines to keep the Oranian ship from firing at us. That's the good news. The bad news is we will have to drop far back before we tear through the last shield layer. Knowing when to back off is an inexact science at best.

"Arcon, estimate the enemy's shield strength," I say.

Arcon calculates his answer in less than thirty seconds. "I estimate eighty-five percent."

"How long will it take to penetrate all the shields?"
"Unknown."

Great. Wait a minute. I see something happening beyond the nose of the Oranian vessel. A large circle of outer space is blurring.

"Open window shields," Silenna says.

She stares through the observation windows. "The

Oranians are opening a wormhole. They are aborting their mission."

Before I can feel relieved, Silenna drops the other shoe.

"When the wormhole opens, we'll be dragged in behind their ship along with a large chunk of the Earth. Our ship and the chunk of Earth will be incinerated. When a starship bends time and space, only the ship that generates the wormhole can pass through. The wormhole acts like a human body. It rejects foreign DNA."

At a more convenient time, I'd like to explain to Silenna the concept of too much information. For the present, I know what I'd do, but it's not my decision to make.

Silenna quickly intervenes: "Divert power from shields to cannon three. Begin rapid firing. Continue for thirty seconds, then drop back to a distance of two miles." She turns to me. "This is all a guess."

I agree with Silenna's plan with one minor exception. I'd say, "I'm improvising" or "I'm calling an audible" to make the troops feel better, but that's just me.

The Oranian ship grows smaller as we reverse trust and back away from it. The rapid-fire beams explode in red circles against the engine shields. As the distance increases, I can't tell if the beams are eating away at the enemy's shield layers.

I can, however, tell that the wormhole in front of the ship is blossoming.

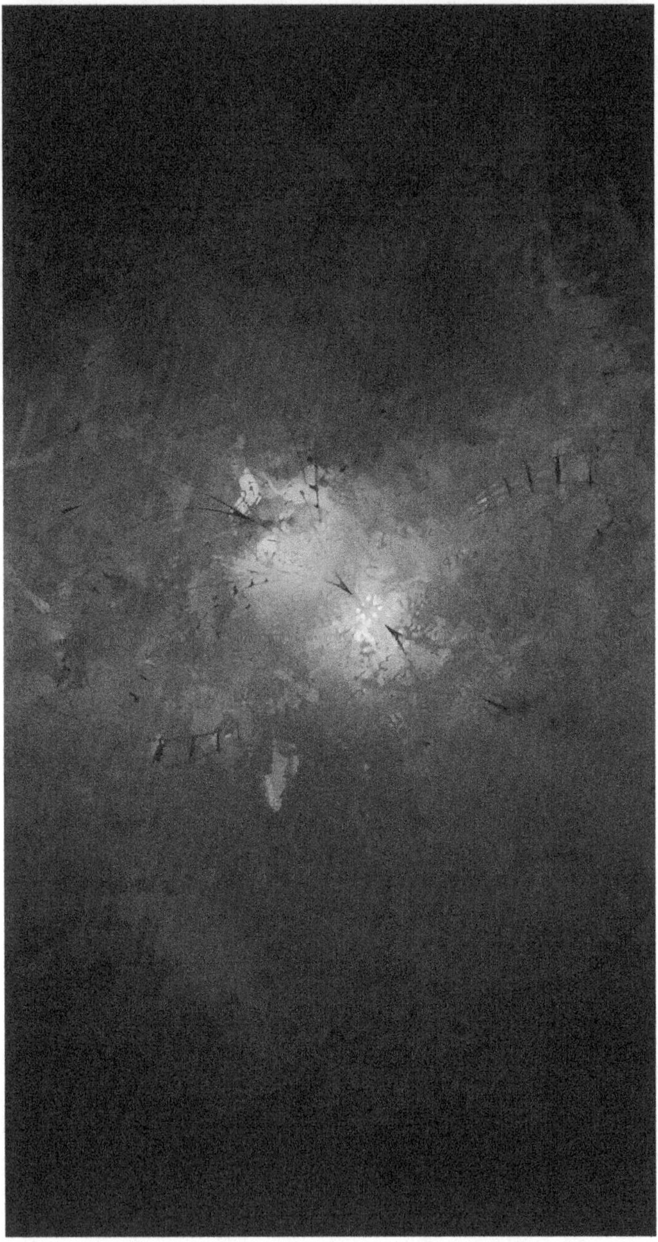

—42—
WHAT WILL BE

"We're moving too slowly," Silenna says through the intercom. "Increase thrust." I feel the ship accelerate. The enemy ship grows smaller.

"Magnify the Oranian ship."

I can now see that the engine shields have been worn down by the pommeling of the red laser bursts. It can't be long until the red fusillade breaches the engine shields.

Minutes pass. The Oranian shields hold stubbornly.

"The Orian Captain is funneling all of the dreadnought's energy to the rear shields and the wormhole," Arcon comments glumly.

I observe Silenna sitting calmly in the seat next to me. Soon, our heavy cannon will run out of energy. There is nothing more we can do except watch. Either the shields will go or we will.

The wormhole keeps expanding. I imagine it will reach operational size any second now.

The view screen is suddenly engulfed in red and yellow.

"Adjust to normal focus," I hear Silenna say. I see Amy touch the back of her hand to the face shield of her helmet.

The Oranian warship ruptures into massive fragments. The force of the red explosion sends pieces shooting off in a full circle into the cruel void of space. Simultaneously two things happen: The burgeoning wormhole blinks out of existence, and, a yellow wave comes hurtling toward us like the blast wave of a nuclear bomb.

"Increase to maximum reverse thrust," Silenna says.

The ship lurches in response. I feel the air pressure in my suit increase as it hyper-inflates for more protection.

As the yellow blast wave pursues us, Silenna comments, "I would have liked to use our main engine less."

Again, too much information. At least she got the conditional and infinitive tenses correct.

I turn to Amy. She turns back to me. We are still holding hands, although now more tightly. "We're going to make it," she tells me. I am reserving judgment.

Our increased speed keeps the blast wave at bay, but it keeps pursuing us like the Hound of the Baskervilles. It won't give up until it engulfs us.

"Change flight angle to forty-five degrees."

"The ship has a thirty-one percent chance of imploding if we make that maneuver in reverse," Arcon warns. "We've never tried it."

"I'll take two out of three chances to the one we have now," Silenna answers. "Do it NOW," Silenna commands the computer.

The ship tilts. We are jerked in the relative direction of "up" like a puppet on a string.

I hear Silenna command the main engine to "shut down" before I black out.

* * *

I awaken to the sight of the verdant Earth juxtaposed with a black-and-white palette of stars. I cannot detect nor can I see through the observation windows any evidence of our ship moving. We seem to be hanging in space like a painting on a wall.

I turn to Amy. She is already awake. "What happened?"

"We survived," Amy answers. Her eyes brighten. "I told you we'd make it."

"How did you know?"

"Because we have a future together that no one can take away."

I'm speechless. And deeply touched.

Silenna turns to us and smiles. Her smile is sincere, but not long-lasting. She tells Arcon to calculate the coordinates to an open field close to where we first landed.

"Let's switch seats," she tells me.

We exchange seats. I am surprised by my reluctance to relinquish the command seat. Aside from the angst, I enjoyed my turn at the helm. Who knows? I may have untapped potential as an interstellar spaceship commander in another life.

"I've input the coordinates," Arcon reports.

Silenna settles into the command seat. "Open window shields. Twenty-second engine burn, then glide to the edge of Earth's atmosphere."

The feeling of claustrophobia subsides. It's a relief to see the open fields of outer space first-hand again. I am becoming accustomed to space travel.

Silenna removes her helmet. Unpinning her multi-colored hair, she shakes her head vigorously. The silver, gold, and black strands fall to her shoulders. She's a beautiful woman cast in pale blue skin and purple eyes with orange pupils. I've grown accustomed to her features in addition to living in a starship.

"You can remove your helmets," she tells us.

Bare-headedness feels liberating. I begin to relax in the absence of world-threatening events. My thoughts go to Philadelphia. How many are dead or injured? How much destruction? We took a measure of revenge, but it won't replace the loss of loved ones, homes, buildings, and livelihoods.

I'm relieved when Silenna interrupts my thoughts.

"Now, we can begin the good work."

I'm not sure if Silenna means to include Amy and me in the "we."

Silenna turns to me. "I mean Arcon and me. Your participation is welcome, of course. I'd never presume."

She's reading my mind again. Maybe she can't help it. Or, maybe she's too tired to tune me out.

"I'm a writer," I tell Silenna. "I can't keep putting my life and my work on hold to help with...whatever."

"Whatever you decide, you will find time to write, Jacob. As you said, you are a writer. Writers write, and now you have some interesting material to add to your collection. Wouldn't you say?"

If my next novel turns out to be a mystery-science-fiction-thriller, I can already hear my publisher screaming at me for changing genres.

"Let's table the discussion," I say to Silenna politely.

Turning to Amy, Silenna says, "Do you have any thoughts about your future?"

"I'm waiting to hear from the Goddard Spaceflight Center about a job," Amy says. She turns to me. "And, I'd like to have a semblance of balance in my life."

"It may take a while for a position to open up at the Goddard Center and it takes time to write a book. I have precious metals aboard the ship that we can barter for currency. If we work together, I think you both deserve a decent salary. I just mention this as food for thought. I'm not trying to persuade you one way or another."

Amy and I exchange a look. It doesn't take a genius to know Silenna is pitching us. I'd go so far as to say she's doing it brazenly.

"Why aren't we traveling faster?" Amy asks.

"I'm keeping our speed relatively slow to conserve energy. We're about a day and a half from Earth. The ship took a beating. It needs repairs."

Amy turns to me before looking intently at Silenna. "What about the situation with my, Uhm, life energy?"

It's almost like Amy can read my mind too. I've been concerned about her life-sustaining capability. I wasn't sure how to broach the subject. I'm glad she brought it up on her own.

"The latest readings from the medical chamber show you are fully healed," Silenna answers. "Your life energy is functioning normally. I don't foresee any dependence on machines to keep you going. If you ask my opinion, your desire to share a life with Jacob played a larger role in your recovery than the med chamber."

Amy and I are delighted at the news. I unstrap to give Amy a Major League hug and kiss. In the absence of mortal danger, my lower back and shoulder assert their need for medical attention.

After celebrating with Amy, I turn to Silenna. "I think I need some time in the med chamber."

"I can see that your posture is off. Let's get you straightened out."

Silenna turns to Amy. "After we take care of Jacob, you and I need to log some serious sleep."

Amy nods in agreement.

Silenna turns to Arcon. "You have command of the ship. Wake me when we enter Earth orbit."

I see our ship picking up speed as the widow shields close.

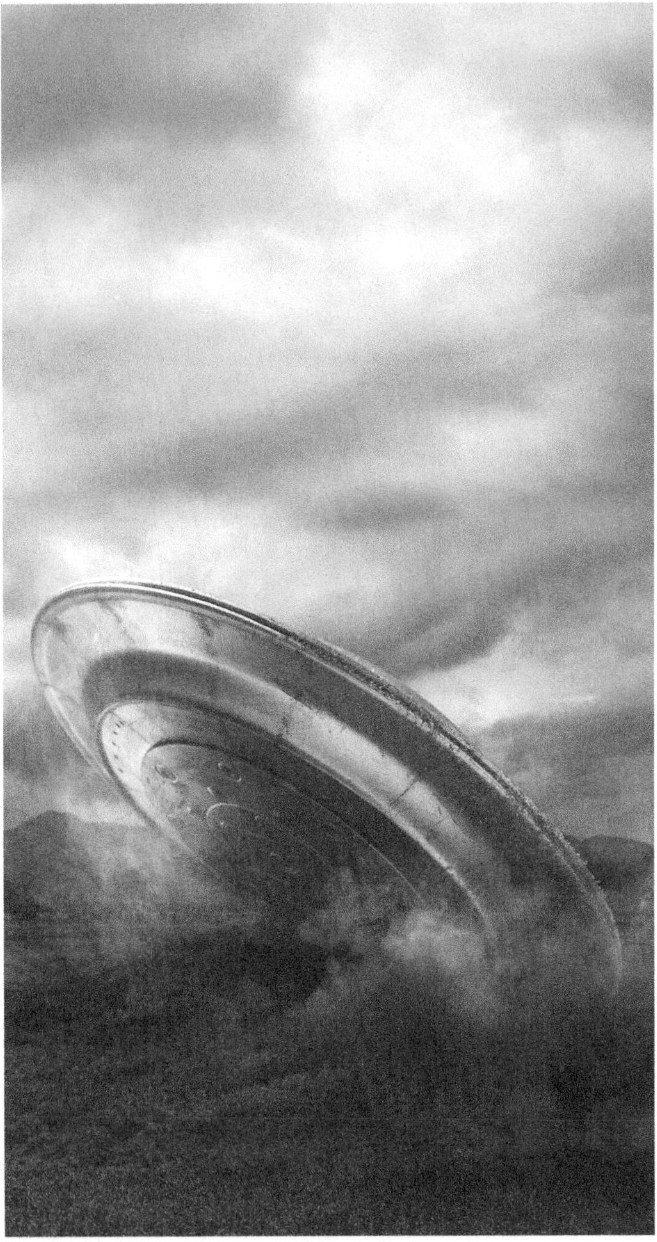

—43—
EARTH

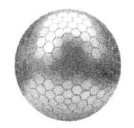

"Raise heat shields," Silenna tells the computer from the command seat. Surrounding her, Amy, Arcon, and I are strapped in our seats. Our exterior view switches to the screen below the windows.

"Fire retro thrusters."

I feel the jolt of the ship's powerful engine. The burn eases our speed down from fifty thousand miles per hour to roughly the speed of sound. The only thing to slow our descent after the burn will be the resistance of Earth's atmosphere.

We are essentially in freefall.

The black void outside changes to light pink. The pink color deepens into red, and then fiery yellow. We are inside a fireball that is ripping the air apart on our descent to Earth. I close my eyes. I'm not thrilled about being inside a fireball.

Minutes later, I hear the pneumatic sounds of the window shields sliding. Silenna tells the computer to "fire maneuvering thrusters."

I open my eyes to a blue sky and clouds.

"Fire thrusters," Silenna repeats.

No discernable response.

"Switch to manual control. Maximum shields."

"What's wrong?" Amy says.

"We've lost engine power. I'm going to dead stick us in for a landing."

The outskirts of Philadelphia lie ahead of us. Our altitude drops rapidly. Crash landing in the city is unthinkable. Half the city is already in flames. I catch a glimpse of the downtown area. It is still standing. The Liberty Bell and countless humans have survived the attack. Thank God our intervention stopped the conflagration before it engulfed the entire city.

It takes less than ten seconds to fly over the city. I'm not sure how Silenna plans to land the ship in one piece going this fast.

Silenna points ahead through the window. "There's our runway."

There is no time to wonder how Silenna plans to land a hurtling flying saucer in a fallow crop field. She works the manual control console on the right-hand side of her seat.

"I'm using gyros to position the ship to an optimal bearing for a rough landing. Prepare for impact."

The field grows larger as we plummet toward it. I feel my straps tighten. The ship shudders violently. I fear it will be torn apart by the concussion of the high-speed crash landing. Silenna has set our containment straps to "max hold" to prevent our necks from snapping on impact.

Seconds later, I feel another impact. This one is less violent than the first. I imagine our shields have bounced us off the improvised runway. I feel the third impact, and then the nose of the ship angles downward.

Finally, we are at rest. I can see that we've plowed into the field at a steep angle. A sliver of the horizon appears across the top of the forward windows.

Silenna immediately sends me down to the engine room again. She gives me instructions to adjust the power flow to the thrusters. Her instructions come through smoothly. Her understanding of the English language continues to improve. Something tells me she will need it. After completing my task, I return to the cockpit.

Silenna gives me an approving nod. "We should have enough power now to use the thrusters to level the ship. Strap in, Jacob."

Silenna manipulates her control console. I hear a loud screech and then a mechanical moan. Gradually, the ship rights itself. We are on the road to recovery. It would be nice to load the entire ship into the med chamber and watch it return to full health. Alas, even Aneleyan technology has its limits.

Before I can ask Amy how she feels, I see three M1 Abrams tanks rumble onto the field about a thousand yards away. The barrels of the tanks acquire a firing position on our ship.

Silenna's straps unravel. She removes her helmet. "Stay here," she tells us. "The shields will deflect their shells if they open fire. Don't come out unless I invite you to."

Five minutes later, I watch Silenna stride out into the open field wearing her spacesuit and carrying her helmet. She's left her hair unfettered. It doesn't hurt to make an attractive appearance when dealing with uptight military types.

The field is blanketed in snow. The sky is overcast with the smoke carried by the wind from the burning city. Someone pops out of the hatch of the middle tank. He is wearing battle fatigues and a matching cap. He holds up a bullhorn. "My name is Howard Johnson. I am a Tank Commander in the 35th Armored Regiment of the United States Army. Identify yourself."

Howard Johnson. Both an innocently normal and a resoundingly famous name. I wonder idly how many recruits have landed KP duty for asking the Colonel if he is related to the illustrious founder of the Howard Johnson hotels. Thanks to my irrepressible curiosity, I've recently read there is only one Howard Johnson hotel left in the world located in Lake George, New York. I make a concerted effort to corral my wandering mind.

Even from a distance of a thousand yards, I can see Colonel Johnson is rattled because Silenna replies to him telepathically with the rest of us looped in.

"My name is Silenna. I come from the planet Aneleya on the far side of this galaxy. I am here for the benefit of the human race. There is no need to aim your guns at us."

"You said 'us'. Are there others with you?"

"Two humans and a sentient being named Arcon."

"Bring out the humans."

"I object to your arrogant tone. Kindly learn some manners, or find someone else to address me."

There is an awkward intermission. I see Colonel Johnson speaking to someone on a smartphone.

Stowing the phone, Johnson says, "Please bring the humans out."

"I will bring them out if you come here to speak with me face-to-face."

"And if I don't?"

"I will leave at a great loss to the people of Earth."

"What about the humans?"

"They will leave with me or stay here depending upon their wishes."

Johnson reverts to his smartphone. At the end of the conversation, he clambers down the rungs on the side of his camouflaged tan tank. As he trudges towards the ship, he suddenly turns sideways to flash a series of hand signals to his men in the tanks. I imagine the signals mean something like: *Don't shoot unless I'm killed or kidnapped.*

Through the observation window, I watch the Colonel make his way across the snow-covered field. He wears a padded grey parka. I'm certain he is wearing body armor underneath. It won't do him any good if he decides to call in ground fire from the tanks. His head is down. He holds the bill of his cap tightly. I gather that tripping and falling on your face in snowy conditions is not a recommended method of representing the United States Army.

As Johnson nears our perimeter, Silenna tells Arcon to lower our defensive energy shield. She raises them after Johnson passes through.

Johnson advances to a spot a few paces from Silenna. He comes to attention and salutes. Making no effort to return the gesture, Silenna gazes at him serenely. Johnson gathers himself. He exhibits no reaction to Silenna's unusual height. He stands about six feet tall. I check the view screen to get a close-up of his face. The Colonel is not a young man, but it's difficult to guess his age behind the reflective silver sunglasses. In the middle of Johnson's cap, there is an insignia of an Armadillo. It occurs to me that I'd feel like an idiot walking around with an Armadillo displayed prominently on my cap. Each to his own.

"Welcome, Colonel Johnson. I always prefer to make new acquaintances face-to-face whenever possible."

"I've come as you requested. Where are the humans?"

Silenna is visibly taken aback by Johnson's bluntness which borders on rudeness.

"Be patient." Silenna's breath clouds as it meets the cold air. She's dropped the telepathy. I can still hear her through her helmet's intercom which she holds with the open end up.

"You seem upset about something," Silenna observes.

"Your actions don't support your claims," Johnson says. "There are two FBI agents who don't have anything nice to say about you."

"I apologize for treating them roughly. I had no time to answer their questions or to meet with their superiors. I had to save the Earth from imminent destruction and the eventual destruction of your entire solar system by a supernova device. I realize I'm making a very bold statement, but I have evidence of the event in a video file.

"I'm sure my superiors will be anxious to review your file, but we have other concerns about your intentions. How do you explain the fact that your ship fired on the city of Philadelphia? How does such a hostile act help the human race?"

Silenna stands with her back to me. I can't see her

expression. I can only wonder why the US Army and likely the Joint Chiefs think we fired on the city.

"We fired on an attacking enemy warship engulfed in a cloud of heavy smoke. I was aware of the possibility of collateral damage. I decided to continue engaging the enemy to prevent a greater loss of lives. I'm deeply sorry for any loss I may have caused."

Colonel Johnson pauses to consider Silenna's response. He removes his cap and brushes a hand over his close-cropped, lead-colored hair. Affixing the cap firmly back, I hear him continue with his questions.

"What happened to the other ship?"

I notice Johnson refers to the Oranian warship as "the other ship" rather than the "enemy ship." It implies that Silenna is allied with the invading ship.

"We followed the Oranian warship into outer space and destroyed it."

Giving the enemy a name should help to verify Silenna's story. I soon find that it doesn't.

"So, you mean to tell me that you saved the Earth, the solar system, and half the city of Philadelphia in one fell swoop?"

"Not all at once," Silenna answers straightforwardly.

"Are you getting this?" Johnson says into his shoulder mic.

"Your suspicious nature is not encouraging," Silenna remarks. She bends closer to her helmet. "Come down, Amy and Jacob. Tell Arcon to stay with the ship."

A few minutes later, Amy and I climb out of an emergency exit on the side of the ship. Wearing our helmets against the cold, we walk around the curving exterior to join Silenna. The snow is about a foot deep.

Our legs are unsteady. We use the side of the ship for balance while our bodies adjust to the pull of gravity. The temperature inside my suit is self-regulating. I feel warm and toasty. Creature comforts are welcome in the middle of yet another crisis.

As we round the curve, I notice a group of Amish people gathered at a distance to our left in the snow. They wear black overcoats, heavy boots, and broad-brimmed straw hats. From the length and grey color of their beards, they look like the elders of the settlement. They may be quietly hoping we are part of the second coming.

Silenna introduces us to the Colonel. I remove my helmet and shake hands as does Amy.

Being the no-nonsense kind of guy he is, Johnson gets right down to business.

"What are you two doing here?"

"Helping," I say.

"That's all you have to say for yourself?"

Amy speaks. "I'm afraid you wouldn't believe us if we told you anything more, sir."

Johnson swivels his head back and forth looking for buried untruths. "Are you being held captive?"

"No, sir." Amy answers.

Johnson looks back at me. I'm pretty sure he has no idea what to think or do at this point. "We volunteered for the mission, sir."

Johnson turns to Silenna. "These benefits to Mankind you talk about. What are they exactly?"

"I bring cures for terminal illnesses and medical devices to heal serious injuries. I will help you to develop a clean energy source to supplement your clean energy initiatives already underway. I am here to speak to the leaders of nations to give them a perspective that will help them to coexist peacefully. I come from a highly advanced race that lived in peace and prosperity for millennia. I hope to create at least some of that here."

Johnson stands in front of us. Speechless. I'm now convinced he doesn't know what to do. He surprises me with his next question.

"I feel this kind of tingly sensation. Are you doing that?"

"It's my energy transmission. It won't hurt you. You may even feel lighter and more cheerful for the next few hours."

Johnson has no more questions at the moment.

"Would you like a tour of my ship," Silenna offers.

"I have no authorization for something like that. My orders are to ask you to meet with a joint committee back at my base."

"That would be inconvenient, Colonel. My ship needs extensive repairs."

"Well, then, I'm not sure where that leaves us. I have a report to file. We'll have to see how all of this proceeds."

Colonel Johnson comes to attention and salutes. "Thank you for the visit. Have a good day."

Johnson turns on his heel and crunches off toward the safety of his tanks.

"Not the warm welcome I was expecting," Silenna says almost inaudibly. "Let's go back inside the ship."

We return to the cockpit. From the command seat, Silenna powers down all non-essential ship functions. I can see from her bearing that the week's extraordinary events have taken quite a toll on her. She turns to Amy and me. "Arcon and I have work to do."

She rises from the command seat. "I'm sure you two can use a little time alone. Let's go, Arcon."

"Talk soon," Arcon says to us.

Silenna gives him a stern look. "Don't be a busybody."

"I was just trying to—"

"I know what you were trying to do."

Seconds later, we are alone in the cockpit. Looking into Amy's eyes, I realize the moment of truth is here. I am semi-prepared for it.

Amy senses the moment too. True to her pragmatic nature, she is the first to speak.

"Let's go over the pros and cons of our decision."

"Makes sense," I say. "You first."

"Okay. While we may be able to make a broader impact by staying with Silenna, there are certain benefits to going our own way. To me, stability and independence are the two biggest factors."

"Not to mention longevity," I add.

"And, while staying with Silenna will no doubt be more exciting and interesting, I'm not a big fan of roller coaster rides."

"I seem to remember swearing off them too."

"What do you want to do, Jacob?"

When I open my mouth to speak, I'm surprised at what comes out. "Whatever life I choose, I want to live it with you."

"Is that a marriage proposal?"

"In a manner of speaking."

Amy rises from her seat to sit on my lap. Garbed in our spacesuits, we are not comfortable. The suits are not designed for marriage proposals or anything in the category of intimate for that matter.

"I'll be kind and say your proposal was tentative."

"Then I'll rephrase it. Amy Goodwin, will you marry me?"

Amy buries her head in my chest. She looks up and kisses me. "Yes."

Looking at her beautiful, freckled face, I'm taken unawares by the elation I feel to know this woman has agreed to spend the rest of her life with me.

"Besides marrying me, what do you want to do?"

Amy's question prompts me to realize that I don't want to go back to my "old life." I've shed it like an old suit of clothes.

I look down at Amy. She's looking back at me a little teary-eyed.

"I'd like to help Silenna. Strike that. I'd like *us* to help Silenna."

Preview

TIME TERMINUS
Expect the Unexpected

A Novella

© 2022 by David B Gittlin

CHAPTER ONE

It had been another long journey from JFK to Heathrow Airport in London. These frequent trips across the pond were beginning to take their toll on him. Peter hadn't slept well on the return flight. The helicopter ride under marginal weather conditions from London to the small town of Kirkwall on the Orkney Islands in Northern Scotland had done little to lift his spirits. And, he had scheduled an appointment with an attorney in Fort Lauderdale in another five days.

Notwithstanding his grueling schedule and the pressures of his new project, Peter remained focused on his important objectives. He intended to dismiss the matter before him as quickly as possible.

"Thank you for seeing me, Mister Alastair."

"My assistant told me your request to see me was urgent. Since you were a friend of my father, I agreed to see you. Please state your business concisely. I have a full schedule ahead of me."

Peter gazed at the man in front of him. He clutched a battered World War II RAF cap in his hands. From his age and attire, he had the look of a retired school teacher. Aside from his longstanding relationship with the family and a reputation for eccentricity, Peter knew the man only by name.

In all of his business dealings, and with the public in general, Peter carefully used proper British English. People had to know, by his bearing and his words, that he was not easily fooled by schemes or empty dreams. People came to him with proposals of every kind. He never wanted the lucky few who made it through to his inner sanctum to think of him as a rube from the backwoods of Scotland. He went so far as to ask the people he saw to speak the King's English to keep meetings on a high level.

"May I take a seat," Shaun Hennessy said.

Peter gestured towards one of the royal blue chairs upholstered in diamond-cut Jacquard fabric in front of his shining blond wooden desk.

Hennessy seated himself as if the chair was made of eggshells. Peter observed Hennessy viewing a row of refurbished photos of the distilling plant. They ranged in age from the 1890s to the present and decorated the wall behind his gleaming desk. Prints of full-page color ads adorned the wall to Peter's right. "Highland Gold— The Gentleman's Drink." "Highland Gold—For Refined Tastes Only." "Highland Gold—The Mark of Success." Peter had thought of the slogans himself. The ads were wildly successful. They appealed to the vanity, snobbery, and sense of self-importance of his target audience.

Peter had purposefully remodeled the offices fronting the distillery with an air of opulence. He regularly met with key government leaders, bankers, and businessmen here. He wanted to impress them with his wealth and power.

Peter drew Hennessy's attention with a hard stare.

Hennessy coughed, and then he began his story. "Two weeks ago, I was on my ATV inspecting the fences bordering my farm. I noticed a mangled sheep in one of the fields. Upon investigating, I found that a pregnant ewe had been hit by a small meteor. In fact, the field revealed signs of a small meteor shower hitting the pasture. Fortunately, the poor female was the only creature that had been hurt. The herd must have scattered quickly."

"Can we get to the point, Shaun?"

"Aye, sir. I'm sorry. Alongside the ewe's body, I found an odd-shaped rock sprinkled with gleaming metal. I couldn't imagine where it had cum' from. Out of curiosity, I took it back to my lab. I don't know if your father ever told you, but I was a physics professor at Cambridge University before retiring to my farm."

Hennessy seemed to wait for a reaction to his previous post in life. Peter showed nothing. He was growing impatient. He had only agreed to grant this man an audience out of respect for his father.

"I'm getting to my point, sir."

"Please do."

"I left the rock in my lab on February twenty-eighth of this year. It was a Monday. I remember the day clearly. I left the lab immediately because I had to drive my wife into town for a doctor's appointment. She was feeling ill. Anyway, I didn't get back to my lab until a week later. We were in shearing season, you see."

Peter nodded. If the story went on without a conclusion for one more minute, he was going to throw Shaun Hennessy out of his office, friend of the family or not.

"Okay. So, when I finally get back to my lab, I notice the date on my calendar reads December fifth of last year. I thought I was havin' a dream. I turn on the classical music station I listen to in the lab, and the news break confirms the date: December fifth.

"Well, you can imagine I was in shock. I left the lab. I sat in the kitchen, wondering if I had the beginnings of dementia. I turned on the television and discovered I had returned to the twenty-eighth of this year again. I repeated the experiment several times with similar results. Each time I returned to the lab, I found it had gone back in time to a different date."

Peter just stared at the man.

"I assure you, Mister Alastair, I am of sound mind and body. I'm not imagining this."

"All right. Let's assume you aren't having hallucinations. Why have you come to me with this?"

"I believe that I can harness the power of the rock to create a time machine. I believe I can reverse the process to change time outside of the lab. I've worked on the formulas using measurements of the wave field the rock emits. I believe I can use the machine to take me to a point in time that I pre-set."

Peter laughed. He couldn't help himself. "Even if what you say is true, I still don't understand why you are here."

"I'm asking you to invest in this project after I prove to you that it works. I can explain the math to you when you have more time. Think of what we can do for the world and ourselves with something like this. The possibilities boggle my mind. This is a once-in-a-millennium opportunity. I'm giving you a chance to get in on the ground floor, and I'm willing to split the notoriety and the profits fifty-fifty."

"It sounds wonderful, Mister Hennessy, but I'm afraid you've come to the wrong place." Peter rose from his desk. "Come. My assistant will show you out."

CHAPTER TWO

Issac Templeton had never seen anything like it. A huge butterfly. Made of glass. With a blue rose painted on each wing. And something like a furnace burning in its belly.

Isaac had parked his silver LC 500 sports car around the corner from the Publix Grocery Store because the mall was busy. He didn't mind the walk in the fresh air in the mild south Florida winter weather. He zipped his sweatshirt against the sudden evening chill. Mentally reviewing his grocery list, Issac turned the corner from the parking lot, and there it was. Fluttering in place, as if it had been waiting for him. He saw himself reflected a hundred times in its bulging, prismatic eyes. Blood red eyes.

Issac screamed, but no sound came from his mouth. He turned to run but found he couldn't move. The thing had paralyzed him.

A sound came from far away. It grew louder until he recognized it. Chimes. Issac's digital alarm. He shot to a sitting position with his heart thudding in his chest.

He took deep breaths to keep it from exploding. The vestiges of sleep slipped away. He had a healthy heart. He had a healthy everything. He was a young man in his prime. The odds of him having a heart attack were practically nil. It had only been another bizarre nightmare that intermittently haunted his dreams.

If confidence bred success and success bred confidence, where were these nightmares coming from? It had to be from the pressure of the business; one of the perks that came tied in a bow on the package of owning and running a law firm without a net. He guessed the worry and anxiety crept up and pounced on him at night when he wasn't looking. It hid from him during the day like a spotted leopard camouflaged by the long grass on an African plain.

Donning a navy-blue silk robe, Issac strolled outside to his penthouse terrace. From thirty floors up at 5 AM, nightlights still glimmered from the surrounding apartment buildings fronting the intercoastal waterway. Speckles of light from the waning half-moon danced on the rippling surface of the waterway below. Issac's thoughts drifted to the meeting awaiting him later in the morning. He routinely handled initial meetings by himself. He only assigned a second lawyer to the account if it proved necessary. He didn't believe in running up a client's bill.

An hour later, Issac enjoyed his drive to downtown Fort Lauderdale. The early hour helped to avoid the brunt of rush-hour traffic. The weather called for another windy day in mid-March with temperatures in the low eighties. Oppressive heat and humidity lurked just around the corner. Issac rode with the convertible top down on his sports car to capitalize on the last of the pleasant weather.

Thoughts of Anna filled his mind. His girlfriend had sounded enthused when they last spoke. He looked forward to having a late dinner with her at an Italian Restaurant in Boca Raton near Le Gallerie Printemps where her paintings were displayed. He thought it would be nice to celebrate with a bottle of wine if Anna had a new sale to announce. He hoped to have an announcement of his own.

After arriving at the office, Issac worked on current case files and fielded phone calls until his first appointment arrived. Peter Alastair showed up at Templeton and Associates at the appointed hour of 11:00 AM. After exchanging pleasantries, Alastair planted himself in a chair opposite Issac. The two men sat in the conference room alone with only the sounds of traffic faintly intruding from the street below his tenth-floor offices. Issac had no intention of ever wasting money on penthouse offices even if he could one day afford them.

Issac took a moment to appraise his would-be client. Alastair wore a charcoal Armani suit with a light blue pocket handkerchief. He wore no jewelry except a sleek gold and silver Movado watch.

Issac owned a few himself. They were stylish without being overly expensive and gaudy. Issac judged Alastair to be a few years older than himself, maybe in his late thirties. He had a handsome face with strong features, although a bit gaunt, and marred by pock marks from adolescent acne. From hazel-blue eyes, he stared at Issac intently. He wore his long red hair pulled back and neatly tied in a ponytail by a gold band. The rest of him contrasted with his unconventional hairstyle. Alastair was clean-shaven. His nails were perfectly manicured. The man projected an air of confidence. He looked fit; a man who lived an affluent and disciplined lifestyle.

"If you don't mind, I always ask prospective clients how they found us." As much as Alastair was interviewing him, Issac was interviewing Alastair to see if he wanted him as a client.

"Since taking over my father's company, I've established my residence and offices here in Fort Lauderdale. I also have offices in New York."

Issac wondered if Alastair meant to impress him with the mention of the New York offices.

"Your name came up repeatedly when I inquired about a lawyer to represent my business interests here."

"I see. And how can we help you?"

"I've recently assumed control of my family business due to the death of my father."

"I'm sorry for your loss."

Alastair brushed by Issac's comment. He assumed Alastair was tired of hearing it.

"I want you to negotiate termination agreements with most of my U.S. distributors. I'll be keeping a few of the better ones for the time being. My company has the right to terminate with a one-year notice. I want to move faster than that."

"Can you tell me a little about your business?"

"I sell only one product: Highland Gold, a twelve-year single-malt-whiskey which I make in Scotland. It tastes as good as a twenty-year-single-malt at a more popular price. Everything is relative in the single-malt business. Our price point is three times that of ordinary brands like Dewars, but we target a more exclusive clientele."

"May I ask why you've made this decision?"

"I'm glad you asked. Understanding my business will give you the necessary sense of urgency." Alastair paused, perhaps to gather his thoughts, and without breaking his intense eye contact.

"You see, my father was a simple man. A frugal man. And a loyal friend. Some of these distribution relationships stretch back generations. My father was a good judge of character. The people he dealt with are honest. Longevity, stability, and loyalty are honorable traditions. The problem, however, with many of these relationships is complacency and stagnation have set in. Some of my customers make a habit of paying as late as ninety days. I'm not in the money lending business.

"Furthermore, the market for single-malts is not exactly flourishing in these changing times. As competition has increased, our market share has decreased. Aggressive marketing is needed to create new retail customers. The most up-to-date business management software and hardware systems must be implemented to maximize marketing campaigns, profitability, accounting, and customer service. I can't tell my distributors how to run their businesses. At the same time, I can't sit by and watch my business go downhill. I've invested a great deal of time and energy to learn how to increase sales in the United States. Now, I'm ready to take matters into my own hands. I'm going to be my own distributor."

Issac had no immediate response. Alastair's plan sounded bold. Would it work? Issac only knew he wouldn't want to attempt it all at once. Only big companies like Coca-Cola and the mega beer brewing companies sold their products vertically. Even by adding its own distribution, Highland Gold would still be a small company. Small companies rarely had the capital to distribute directly to retailers.

"Your business is your business," Issac said. "I'm just wondering if it would make sense to test your plan with one or two distributors first."

"May I call you Issac?"

"Of course."

"I have already tested the concept. A year ago, I replaced a distributor that wasn't achieving what I expected from this market. I rented a warehouse for a year and set up my operation. I had to pay too much for the early termination of the distribution contract because I employed a weak attorney to handle the negotiations. That's why I'm here, by the way. In the past year, I've learned invaluable lessons about hands-on, direct distribution. If you'll allow me to pat myself on the back, the results of my efforts are paying off handsomely. As a result, I'm building my own warehouse near Port Everglades. I'm ready to open more distribution centers across the country. As I mentioned, my father was a frugal man. He lived a comfortable and simple life until he fell ill. He saved most of the money he made from the business. Thanks to him, I have the resources to roll out my plan."

"Is your mother alive?"

"She died two years ago. I have two sisters, but they have nothing to do with the business. They were provided for in my father's Will."

"Do your lenders have to approve the plan?"

"They already have."

Issac decided he liked what he was hearing. "Well, then, it sounds like we can get started if you are ready to engage my firm, subject to a routine credit check."

"You will find my company's financial standing is rock solid. I'm prepared to engage your firm as long as you handle all of the negotiations."

"I will handle all of your matters personally. I'll prepare an engagement letter with all of the details. I will have it couriered to your offices tomorrow. I'll need you to provide me with documentation confirming your ownership of the business and trademark information. Once we get the engagement letter signed and the requested documentation, we'll be in business."

Alastair bent down and produced two folders from his briefcase. Handing them to Issac, he said, "I believe this is all of it."

Issac smiled. "You are a decisive man, Mister Alastair. Welcome to Templeton and Associates."

He watched Alastair leave the office. Confidence breeds success, and success breeds confidence, Issac thought. Alastair exuded both in spades. He enjoyed working with people like Alastair, as long as they weren't too arrogant. He had read that a person makes their future with their every thought and action. It appeared that Peter Alastair subscribed to the philosophy, and so did Issac.

ABOUT THE AUTHOR

After a career in marketing and business communications, David Gittlin began writing short stories and screenplays. He now writes novels and posts regularly to his blog. To date, Gittlin has authored three novels and four novellas including the Silver Sphere Series. He lives in Florida with his wife and daughter.

www.davidgittlin.com

www.davidgittlin.net/novels

Made in the USA
Monee, IL
28 August 2024